MYSTERIOUS WAYS

A NOVEL BY

Terry W. Burns

RIVEROAK®
Good News in Fiction

An Imprint of Cook Communications Ministries
COLORADO SPRINGS, COLORADO • PARIS, ONTARIO
KINGSWAY COMMUNICATIONS LTD
EASTBOURNE, ENGLAND

RiverOak® is an imprint of
Cook Communications Ministries, Colorado Springs, CO 80918
Cook Communications, Paris, Ontario
Kingsway Communications Ltd, Eastbourne, England

MYSTERIOUS WAYS
© 2005 by Terry W. Burns

Cover Design by: Jeffrey P. Barnes
Cover Illustration by: Ron Adair

First Printing, 2005
Printed in the United States of America
2 3 4 5 6 7 8 9 10 Printing/Year 09 08 07 06 05

Unless otherwise noted, Scripture quotations are taken from the King James Version.

ISBN 1-58919-027-0

I lovingly dedicate this book to my wife, Saundra, whose
love and support makes my writing possible,
Judy Vincent who did the first editing on the book,
and to my editor Jeff Dunn who saw the
promise in my stories.

One

Central Texas, late 1860s

*W*hat I need is a disguise.

Amos Taylor hooked a leg across his saddle horn as he looked across the field at the little country church, a small, white building with a steep-pitched roof that led up to the spire on the front. An idea formed in his head, and the more he thought on it the more he liked it. In back of the church a black-frocked suit and a white clerical collar and shirt, the standard uniform of a country parson, hung on the clothesline. *How's that for timing?* Amos thought.

Amos rode over to a young boy skipping rocks across a small stream. "Where ya live, boy?" It wouldn't do for the boy to live at the parsonage.

The towheaded youngster looked up, all freckles and grin. He had a rag tied on his big toe to cover some recent scrape. "Over yonder." He pointed across the field.

Excellent. "You wanna make a dime?"

The boy looked at him appraisingly. "Do frogs bump their bottom when they jump?"

"Is that a yes?"

The boy nodded vigorously, and Amos fished the promised coin out of his pocket. He held it, his hand resting on his saddle horn. The youngster devoured it with his eyes. "I want to surprise a friend of mine. You know the lady that lives in that house over there?"

The boy fidgeted, not liking having to stand still, but his eyes never left the coin. "The preacher's wife? We don't go to that church, but I know her."

"If I give you the money, will you go over there, pluck a handful of those wild flowers, and take them to her? Tell her a friend sent you with them."

"Who should I say?"

"Just a friend."

"I can do that." A grubby hand stretched forth for the coin.

Amos tucked it into the boy's hand. "Take them to the front door, son. Flowers oughta be delivered to the front door."

He was talking to the boy's back. The youngster was already halfway to a growth of pretty wildflowers: reds, yellows, and blues in happy confusion.

Amos watched as the young man gathered and arranged a bunch of them, tried to slick down his unruly hair, straightened his rumpled clothing, and approached the door. He was taking his mission very seriously.

As the youngster knocked on the front door, Amos rode into the backyard to liberate the suit, shirt, and collar from the clothesline. It took but a minute to tuck the garments into his saddlebags and head out of town. *The perfect disguise*, he thought.

Judy Valentine held a delicately scented handkerchief to her nose. It helped keep the ever-present dust cloud inside the Wells Fargo coach bearable. The visit to see family in Boston had been pleasant, but it felt good to be going home again.

Home, she thought. *They just don't understand*. Her family had been very difficult when the time came to leave. They did not understand her desire to return to this untamed region, and certainly would not have understood her thinking of it as home.

They wouldn't have seen her life back in Boston as confining or regimented either. To them it was a proper, organized existence. She had felt exactly the same way until she came out West to visit her Aunt Helen and Uncle John. She was surprised to find that from the moment she stepped from the stagecoach, the wide-open land that stretched as far as she could see removed any boundaries in her mind and freed her spirit. She loved it.

Now almost back to her adopted home, she looked out over the flowing grass of the prairie. Soon the coach would make the turn by Saddle Rock. From there it would be a relatively short trip on in to Quiet Valley. She smiled and smoothed some wrinkles from her skirt. *I'll be home soon*, she thought again.

Amos rode deep into the hill country before he determined it would be safe to pull a job. He watched the Wells Fargo coach round the turn chased by a cloud of dust. It would pass under Saddle Rock in a matter of minutes.

He had been careful in his approach, as it was hard to move secretly in this country. Any motion produced this cloud, a tan, highly visible marker that would remain in the air indicating the path of those who had made it. He removed his hat to peek gingerly over the top, watching the stage slow up to make the turn. He heard the shotgun guard yell, "You better rein 'em in, Slim; you're gonna slide us into that rock."

Slim was equal to the task, and the bright red coach swung neatly around the turn, yellow wheels spraying gravel. As it passed underneath, Amos slipped a couple of pebbles into his mouth to disguise his voice and adjusted the red print bandanna over his face. Then he took a deep breath, coiled, and jumped. He hit and rolled on top of the coach, moccasined feet quickly finding purchase, then he slipped up behind the surprised pair at the front.

"You're doing right well handling that team, but you'd best pull 'em up now."

Looking back over his shoulder in surprise at the Colt aimed at his back, Slim leaned back into the reins, and put his foot on the brake lever. He applied gentle pressure, then pushed harder. The rear wheels finally locked, and the coach slid to a stop. Inside the passengers bounced around like rocks in a washtub. The pair on top tossed their weapons to the ground.

There was little sound except the horses blowing and stamping their impatience at being stopped at a place they knew was not proper. A couple of them voiced a shrill objection. Amos leaned over the side, "You people try anything, and you'll find you're looking smack-dab into the sun. I'll drop you like a bad habit before you get me spotted. Now come out of there."

The pronouncement had its desired effect, and the passengers filed out as docile as lambs. A tall, distinguished man in a dark suit and frilly shirt that marked him as a gambler stepped out casually. He turned, but did not look up as he reached out to offer his hand to someone still inside the coach.

Amos got his first look at the lone female among the group. She had on a light blue traveling suit and hat and wore crisp white gloves. A light scent of lilac wafted up into Amos's nostrils as she stood beneath him in the doorway. Without thinking, he inhaled as much of the sweet nectar as he could, leaning over and nearly losing his balance in the process. The heady aroma made him a little lightheaded. He shook it off as the gambler helped the young woman down and led her a half-dozen steps away from the coach.

She walked with a distinctly feminine sway and a light easy grace, not obvious or provocative, but Amos could tell she was a woman accustomed to being looked at. Still, he had no doubt she was a lady.

The pair stopped and turned to face the coach as the man released her hand. He opened his coat in an exaggerated gesture to show he wasn't armed. They both raised their hands. The young woman tossed her head to get her long chestnut hair off her shoulder. All the while she regarded Amos with soft brown eyes, curious but unafraid.

A short, mousy-looking character in a loud brown and orange plaid suit emerged, lost his equilibrium on the step, flailing and nearly falling. The smell of cheap whiskey and body odor replaced the delicate lilac scent as the little man fought for balance in the doorway. At the end of the clownlike run, he stumbled and would have gone down on his face if the gambler hadn't put out a hand to steady him. Amos shook his head in disgust; nobody but a drummer would wear an ugly suit like that.

"Fine, just fine," Amos said. "Everybody is showing uncommon good sense."

He turned his full attention back to the two still on top, motioned with his pistol barrel and said, "Is that all of them?"

Slim glared at him. "Yes."

"If there's anybody hiding down there to take a potshot at me, you better know I'm gonna shoot you first."

Slim's face clouded up, insulted at his word being questioned. "There's nobody down there."

Amos motioned again with the pistol. "All right, you two get down."

The two scrambled down. They stopped and looked up as he waved them over to the others. "Very good, now kindly come forward one at a time and toss your valuables through the window into the coach."

"Dumbest holdup I ever saw," the guard murmured as he complied, then said louder as he shaded his eyes to look into the sun at Amos, "You new at this?"

Amos didn't hide his amusement. "I reckon I might not be doing it the usual way, but nobody's been shot, have they? Not yet anyway."

One at a time they made the move to the coach. When the lady started forward, Amos stopped her with an uplifted hand. "Not you, ma'am. It ain't in me to rob anybody as pretty as you."

Judy nodded her head slightly to accept the compliment, then held her place. She pursed her lips as she thought about the irony of it all. As much as she loved it out here, she had been compelled to accept the fact that there would be few men with the manners she was accustomed to back East. But here she had finally met a man with some manners ... and he was busy robbing them.

The shotgun guard broke into her thoughts by speaking to the masked man in a surly voice. "You better be almighty careful when you climb down to get that stuff outta the coach."

"You still don't get it, do you?" Amos slipped quickly into the driver's seat and released the brake. "I'm taking coach and all."

"*What?* You can't leave us out here," several of them yelled as they started toward the coach. His gun swung and covered them. They froze awkwardly in their tracks, looking like a set of poorly conceived statues.

Two

Amos swung the pistol back and forth in a tight arc and spoke in a quiet, even voice. "How about you move back a step or two? We're getting along so well that I'd hate for this little meeting to turn nasty. Matter of fact, I think all of you best get down on your bellies, hands behind your heads. Not you, ma'am, though I'd admire for you to step over there and have a seat on that rock."

Judy walked over to where he had pointed, casually, as if she were at home in someone's parlor. Still, she clutched her handbag tightly as if she feared he might change his mind. Her pulse raced. *Isn't this exciting? Who would have thought a holdup would be so—so—stimulating!*

A shiver ran through her as she tried to interpret what she was feeling. It wasn't fear, although the stranger certainly looked dangerous holding his gun on them. Yet, as she examined her deepest feelings, what she found was not fear, but excitement.

She reached the rock he had indicated, turned, and sat, composed her hands around her handbag in her lap as she smoothed out her skirt. She regarded him frankly. *It's his eyes. They cut straight into a person, yet there's almost a glint of humor in them. It's as if they are saying ... saying ... oh my.* Judy began to fan herself with her purse.

Amos turned his attention to the young woman again, touching his hand briefly to the brim of his hat. "Don't fret your pretty head, ma'am. I'm just gonna take this coach down the trail a bit. It's a nice day, and I reckon you'll find it a pleasant walk. It won't be far."

A smile toyed with the corners of her lips, but before she could respond he turned, whipped up the team, and left her and the other passengers choking in a cloud of dust.

Judy watched the coach disappear down the road. She felt relief that nobody had been hurt, yet at the same time she experienced a strange disappointment at the disappearance of the masked man. *I must be losing my mind.*

Amos laughed as he pulled down the bandanna covering his lower face. "That's got to be the slickest job I've pulled yet."

As promised, he pulled up several miles down the road. He hefted the strongbox over the side to let it fall, then quickly followed it to the ground. It took two shots to dispose of the lock, but then it opened to show a generous amount of cash and some negotiable papers. He tossed the papers aside. He didn't need them; they'd be too difficult to do anything with. He determined to take just the cash.

Inside the coach he went through the passengers' personal belongings. A fine leather wallet caught his eye, and he pulled it first.

"Old son!" he whistled through his teeth. "You go mighty well heeled. Nobody carries that much cash. You must have just won a really big pot." The pictures indicated it belonged to the man he had apparently pegged correctly as a gambler. Amos left the pictures but kept the wallet.

He quickly went through the rest of the items in the coach, then tied the team off in the shady little grove where he had hidden his horse. He began to carry out the rest of his plan, which was simply to hide in plain sight. Amos couldn't help but chuckle. People don't think about what's right in front of their noses.

He took the parson's outfit out of the saddlebags and shook the wrinkles out of it as best as he could. He wished he could take a bath before he put on fresh clothes. He stretched out his full six-foot-two frame and pushed his hands up as if reaching for a cloud.

It was a long, hard stretch; then he released it so very slowly to keep from getting a cramp. He emptied a little water from his canteen into his hand and used it to slick back the dark brown hair that matched the fur on his chest and the thick fringe under his nose.

He pulled on the pants and the white shirt, then fastened the clerical collar. *Aaacccccckkkk, how do they wear these things?* It felt as if his neck were locked in a vise. He pulled at the collar with his forefinger, trying to loosen the fit, then pulled his good boots from his saddlebags. They were far from new but were routinely kept blacked and polished. He grunted as he pulled them on, then stood to stomp them into a good fit. The flat-brimmed black felt hat completed the picture.

A smile came over his face as he slipped into the coat. He tried to give himself the once-over in a small metal shaving mirror, but he couldn't see enough to tell what he really looked like in his new garb. It didn't matter; nobody would give him a second thought in that getup. He stretched his neck. *Guess for what I got from this job I can learn to live with this collar.*

The smile changed into the one that had always been one of his best features. He rubbed his teeth with the tip of his forefinger. He knew exactly how disarming a nice, sincere smile could be in his line of work.

He slipped into the saddle, turned the horse, and circled back around. He rode barely below the ridgeline until he reached a point well behind the group on the road. There he turned Biscuit-eater around to ride back toward them as if on a leisurely ride. As he caught up, he put on the practiced smile and touched his hand to the brim of his hat. "Howdy, folks, kinda hot to be out for a walk, ain't it?"

The people began to complain all at the same time; that is, all except Judy. She stood off to the side, quite above the whole process. She checked her face in a small mirror and patted her hair into place.

Her manner clearly said it was beneath her to have to think about it at all. She saw no reason to be inconvenienced whatsoever. She smiled, *This is men's business, so I'll just let them sort out all of this foolishness.*

Finally, Amos, in his best pastoral garb and manner, waved them into silence. "Whoa, whoa, I think I've got it. This character held you up and ran off with the stagecoach? What nerve." He gestured toward the two in work clothes. "I take it one of you two is the driver?"

Slim said, "Reckon that's me."

"Well, how about you climb up here behind me, and we'll go to town. These other folks can sit down and get a little rest until you can get back for them."

Slim walked toward him. "We may not have to go that far. That jasper said he'd leave the coach down the road a stretch."

"Even better. Here's my canteen, ma'am." He rode over and leaned down to offer the burlap-wrapped container. "Sorry I ain't got no silver cup for you to drink out of."

"Thank you, this will be fine." Judy's eyes met his. He looked so familiar. She knew they had never met before, yet something about him nagged at her.

They both retained their grip on the canteen for a moment, eyes continuing to hold each other. "I'm right sorry for your troubles, ma'am. If I'd been here earlier maybe I might have been able to do something."

How chivalrous. Yet another man with manners after all. She didn't respond aloud but simply gave a small incline of her head to acknowledge the statement. That broke the spell and he released the canteen to sit upright. She analyzed him. He certainly didn't appear to have a woman to look after him, in fact, he looked like an unmade bed. His clothes appeared clean enough, but they needed ironing in the worst possible way. She was sure he must carry them stuffed into his saddle-bags. Still, she admitted he wasn't bad looking.

He turned to ride back to the men, and she shook it off. *Girl, what's the matter with you? Here you are swooning over every man you meet today.*

"You might have been able to do something?" Slim said. "Ain't you some kind of preacher or something?"

"I am."

He snickered. "I don't know what good a preacher would have done."

Amos pulled back his coat to reveal the forty-five strapped on his hip. "I don't believe God requires me to go wandering around unprotected. Well, climb up here, Slim, and let's go get these folks something to ride in."

Slim put a foot in the stirrup, they clasped forearms as leverage, and the big man stepped up behind him. Then Amos realized what he had done.

Perspiration broke out on his forehead. *I can't believe I did that. Nobody said their name 'ceptin when I was here before. They'll know there is no way in the world I would know Slim's.*

Three

Amos glanced from face to face, his smile pasted on. Nobody seemed to notice. Lady Luck had given him another big grin.

Amos carried Slim to get the coach, and they rushed back to pick up the folks. He rode along with them to town. Slim and Wilbur, the shotgun guard, set up a commotion as soon as the coach hit Quiet Valley. People from the stores and saloons filtered into the street. As the stage pulled up in front of the Wells Fargo office, the sheriff came out to see what was happening.

He was a huge man with a badge pinned above the pocket. His once-dark hair, now streaked with gray, peeked out from under a sweat-stained tan hat. He wore his pistol high on his hip and slightly behind him. His face was all business.

Slim spotted him and said, "We was held up, Sheriff Wilson, out by Saddle Rock."

"How many were there?"

"Just one. Cool customer. Ugly as sin, and on us before we knew he was around."

"That's right," the guard said. "Ugly."

Amos squirmed. *Ugly? Who you calling ugly?*

Slim glared at the guard. "I'm telling this."

"Then get on with it."

"One of you better get on with it," the sheriff snapped.

Slim continued. "You won't believe it, Sheriff, but he stole coach and all. We'd have had to walk for miles if this stranger hadn't come along and gimme a lift to get the coach back."

The peace officer's gunmetal gray eyes came to rest on Amos. Amos squirmed inside his clothes. He had seen eyes like that before, only the last time he had seen them, they had been staring out at him from under a rock.

"That you?" the sheriff said in a voice cold as a Panhandle norther.

"Yes sir, Amos Taylor, late of Denver, Colorado. Glad I could help out."

Those eyes penetrated clear to Amos's soul as the sheriff added, "Don't reckon you saw this character?"

"All I saw was these poor souls having to walk in the hot sun."

"Shame you didn't get there a little quicker."

"Funny you should say that, Sheriff. I was saying the same thing to Miss ... ahhhh ... Miss ..."

Judy stepped forward, and all the hats came off as she introduced herself. "Valentine. Judy Valentine."

"I'm sorry, Miss Valentine," Amos said, "it was rude of me not to introduce myself out there."

"It's all right; you were busy."

"Let's get back on the subject," the sheriff said. "You can make your play for Miss Valentine later."

Amos felt his color rise, more so after he saw her hide a small smile behind a gloved hand. He stretched his neck inside his collar as he wondered why he was reacting to her so strongly; she was nothing to him. "Sure thing, Sheriff. I take it you're about to put a posse into the field?"

Safely hidden behind her hand, Judy fought back a laugh. *Is he blushing? Surely not.*

The sheriff stepped in front of Amos, blocking her vision. "You can bet the ranch on that one, and I'll be wanting you with us."

"That's what I was about to suggest." Amos gestured down the road with his hat before he returned it to his head. "I can show you where I found these people, and where the coach was left."

"All right, let's get to it."

Judy said, "Are you through with me?"

Sheriff Wilson seemed to have forgotten she was there. He looked puzzled for a moment, then responded, "Yes, ma'am."

"Then I am eager to get over to my Uncle John's place."

"Yes, ma'am; I'll see your luggage is sent over." He assigned the task to a man with a look and a jerk of his thumb.

The men all touched their hat brims, murmuring pleasantries, then paused to watch appreciably as she began the short walk to the house.

It took only minutes to raise a posse of twenty men. The group included John Lightfoot, a half Kiowa, well known for his tracking skills. A short, stocky man, his dark face looked like leather and had more lines than a shrunken apple. His long black hair, caught up in thick braids, framed a pair of flat black eyes. They peered out from under a floppy black hat. His features made his age impossible to gauge.

The tracker made Amos more than a little nervous. He hid his anxiety as the group rode by where the coach had been left. A little farther down the road Amos pulled up and said, "This ain't right. We've come too far."

They turned around, and Amos led them back. Now the

whole posse had passed twice over whatever tracks might have been left at the site. It would have to do.

"This is it," he said. "I didn't recognize it coming from the back side."

"Too bad," Lightfoot said. "Now tracks are all trampled." If the tracker was suspicious, his stoic features gave no sign of it.

"Sorry about that," Amos lied. "Can you make them out?"

"Don't worry about Lightfoot," the sheriff said. "He's the best there is. He can track a red ant across a rock bed."

That was the last thing Amos wanted to hear. He became even more nervous as it immediately became apparent that Lightfoot *was* every bit as good as the sheriff had said. Lightfoot dismounted and worked his way around the tracks. He quickly found where Biscuit-eater had been left while Amos pulled off the robbery at the stagecoach. "He wears moccasins," Lightfoot said. "He left his horse here."

Lightfoot followed the tracks. "He has ridden all over this area. I cannot tell which tracks came first, when he left, why he rode all over this place. These tracks make no sense." He continued to look around.

He searched the area thoroughly and then came back to the posse.

"You find anything?" the sheriff asked.

Lightfoot shook his head slowly. "I do not know. I find tracks. I trail him to this rock. He followed the group on the road for a while, I do not know why. He went ahead of them and behind them, mixed his tracks with the tracks of the road. I cannot tell you which direction he rode when he left. The tracks are new, they are old, they come, they go, they are everywhere and make no sense. I think he is ghost rider.

He comes and goes at will. I have never tried to track such as he."

Amos tried to disguise a sigh of relief. As long as Lightfoot didn't put it together that the reason the tracks didn't add up was because the horse that made them still stood among the group, he'd be all right. It was a long shot, but it seemed to be working. Still, Amos tried his best to keep most of the group between him and the tracker.

The sheriff removed his hat to wipe his forehead with the back of his hand. The heat had begun to work on all of them. "I'm surprised, Lightfoot. You've never had anybody lose you before."

"I've never tried to track a ghost before. The tracks are jumbled. They come, they go, they disappear."

"Ain't no such thing as a ghost, Lightfoot, but he didn't come into Quiet Valley, or I'd have seen him. If you didn't see where he got off this road, it has to be because he went back to Three Forks. When we get back to town, I'll wire a description to the sheriff there."

John Daniels sat on the porch smoking his pipe. When his niece, Judy, had left to visit her family back in Boston, he wasn't at all sure she would come back. He was inordinately pleased to see her walking toward him now.

John was a habitually pleasant man with unruly gray hair and thick eyebrows that made him look like he was peering out from under a bush. His rumpled clothing had been a long-standing source of irritation to his wife. She continually got onto him for wearing them several days in a row while freshly ironed clothes hung in the closet.

"But I just got them broke in where they're comfortable," he'd say. She didn't go for that excuse.

When he saw his niece walking up, he said what he had been thinking. "Judy, I can't tell you how glad I am to see you. I wasn't sure you'd come back."

His wife, Helen, came bursting through the door to envelop Judy in a hug. "Of course she came back," she said as she pushed Judy out to arm's length where she could look at her. "This is her home now."

"Yes," Judy agreed. "I was surprised to find that was true. I didn't realize it until I started back and found out how eager I was to return."

John motioned for her to take a seat on the porch. "This country does sorta grow on a person."

The ladies sat, and John resumed his seat, struggling to get his pipe going again. "Did you have an eventful trip?" Helen asked Judy. "Tell us about the family."

"That'll have to wait; you'll never believe what happened. We were held up."

John's eyebrows went up. "The stage? Held up, you say?" The match burned down to his finger. "Yeow!" He shook his hand, and blew on his thumb and forefinger.

"How terrible." Helen's face became a mask of concern.

"Actually it wasn't. The man was very nice, in fact more than that, quite charming and chivalrous. I found it all very exciting."

"You're talking about an outlaw as if he was somebody coming to court you," John said. "I don't understand what's going on."

"Yes, I know. It's silly, but it *was* the most thrilling thing that has ever happened to me."

Helen patted her on the hand. "You have led a rather sheltered life, but such thoughts are quite unseemly, my dear."

"Oh no, I'm having no such thoughts. I just didn't know

quite how to react, I suppose. One shouldn't look upon a criminal activity as an adventure, I suppose, but it was really something to experience."

The posse rode back to Quiet Valley where it stopped in front of the rough lumber saloon. They dismounted, used their hats to slap the dust off their clothes as best as they could, then went inside.

The saloon was more than a place to get a drink; in fact, many of those who hung out there didn't even imbibe. No, in small towns west of the Mississippi, it was communications central, offered the only entertainment in town, and often doubled as a courthouse or even housed the church on Sunday. It was a known thing, when men hit a town; the saloon was the first place they'd go to find out what was going on.

The men from the posse stepped up in unison to the bar as the bartender poured drinks. Two dozen sets of spurs ching-ching'd a silvery counterpoint to the tin sound of the piano in the corner. The bartender automatically set a sarsaparilla in front of Amos, who barely remembered his disguise in time. He had come within a hair's breadth of telling him it wasn't what he wanted and ordering red-eye instead.

Amos looked oddly out of place, one black-suited "parson" in the middle of a solid row of dusty cowboys, each of whom expressed his personal individuality by wearing the exact same nondescript garb, the uniform of the working cowhand.

Each stood with one foot on the rail, hat pushed back, shot glass or mug in his left hand, with his gun hand free. No one expected any trouble; it was just how it was done. They moved in unison, as if the whole thing had been choreographed in a Kansas City dance hall.

The bartender was a fat little man who was obviously trying in vain to cover his receding hairline by combing his remaining thin hair up over the top of his head. He leaned on the bar and toyed with the point of his waxed black mustache. "What'd you find, Sheriff?"

Wilson tossed a drink down before responding, shoving his glass back toward the bartender. "Not much, Jack. Lightfoot here figures it's a ghost. I think he either went back to Three Forks, or hid in the hills somewhere. I guess right now I figure it to be the latter."

Lightfoot nursed a glass of water at the end of the bar. As an Indian, he was prohibited by law from joining the men in a round of drinks. "If he had left tracks into the hills, I would have found them." Lightfoot said as he pulled himself up to his full height, upset at the challenge to his tracking ability.

"Don't get your back up now," the sheriff said, holding up a big hand in a conciliatory gesture. "Stands to reason there'd be somebody come along someday you couldn't track. Reckon that time has come, that's all."

Lightfoot glowered, the only discernable expression that had been on his stoic face all day. "Humans leave tracks. Only ghosts can leave them and then stop leaving them at will."

The sheriff smirked slightly, enjoying the uncharacteristic reaction he had provoked. "Yeah, well, be that as it may, I guess I best get over and wire that description. Reckon I'll see you in church Sunday, Parson? When we get a circuit rider through, we generally use our little schoolhouse for services. I'm really looking forward to it."

"Oh, well, I wasn't ... I mean, I'm only passing through."

The sheriff stopped at the door, turned to face him with concern on his face. "You ain't gonna have services? What kind of preacher is it that'll come to a town and not preach to the people there?"

Amos didn't like the look the sheriff gave him. It wouldn't do to have him start to wonder about things. "I just hadn't planned on it. I'm sorry; I didn't realize there wasn't a regular church here. One would think a town this size would have one. Of course, I'll be happy to hold services."

The suspicion left the sheriff's eyes. "That's mighty fine, Parson. Like I said, I'll look forward to it. Be pleased if you'd take supper with the missus and me tonight. Say about six? Anybody can point the place out to you."

"Be proud to, Sheriff."

He watched the big man go through the swinging doors, blocking out the light as he exited. He released the air he hadn't realized he was holding as he decided he'd better hotfoot it out of there. He studied his drink, and his heart sank as the truth of the situation dawned on him. If he ran, the posse would be on his trail at first light and would run him to ground in no time. *I took cards in this game; reckon I have to play out the hand.* He tossed down the rest of the sarsaparilla as if it were hard liquor. *What on earth have I gotten myself into? I've never even been to church, much less preached a sermon.*

Four

Sunday inched closer and closer, yet Amos still didn't have the slightest clue as to how to hold a church service. But he ate well, very well indeed. Feeding a preacher appeared to be not just a duty but a privilege, one that people in town fought over.

If somebody asked him to lunch or to supper, and he'd already been spoken for, they were actually disappointed. They immediately tried to get the next available opening. Amos hadn't been prepared for that kind of a reception, and he found it quite a pleasant surprise.

As a matter of fact, he hadn't had to part with a dime of his newfound wealth yet. Most of it lay buried outside of town along with his so-called work clothes. It wouldn't do to have somebody stumble across that stuff in his room.

No doubt about it, little time remained before the clock ran out. He could sneak out of town in the dead of night, pick up the buried stuff, and run for it. He sighed. *But they'd almost certainly put two and two together, and it would add up to five—five years in the state penitentiary, that is. No, I still have to play out the hand.*

He thought about all of this as he sat in a chair on the porch of the hotel and looked the town over. It wasn't much as towns went, a dozen board-front buildings facing either side of a dirt street. All had board sidewalks in front paralleled by hitching rails made of rough cedar posts, water troughs standing behind several of them. The hotel and the bank had balconies shading the boardwalk, supported by sturdy posts. A sign pointed to Doc Bledsoe's office up the stairs, and another set of stairs led to Colonel Steffen's Land and Investment office. The bank and the jail were more imposing buildings made of red brick.

The jail caught Amos's attention now. Directly across from him, he noticed for the first time an old black man sweeping out the building. He knew who the old man was; he'd heard it around. His name was Joseph Washington, and one would have to say he was definitely black and white. His ebony skin made his white hair, beard, and eyebrows stand out as if they were lit up from within.

Amos had already heard that the man had been completely blind for years, and as he watched him work, he wondered how he knew whether the place even needed sweeping, or even more to the point, whether his sweeping got the job done or not.

The old man hummed as he went about his task, and coughed as the dust flew around him. His spare frame rattled around inside baggy black cord pants, faded until they were more of a charcoal color, and a once-red shirt that now appeared mostly pink.

Joseph worked in the jail in exchange for room and board in the back of the building. He wasn't responsible for the prisoners; the sheriff and his deputies handled that duty. Joseph cooked and helped out around the place. Amos also knew the old man acted as something of an unofficial jail chaplain, testifying to those who were trapped in those cells and couldn't get away from him.

Amos pitied the pour souls, cringing back there in the dark, ducking a barrage of Scriptures and hymns. What a fate, yet maybe he could pick up something from the old man he could use for a sermon. He got up and walked over casually as the old man went back inside.

As he entered the dark jail, Amos saw Joseph preparing lunch in the rear of the building. It was the standard fare; beans and cornbread.

"Joseph, my name is Amos Taylor."

Joseph turned in his general direction. "Yassah, I's heard about you."

He was fascinated watching the old man. "I don't mean to make light of your situation, but I really don't see how a man can cook without seeing what he's doing. How do you know when things are done?"

Before he could answer, one of the prisoners shouted from the next room where the cells were located. "He smells it burning, that's how."

Amos looked back into the dark cellblock, but he couldn't see who spoke.

Joseph laughed. "In a way he's right, Massa Amos. I cooks mostly by nose." He took a wooden spoon and gently patted the inside of a pot. "Hmmmm, no water sound, just beans. These needs water." He added water to the pot until he could feel it near the rim.

Amos pulled a broom straw from a small container by the stove. "I uses a broom straw to see if the cornbread is ready. I can tell by the feel, by how stiff it is. This is about ready." He set it off the stove. "If I cooks some kind of side-meat, I has to go by the smell. I tries to cook the beans just long enough, but sometimes my nose tells me they're cooking too fast too."

Joseph turned in the general direction of the prisoner who

had yelled out and raised his voice, "But these men *are* in here to be punished, and I tries to do my part."

There was some sort of muted grumbling from the back.

"I'd have never guessed a guy could cook without seeing," Amos said.

"Naw sah, I suspect not," said the old man as he wiped his hands on his apron, "but you didn't come over here to discuss my cooking."

"Me?" Amos raised his eyebrows and manufactured a surprised look as he put a hand on his chest. "No, I just stopped in to see the sheriff."

Joseph opened the grate on the big wood stove and used a poker to cut the fire down under the beans. The smell of the burning mesquite wood mingled with the odor of the nearly done beans to make Amos's mouth water.

"How do you know you stirred that fire down enough?"

"Felt the heat, Massa Amos, that's how I does it. Let's step into the front office where we can talk in private."

That suits me. Amos followed him. Now to see if he could cleverly work the conversation around to something he could use on Sunday.

They walked into the office. Joseph poured two cups of coffee, filling them almost to the brim, and set them on the desk without spilling a drop. Just before Amos could ask him how he did that, Joseph turned to him. Something came over his features. The shuffling, deferential black man disappeared. His face took on a confidence, his voice an educated tone, as he said, "Excuse me, Mister, but you just aren't a preacher."

Five

─────────

W ha ..." Amos jumped and sloshed hot coffee into his lap, but that wasn't uppermost on his mind. He was in trouble, big trouble.

Joseph's mannerisms had changed completely. He was in the driver's seat, and he knew it. "Don't bother to deny it," Joseph said. He stood by the little potbellied stove sipping coffee. He looked directly at Amos with a disconcerting gaze, even though Amos knew he couldn't see him. "I also calculate you're the mysterious bandit as well. I think that's why the tracks don't make any sense. Nobody has bothered to take a look at the tracks your horse makes."

Amos was too dumbfounded to talk. "You ... you ... you're ba-barking up the wrong tree." He brushed his lap futilely and made a concerted effort to compose himself. Slower and calmer he said, "Even if you were right, I don't see how a blind man could prove such a thing."

The wry smile on the old man's face told Amos that Joseph could sense his discomfort and rather enjoyed it.

Joseph said, "People who don't have their vision aren't the only ones who are blind. They don't see what is right in front of their faces because a man of the cloth is above suspicion. If I tell them you aren't a preacher, it would take no time at all for them to do the rest."

"What you planning on doing?"

"Nothing at present. I had a long talk with the Lord about it. You see, I'm blessed that way. Most people see my blindness as a curse and feel sorry for me. It is an inconvenience at times, but in return I get to go to God in something much like a big black room totally apart from the entire world. It's just Him and me in there, and I can come out totally secure that I know what He wants me to do."

Obviously, the old man had gone around the bend, but Amos saw no alternative but to humor him. Either that or he had to knock him in the head and make a run for it. In a snap decision he decided he'd better find out what the old man had in mind before he did anything drastic.

Joseph was way ahead of him. "You're sitting there trying to figure out what God told me to do."

Amos slipped the rawhide loop restraining the hammer of his gun. "Maybe. What if I am?"

"God *is* using you here in Quiet Valley. There's a revival going on in this community, and it's because of you."

Amos shook his head negatively and waved his left hand as if trying to ward off the accusation. His right hand stayed on the butt of his gun. "Now wait a minute; I ain't done nothing to make people feel that way."

If Joseph felt any defensiveness, there was no sign of it in his voice. "No, you haven't, but simply knowing you are here has put religion on their minds. Bibles have come out of drawers, and people have started acting more charitable toward each other. It's very true that it isn't your doing; you are deceiving these people, but in spite of your evil intentions God is using you."

Amos knew that nobody ever used him, but if the old fool

wanted to think that way, particularly if it made him keep his mouth shut, he would play along.

"You don't believe that, of course. You figure I'm crazy, but will play along with me as long as I keep quiet."

Whaaat? Amos began to figure the old man for some kind of mind reader, the way he kept coming up with what he was thinking.

"Whatever you have in mind, as long as it serves God's purposes, I'll help you."

"You want me to believe you're serious?" Amos still toyed with the handle of his Colt, continued evidence of the thoughts playing through his mind.

"You want to know how I justify it to myself." He raised one hand, and then let it fall into his lap. "You probably aren't a Bible reader, but if you looked over in Philippians, you would see that it says something like, 'Whether it's in pretense or in truth, Christ is preached; and I therein do rejoice.'"

"You figuring I know what that means?"

"No, I know you don't, but I'll tell you. That was the apostle Paul talking about people who preached in early times. Many preached out of ambition or for selfish purposes, but he said that regardless of the motives, the only important thing was the fact that Christ was being preached."

"And that told you to help me, even though you know I don't believe that stuff?"

"It did. If it was good enough for Paul, it's good enough for me."

Amos let go of the gun. There was no longer any doubt in his mind that the old man was totally crazy but he was also sure the old fool believed in what he was saying too strongly to be a threat right now. "What I think is that you people can read those old words that don't make no sense at all and make them say whatever you want them to say."

"What you think doesn't matter to me right now. As long as God wants me to do so, I'll help. I figure you need it. For example, I suspect you don't have the slightest idea of how to conduct a service or write a sermon."

So much for Amos's cleverly working him around to the subject. "No, you're right. I kinda had in mind to get an idea from you."

"I can do better than that." Joseph pulled an old box from a drawer. It contained a bunch of folded papers. "Before I completely lost my vision I used to write sermons. I always wanted to preach, but of course a white congregation wouldn't sit still for it, and I'm the only black man in these parts."

"That's why you act like a field hand in public?"

Joseph chuckled. "I had hoped I wasn't going *that* far with it, but yes. I fled the South as a youth and got a job as a house-man for an English professor at a high-class northern school. He enjoyed tutoring me at home, so I probably have the equivalent of a college education."

"Why do you hide it?"

"The West is far less bigoted than the Deep South, but even here if whites think a black man is trying to act superior, they just can't help reacting to it. I don't hold it against anybody, it's just the times, but I don't provoke it either."

"Amazing. It takes some getting used to, you talking like a Southern darkie one minute, and some northern banker the next. But don't you think you're overdoing it?"

"You tell me. As I said, I grew up on a school campus; my recollection of the plantation days are pretty shaky."

"Sounds to me like you're overplaying your hand, but it

looks like everyone is buying it, so I guess you're doing all right."

Joseph ran his hand over the papers lovingly. "Getting back to the sermons: I've continued to write them, but I can't guarantee they can be read, as I can no longer see to make them legible. I use my other hand as a marker to try and keep the words straight, but I may be wasting my time."

"You haven't asked anybody to tell you whether you're writing something people can read or not?"

"No one has seen these but me, and now you."

So no one was likely to jump up and yell that Amos was a crook if he presented one at church as his own? *What luck!* Amos said, "Let me look and see if I can find one of the newer ones." He reached for the box, but Joseph didn't release it.

"No, let me. I know where the last one is." Joseph felt around in the box, found his place, and pulled one out. "Here, this is the latest."

"Lemme look." Amos opened it up and glanced down through it. "Well, it's a scrawl, all right, but with a little work I think I can make the words out. You write on top of yourself at times, but not as bad as you might think."

"That's such a relief. I was really afraid the effort had been totally wasted."

Amos ran his fingers through the contents. "All right, so all I need to do is go through here and find a sermon I think I can get through without messing up too bad, then go practice it, right?"

Joseph let go of the box reluctantly. He seemed to be doing it under protest. "You look over one tonight. Tomorrow we'll ride out of town somewhere and you can practice it on me. Now, for the service itself, I suggest you go to Mrs. McAfee and ask her if she'll lead the singing."

"Who's Mrs. McAfee?"

"Widow lady. Big woman with a strong, fine voice, and there is nothing that would please her more. Miss Valentine can play the piano if you'd care to ask her."

Amos got out a little stub of a pencil and wrote on the back of an envelope. "Miss Valentine? The lady that was on the stage?"

"Yes, the one you so gallantly saved. Saved from yourself, that is."

Amos smiled as he realized that meant he'd get to see her again. Amos licked the point of the pencil and made the notation. "All right, I'll ask them. What else?"

"Jed Bigelow over at the bank, and Sam Witherspoon at the general store generally act as deacons when a circuit rider comes through. They'd be that full time if we had a real church. Anyway, they'll be happy to act in that capacity. You can call on them to pray since I expect you aren't too good at it. They'll also pass the plate."

Amos frowned, "Pass the plate?"

"You've never even been to a church, have you? I can't help but wonder if I'm doing the right thing. Still, I have to trust that God knows what He's doing."

The old man let out a sigh. "They will pass an offering plate and give you money for the pleasure of having you defraud them. You won't have to hold a gun on them or anything. And they'll go away feeling better after they've done it."

He raised his hands in a futile gesture, then let them fall as he sighed. "Under the circumstances, I know that's not right, but everyone would know something was wrong if it didn't happen. At any rate, you need to ask those two gentlemen to help."

Amazing. Free room and board, and now they're going to give me money as well? This is too good to be true. It's the best dodge I've come across yet.

Six

Marcie McDonald, daughter of the co-owner of the M Bar B ranch, came barreling into town with her pony at a dead run. She had only two speeds, full out or dead stop. The sheriff waved his hat for her to slow down as she sped by. She responded with a wave and a show of some of the whitest teeth in the territory. They appeared even brighter surrounded by her tan face, flecked with a million freckles her mother had always told her were angel kisses.

Marcie could ride and rope with the best of them, and wore tight pants that turned every head on the street. The women cluck-clucked because ladies were not supposed to wear pants, and the men looked because, well, there was no doubt why they looked.

She slid the little horse to a stop so fast that he nearly sat down, hopping off his back in the same motion to tie him to the hitching rail at the Daniels' house. Her best friend Judy sat on the porch.

"Marcie, some day you're going to run somebody down in the street." Judy's smile said the scolding was not serious.

"I try my best." Marcie bounced up the step to flop down in the rocker beside her friend. "Besides, I was in a hurry."

"Why?"

She sat forward and put a hand on the arm of Judy's chair

to stop it from rocking. "You know why. In a holdup? Face to face with a genuine desperado? And you sit there like Sunday-go-to-meeting? I want to know all the details."

Judy's reserve broke, and she became as animated as her friend. "Oh, Marcie, it was delicious. He was dark, and mysterious, and had eyes like a pirate or something."

"Weren't you afraid?"

"No, that's what's so amazing. It was as if he sent me a message with those eyes. I knew I had nothing to fear from him. He was absolutely charming, and had wonderful manners."

"We don't get much of that around here."

"How true, and his voice was soft and smooth, and he just sort of drawled the words."

"Oh, I'm so jealous."

"You're jealous of my being held up? People would think we were both crazy."

"Wouldn't they though?" Both erupted in laughter.

Sunday. Excitement sparked in the air like static electricity. People paraded around like a flock of peacocks in their best finery, greeting one another, seeing and being seen. Amos figured the hullabaloo didn't have as much to do with going to church as it did the opportunity to get dressed up and do something different for a change.

The air in the church presented a nasal bouquet. The ladies smelled of perfume, and the men had fresh haircuts splashed with spicy hair tonic. The floral scents all blended together into a sweet aroma impossible to classify. Amos sucked up a nose-full as everyone settled into their places.

It wasn't a full-time church. The blacksmith, Jeff Walker, had designed it as a combination school/meeting house/church/courtroom all in one. He had made the tables that the children worked on in school to swing to the rear to make backs on the benches. They were in the bench configuration at present, and they performed that role nicely.

Amos looked over the people as they settled into their places. *Pass the plate, eh? Well, if they're going to pay for a show, I'll certainly give them one.* He paced the floor behind the crowd, getting ready to make his entrance.

Mrs. McAfee opened the service and led those assembled in several old favorites, as Judy played the piano.

Mrs. McAfee turned out to be a generous-sized woman who used no music, so she obviously knew the songs by heart. Her rust-colored dress and matching hat adorned with a single big feather put Amos in mind of a large setting hen, cackling instead of singing.

Instead of thinking about what he would be speaking on, Amos found his attention wandering to Judy as she played. Dressed more simply than she had been on the stagecoach, she wore a long brown skirt and a white blouse with frilly lace down the front. She was a pretty lady, and he wondered what he'd have to do to get her interest. He forced his mind back to the business at hand. A rolling stone like him had no business paying heed to such things.

After the hymn singing, banker Bigelow stepped to the front. A rotund man with pork-chop sideburns, he had jowls that jiggled when he shook his head, making a point. He nevertheless presented a very dignified picture.

Bigelow began to pray, and pray, and pray ... on and on ...

Amos thought the man would never quit. Still he had to admit it worked out well when he saw the amount of money going into that plate.

So far he'd been able to duck praying except when he went for a meal. Everybody always wanted the preacher to return thanks. Fortunately, he had heard the same old tired prayer at the boarding house where he used to live to the degree that he could parrot it as well as the lady who ran the place.

Finally it came time for him to perform. Joseph had prepared him well, and Amos strode up the aisle to the front feeling very confident. He did wish Joseph could have been there, but the old man wouldn't come. He said he knew his place.

Amos took hold of the podium in both hands, Joseph's notes in front of him. He looked over the group, taking charge of them with his eyes. Only then did he look down to read.

"I'll be taking my text this morning from 1 Corinthians 13:13: 'And now abideth faith, hope, charity, these three; but the greatest of these is charity.' This chapter is known as the love chapter, and the use of the word 'charity' is best translated as the word 'love.'"

He went through some of the verses Joseph had given him, substituting the word "love" for the word "charity" as the old man had suggested. He paced the front and explained the passages as they had been explained in the paper.

He'd always been able to handle a group of people in a convincing manner, but now he used the power of his voice as Joseph had shown him to do. He brought it up from deep down in his diaphragm and put a quiver into it to get the full effect. It echoed back from the back of the room at the end of each sentence. He knew it sounded good.

He went on to quote verse 3, "And though I bestow all my goods to feed the poor, and though I give my body to be burned, and have not charity, it profiteth me nothing."

There, he thought, *that ought to keep the free meals coming.* He kept pounding on love thy neighbor and applying the Golden Rule.

"I'd like to finish up by going to John 15:17: 'These things

I command you, that ye love one another.' That says it all. We need to concentrate in the coming week on being charitable and loving one another." Amos looked over at the storekeeper. "Mr. Witherspoon, will you dismiss us?"

Witherspoon prayed from where he was, a much shorter prayer. Amos thought he was probably starting to get hungry. While the merchant prayed, Amos moved silently to the back door as Joseph had instructed, to be ready to shake hands with everyone as they left. As they did so, they all said complimentary things about the message. Amos knew that would please Joseph.

Judy came out toward the end of the line. Amos said, "Thank you, Miss Valentine. You did a mighty fine job on the piano."

"You are quite welcome, and I was very impressed with your message as well. It was a fine sermon. You know, I don't know if anybody has ever mentioned it or not, but you sound much more refined when you are preaching than you do in your everyday talk."

He realized that he had better start paying attention, before she started getting suspicious of him. It was hard to read the words of someone else without it sounding like him though. He put it out of his mind. They weren't likely to put the words together with the old man since he was an illiterate Negro, as far as the people in town knew. "Yes, people have said that on occasion. All I can figure is I do a better job with words if I have the time to write them out, and study on them, instead of pulling them right off the top of my head."

"Interesting. Well, however it works, it was a wonderful message."

Bigelow echoed the sentiment from behind her, "It was a wonderful message indeed." With his handshake, he pressed the offering into the hand Amos offered. As the banker stood last in line, the con man began to relax, thinking he had pulled it off. Then Bigelow said, "Yes, a fine message, Brother Amos, but I was most surprised that you didn't have an altar call."

Altar call? What's that? Joseph didn't tell me anything about no alter call. He said, "I just figured this to be kind of a get-acquainted meeting. I felt it could wait."

"I see. Interesting. I didn't know preachers ever passed up an opportunity to win souls."

Win soles? What does the bottom of my boots have to do with anything? It may be important though, so I reckon Joseph and I have a lot more talking to do. "Normally I wouldn't pass up the chance either. I just followed what the spirit told me to do." He knew a guy could do anything as long as the spirit told him to do it, whatever the spirit was.

Bigelow looked unconvinced, but let it pass. "Perhaps you're right. Well, we do have some likely candidates for conversion here, Parson. I'm sure before you leave town that you'll treat us to a little hell-fire and damnation and see if we can't make them get right, eh?" He poked Amos in the ribs with his elbow and winked.

To Amos it was as if the banker spoke some sort of foreign language. "I'm sure I will."

The Carson family had invited him for Sunday dinner, but it would have to wait. Amos rushed directly over to the jail. As soon as he saw Joseph, he immediately said, "What's an altar call?"

Joseph stopped shelling peas into the bowl in front of him, "Something you aren't entitled to do since you aren't ordained."

Amos opened the restraining collar. "Well, I'm going to have to do it or get out of town."

"All right." He went back to his peas as he considered his answer. "Actually, I suppose it isn't a preacher who saves anyone, but God Himself. A servant of the Lord can only show how, then when it gets right down to it, it's between the sinner and the Lord."

"Whatever. You know I don't understand any of that stuff. You gonna show me how to do it or not?"

"In for a penny, in for a pound. I think I can come up with a compromise that'll work and not be too hard on my conscience."

"And I've been asked to serve up a little hell-fire and damnation."

"That one is easy enough. Plenty of that in the box."

"So I've got no problem at all. I only have to take words somebody else wrote, make people think they're mine and I know what I'm talking about, and deliver them like I believe 'em heart and soul?"

"That's about it."

"Well, that's no big deal for a high-stepper like me."

"If you say so."

Seven

Judy and Marcie walked home together after the services. Judy's mother would have said they were "lollygagging." The exaggerated slowness of their pace made their skirts sway in unison.

"What do you think about the new preacher?" Marcie glanced at her friend.

Judy measured her words. "He's nice. He rescued us after the holdup, you know."

"So you said. That isn't much. Why do you make me drag it out of you?"

Judy busied herself smoothing imaginary wrinkles from her skirt. "What can I say? He has this ability to put people at ease. It was the most amazing thing. From the very first moment I met him, I had this overwhelming feeling we had met before, which of course we couldn't have. That must be a very useful gift in his profession."

Marcie stopped and turned to face her friend as she caught up both of Judy's hands in her own. "You aren't interested in him? He's very cute."

Judy shook her head, affecting an air of indifference. "Don't be silly. He's a man of the cloth. His only interest in me is as a member of his flock."

Marcie smirked, "I saw the way he looked at you, and he wasn't thinking about the condition of your soul."

Judy pulled away. "Oh pooh, I don't even think preachers marry."

"I think it depends on what branch or, oh that's not the right word ..."

"Denomination?"

Marcie nodded and pointed a finger. "Yes, I think that's it. It depends on what denomination he is."

Mischief shone in Judy's eyes. "If I didn't know better, I'd think you were interested yourself."

Marcie blushed, but it could hardly be seen for her tan face. "Now you're the one being silly; you know I'm spoken for."

"I'm just teasing, but it doesn't matter. I don't think of him like that. Now come on, we had better get on home before Helen starts to worry."

"Like anything could happen in this hayseed town."

Amos had gotten up in a good mood. It still lingered. This was a sweet deal, no doubt about it. There couldn't be any better cover for him to work out of. He just had to be sure he didn't pull anything too close to home.

He had been ready for his next job for some time, waiting for all the pieces to fall into place. He had targeted two brothers in a neighboring town who were arrogant enough to think they could see something nobody else could see, rich enough to be worth the time, and greedy enough to bite at the bait he would offer.

The Prescott brothers, Marcel and Leroy, fit the bill to the letter, but they couldn't be approached directly. Amos knew that wouldn't work. No, for this dodge to work they'd have to sniff out the opportunity themselves and spring their own trap, or they wouldn't go for it at all. They had to think they were taking *him* for a ride.

The things they owned was the main key to the whole dodge, and between them they pretty much owned the little town of Dustin, Texas. They had the bank, a big ranch, the hotel, two saloons, and the town newspaper. Rumors of railroad expansion had started to circulate all over the state, and that was what Amos had been waiting for in order to set his carefully crafted little plan in motion.

To work, it had to be carried out quickly, in little more than an overnight stay in town, and executed flawlessly. Amos knew he was just the guy to get it done.

Amos rode into town slowly, the few people in evidence on the boardwalks eying him curiously. It was a board front town not unlike most every other he had ridden into except most of these fronts had the name Prescott on them. Amos wondered why the name of the town itself wasn't Prescott and decided it wouldn't be long before it would be.

The hotel was the only two-story building, with a porch down the entire front and a railing for those who came out on it from the second floor. He dismounted, tied his horse with a quick flick of his wrist that wrapped the reins around the post several times, and entered the hotel. He arranged for his horse to be taken to the stables later that evening, then focused on his plan. Success involved a series of steps, each building on the other. Step one was getting settled into a room.

He checked in under an alias, purposefully evasive and mysterious. He was sure he had raised the curiosity of the desk clerk. He counted on it. It was necessary before the plan could progress further.

He knew people like the Prescott brothers wouldn't like anything going on in their town they didn't know about, particularly some stranger on unknown business. That had to add up to the desk clerk looking through his stuff. Amos counted on that as well.

His valise now held a set of carefully manufactured surveyor's field notes. The notes very strongly suggested three proposed routes for a new railroad. He hid the valise behind the bed where it was sure to be found. The bait was in the trap.

Amos picked a loose thread off his new blue suit as he headed down to the hotel bar. Stage two of the plan required him to get falling-down, loose-mouth drunk, or at least appear to be. He needed a place to sit where he could dispose of drinks and appear to be drinking much more than he really was. A large and very ugly potted plant in the corner fit the bill. The alcohol he was about to dump in there wasn't going to do that monstrosity any good, but it would be a small loss.

An hour later, the plant had consumed five drinks. Amos had actually nursed down maybe a total of one. He started weaving in his chair. He'd played this scene before, and he was good at it. Out of the corner of his eye he saw Marcel Prescott in the lobby talking with the desk clerk. The clerk's hands were animated, but they soon came to bear, pointing out Amos in the adjoining bar. The bait was taken. Now to set the hook.

Prescott had jet-black hair and a black, heavily waxed mustache. The buttons on his vest strained at their task, yet he didn't give the impression of being fat. He approached the table and said, "Mr. Smith?"

"No, i'sh Jim Anderson." Amos made an exaggerated effort to snap his fingers and failed. He made an effort to put a finger in front of his lips to indicate silence, but missed by half his mouth. "I forgot. Thesh trip I'm going by that name. Sssshhh. Don't let it get out."

Amos made another exaggerated gesture, motioning toward the chair, mimicking the act of nearly losing his seat in the process. "Be my guesh."

Two hours of carefully manipulated slips and maneuvering, and Amos managed to have the big man convinced he was an advance man for the railroad, capable of determining the route it would take. It was obvious that Prescott knew how much money was at stake to him, as well as to the town he owned so much of, if the route went across his land. Sure that he had dangled the bait successfully, Amos went to bed.

The following morning Prescott was waiting for him in the lobby. He offered Amos his hand and said, "Good morning, Jim."

Amos took the hand reluctantly, feigning consternation. "Did you call me 'Jim'?"

"Yes, you took me into your confidence last night."

Amos pulled his hand away, retrieved a handkerchief from his coat pocket, and began to wipe at perspiration that didn't exist. "I shouldn't have done that. I'm involved in something that's highly secret."

"Yes, you confided that to me as well."

Amos worked at looking totally distraught. "Oh my, I'm gonna get fired for sure."

Prescott smiled benignly and touched Amos on the arm reassuringly. "Not at all; nobody ever needs to know." He restrained a smile that tugged at the corners of his mouth. Every man had his price, and there was nothing he enjoyed more than finding the price of supposedly upright men and making a profit on it. The price was generally smaller than one would suppose, much smaller. He eyeballed the nervous man in front of him and decided the man would be easier to shear than a spring lamb.

"You'd do that for me?" Amos made his voice border on an outright whine.

"For a consideration."

"What kind of consideration?" Time to dangle the bait slowly, let him set his own hook. Amos could lose him now by overplaying his hand.

"I know you have the power to say which of the three routes marked on your map the railroad will take." Prescott removed the cigar from his mouth and leaned over to take Amos into his confidence. "I'd like to make a case for that middle route."

Amos shook his head. "That middle route is the worst of the three."

"What would we have to do to make it more attractive?"

Amos shrugged his shoulders, "A passel of dirt work, and a trestle over that big gorge so the railroad wouldn't have to do it."

It was Prescott's turn to shake his head. "That would be very expensive. How about if I just made it more attractive to you personally instead?"

"Are you talking about a bribe?" Amos tried to look as offended as he could. "Sir, I'm insulted."

"Would a thousand dollars insult you?"

"That's almost a year's pay, but it'd surely cost me my job when the construction crew made it out here and found out what I'd done."

"But it would be too late to change direction then, wouldn't it?"

"I'm afraid so."

"I thought it might. Then it is just a matter of what it would take to assuage your delicate conscience. Say two thousand dollars? Then you'd have two whole years to find another job."

"This is a good job. I don't know I could find a better one, certainly not after the word got out." Amos was taking a big risk here. If he jumped the price too high, it could ruin the whole deal.

Prescott jerked the cigar from his mouth. "Oh bother, I'll go as high as five thousand, but that's my last offer."

"Sold."

Eight

*F*ive thousand bucks." Amos whispered it to himself as he put the money into his hiding place. That was a suitable road stake. A couple of months for things to cool down, and he'd be Mexico bound. He felt a few years down there, lying in the sun, was exactly what he needed.

The Mexico beach dream was a favorite of his; clear blue water, white pristine sand, and soft tropical breezes. It always included a beautiful senorita to serve him cool drinks and attend to his every desire, and generally it entailed a couple more shapely beauties performing a native dance. *Or maybe Judy?* He wondered how she'd look in one of those Spanish dancer costumes.

He forced himself back to reality. She didn't have any interest in him, and he had no business being interested in her. *I gotta find a way to get out of here.*

The town was quiet as he rode back into Quiet Valley. He saw Joseph making his way down the boardwalk toward the jail, taking periodic references with his cane. The old man seemed totally confident inside his world, the confines of the jail. He was less confident outside where things did not stay in place, and very dependent if he got into an environment he didn't know at all.

A shopkeeper spoke to the old man, "Hello, Joseph."

"Massa Witherspoon, fine day, sah. How is you and yours keeping?" Joseph hunched his shoulders, adopted an ingratiating posture.

"Just fine, Joseph, and you?"

"The Lord is mighty good about taking care of my needs, thank you, sah."

"Fine, Joseph, fine." Witherspoon moved back inside, and the old man continued down the walk.

"You should have been on the stage; you give quite a performance."

"That you, Massa Amos?"

"You know it is."

The old man broke into a wide grin. "You been out riding, Massa Amos?" They went into the jail where Joseph dropped the shuffling steps and walked confidently to hang up his cane.

Amos still hadn't gotten used to watching the sudden transition. "You take me to raise? I been playing cards out at the KY ranch."

"Likely story. You want some coffee?"

He'd have some if it'd make Joseph quit asking questions. "Sure, why not?" He moved over to take the cup, and pull up a chair near the desk.

They had barely gotten seated with the coffee when the sheriff came in with a handful of WANTED posters tucked under his arm.

"Anything new, Sheriff?" Joseph asked.

The sheriff tossed them on the desk and hung up his hat. "Mostly updates on people we've already got. Do have a telegram here from the Prescott brothers over in Dustin."

Amos choked on his coffee. The sheriff stopped to pound him on the back. "You gotta be careful with that coffee,

Preacher. Joseph makes it strong enough to walk around on its own."

"What's their problem?" Amos croaked hoarsely.

The sheriff stopped. "Who?"

"You were talking about the Prescott brothers."

He shuffled through the posters to come up with the one he wanted. "Oh yeah, seems some yahoo held up the bank over there and got away with over fifty thousand dollars."

Amos jumped, then occupied himself wiping hot coffee from his shirtfront with his bandanna. *A bank? Fifty thousand? What a bunch of bull.* "Any idea who did it?" He tried to sound unconcerned.

"Some guy by the name of Jim Anderson," the sheriff read. "Says here he was in town posing as a railroad man, using the name of Smith."

"Sounds like a man who didn't have a lot of imagination."

"Now that's a fact, Preacher; it sure is. You'd think almost anybody could come up with a more original name than that. Well, we got nobody new in town, but I'll keep an eye out." He looked over at the old man. "Joseph, you're mighty quiet today. Got something on your mind?"

"Naw sah, Sheriff, got no business messing in the affairs of white folks."

The old man shuffled toward the back of the building. The sheriff smiled at his retreating back. "It's a game he plays, Preacher. He's the perfect darkie if there's anybody around, just what everybody expects him to be. Would you guess he's probably the best-educated man in town? He plays his part so well most people don't even suspect."

"I'm surprised he told you."

"We're together too much; he just let it slip." He rocked back to put his feet up on his desk.

"Why does he go to so much trouble?"

"He doesn't want folks thinking he's uppity. There are those who would make it mighty hard on him."

"Would they really?"

"I don't know, maybe. But as long as he thinks they will, I guess that's what matters."

"Why what matters, Sheriff?"

"Nothing, Joseph. We were just discussing the preacher's new congregation."

Amos hadn't even heard the old man come back in. He caught his breath as he looked into the sightless eyes. He wondered what the old man knew. Or thought he knew.

Joseph was sitting out back enjoying the sun when Judy approached him. He got to his feet quickly, pulling off his hat. "Good day, Miss Judy."

"You amaze me, Joseph. How in the world did you know it was me?"

"Your scent, Miss Judy. Don't rightly know the name, but I knows it when I smells it."

"Astonishing." Judy and Joseph had been friends almost from the day she arrived. Even at that, he was constantly surprising her. She had shared much with the old man and had found any advice he gave her sound as a five-dollar gold piece.

"Let's go inside, Miss Judy. It's too dusty for me to ask you to sit out here."

"No, it's beautiful out, and this is an old frock. I'll just sit on this bench next to you." She smiled and shook her head as he affected the shuffling walk that he did automatically when he thought someone was watching. "And you can drop your Old Black Joe routine. There's nobody around, and you know I know better."

"No, Miss Judy, I'll sit on this stump." She started to object, but he held up a hand. "It's not you, child; I know there's not a bigoted bone in your body. But you can't understand how it is for me. If I sat over there by you, talking uppity, and somebody came around the corner unexpectedly, it could get bad."

"But I'd tell them ..."

"There'd be no telling anybody anything, Miss Judy. It's just how things are." He listened for her to be seated before he sat back down. "But you didn't come over here for this; you have something on your mind." It was a statement of fact.

"Yes, something is disturbing me. Can we talk about it?"

"Miss Judy, you know you can tell me anything."

She couldn't stay seated. She jumped to her feet and he followed suit. "Yes, I know I can. This is rather personal, though. But sit down, Joseph, I just need to pace a bit."

He sat reluctantly. "Haven't I always kept your confidences?"

"Of course you have. I just don't know how to ..." She stared out at the gently rolling countryside, having trouble composing her thoughts into words.

He understood. "Take your time, Miss Judy. I got all day."

She continued to look off into the distance. As far as she could see was flat prairie occupied only by knee-high sagebrush. Many thought it a barren sight, but she loved it. She forced her attention to squeezing out the words. "I'm having disturbing thoughts about a man."

Joseph cocked his head. "My, my."

She turned quickly toward him. "Oh, nothing improper or anything like that. I just can't get him off my mind."

Joseph gave a soft chuckle. "Nothing wrong with that, Miss Judy. You're at that age."

"But I've met him only once, and I couldn't even see his face then."

Joseph frowned. He had a way of looking at people that made them forget he couldn't see them. "I don't understand."

Judy's eyes dropped to the hands wringing her hanky in her lap. She seemed to have to force the words out. "I can't get the man who held up the stagecoach out of my thoughts."

"Ohhhhh." Joseph thought carefully; this had to be handled exactly right. "Miss Judy, it's not my place to lecture you, but I think you're just a little attracted to the danger in him. Most of us are, you know. We don't want to be genuinely scared, but a little bit of a thrill can be quite exciting."

She shook her head slowly, the intense feelings playing in her mind written on her pretty features. "I thought that too, but I can't quit thinking about it ... about him. Thinking about a bad man like that, it's a terrible thing. I'm so ashamed."

"Nothing to be ashamed of, Miss Judy. It's perfectly natural. You'll put it behind you soon enough."

Her eyes came up slowly. "I thought I might go talk to that new preacher about it." She laid the thought out tentatively, testing it on Joseph.

Joseph got choked and began to cough. She stepped over to pound him on the back.

"Sorry, swallowed wrong," Joseph sputtered. "I don't think that's such a good idea, talking to that preacher."

"Why not? Isn't that what a minister is supposed to do?"

"Well, yes, but ..."

The coughing spell over, she took a few steps away from him, her back still turned toward him as her hands rose in an exasperated gesture. "I'm surprised, Joseph. I expected you to tell me to go see him."

Joseph pulled a rag from his pocket and used it to wipe his forehead. "It's just that he's new in town and all. He doesn't know us, and we don't know him. I think it's best we let him get settled in before we start unloading our troubles on him."

"Are you all right, Joseph?" Something in his voice disturbed her. She turned and stepped over to put a hand on the old man's forehead.

He let out a small sigh; the hand was cool, soft, and silky. He relaxed. "Just not over that coughing spell yet."

"Well, maybe you're right about not talking to him; you usually are. It's just that I felt like I formed a bond with him immediately, like I had already known him or something."

"Things ain't always what they seem, Miss Judy. I think it's best to wait a while."

"If you say so."

Nine

Amos walked into the sheriff's office to find Joseph sitting in a chair by the wall. The chair leaned precariously back against the wall and Joseph's chin rested on his chest. Gentle, almost inaudible snoring sounds came from under the hat pushed down over his eyes.

"Joseph?" Amos said with mischievous force.

The old man jerked awake and came to his feet, pulling the hat from his face to hold it in both hands. "Massa Amos, the sheriff ain't here."

Amos smiled. "You can drop the act; I'm alone."

Joseph put the hat back on his head, displeasure on his face. "I wish you wouldn't sneak up on me like that."

"It's not like I wasn't making plenty of noise; you were really out. Where's the sheriff?"

The sudden awakening still had Joseph a bit out of sorts and he banged around the room straightening up. He swung a hand in a wide gesture, "He's out riding the hills, looking for you; only he doesn't know he's looking for you. Don't you feel bad about that?"

"What I'd feel bad about would be if he *did* know he was looking for me. You haven't changed your mind on our little deal, have you?" Amos took a seat opposite where the old man stood.

The agitation in Joseph's voice came down a notch. "Not until the Lord tells me differently. He must see something in you that I just can't quite make out." He looked down, realized the voice came from a lower point now, and knew Amos had taken a chair.

Amos nodded. "Good. Because I don't think I'm ready to go on the run right now, but don't worry, I'll get out of here as soon as I can. Then you can quit worrying about it all."

Joseph shook his head slowly, "No you won't."

"I won't what?"

"Leave. Whatever God has in mind for you is here. If you try to leave, our deal is off, and I *will* tell the sheriff about you."

Amos released a frustrated sigh; this was wearing on him. He rocked his head back as if looking at the ceiling, but he closed his eyes. He didn't feel up to this verbal sparring. "You're kidding."

"You keep saying that. Rest assured I never kid about God's work." Joseph came over to sit down beside him. The old man walked directly to a chair, and when he put out a hand to check, it was there.

Amos watched his progress. He considered moving a few things around one day, just to see what happened. "You're saying I'm stuck here?"

Joseph sat down. "Until God tells me otherwise."

Amos racked his brain; there had to be some answer to this, some way to get the old man off his back. "What if He tells *me* I can go?"

Joseph nodded. "If I thought He really had spoken to you, and felt you really believed it, it would be great. However, I'd know if it was real, believe me."

"You know, I think you would."

The young girl with the thick spectacles was vigorously massacring the piece she was playing on the piano. Not even close to matching the *tock-tock-tock* of the metronome, even she was aware enough of her shortcoming to glance up at her teacher. Judy had one hand on the piano and her eyes were on the sheet music, but her mind wandered.

Relieved to escape criticism for her errors, the little girl played on.

Images played across Judy's mind. Maybe Marcie was right; the young preacher was quite handsome. Then in a moment the image of the young outlaw replaced it. Her thoughts continually went back and forth between them.

She felt the thoughts running through her head to be silly. She was a respectable woman and had no business thinking about a brigand and a scoundrel. She told herself she was merely reacting to the excitement of the moment. But then her thoughts turned to Pastor Taylor. He had such a pretty smile, and he was so polite. When she thought of him she felt … actually … nothing. The reverend was not exciting. He faded, and the masked man began to come back …

She forced her mind back to the music lesson. Thinking of the two confused her. "Polly, what on earth are you playing?"

Ten

How come I can get everybody in the world to believe everything I say but I can't lie to you for a minute?" The irritation rang clear in Amos's voice.

"I'd tell you but you wouldn't understand." Joseph lifted one hand in a gesture of resignation. "You'll come to understand, though. At any rate, I can't stay hitched to our deal if you continue robbing people. You're going to have to give up the money from the robbery."

Amos jumped to his feet shouting. "In a pig's eye. I'll go pick up the money and go on the run first." *Calm down, calm down,* he told himself. He paced the office, agitated and upset. This was getting him nowhere.

The tirade left the old man unaffected. "They'd have you here in jail by nightfall. You know I'm telling the truth."

Amos forced himself to come to a stop. "You're saying I don't have any choice?"

"You haven't had any choice since God decided to take a hand in your life."

Amos eased into a chair, then sat there thinking quietly. There had to be another way out. He quietly slipped the restraining thong off the hammer of his gun.

Joseph said in a soft gentle voice, "I've lived a long time. I've found over the years that the best way to resist temptation is to try to avoid situations where temptation might occur. With that in mind, I've decided to keep you from being tempted in regard to me."

Amos slipped the weapon from the holster very slowly so it wouldn't make a noise to alert the old man. "I don't understand, not that that's anything new."

If Joseph knew he was in danger he gave no sign of it. "Sooner or later you'll get around to thinking that since I'm the only one who knows your secret, all you have to do is get rid of me."

A crooked smile came to the con man's face. He had news for the old fool: he had already thought about that. He looked out the window. There was no one on the street. There couldn't be any hesitation once he cocked the weapon.

"You're a scoundrel, all right, but I don't believe that's your style. Still, I don't want you burdened with even having it cross your mind."

You're too late on that one. I always thought I could never do this, but it looks like I'm not going to have any choice. He aimed the weapon at the center of the old man's chest, but still didn't cock it. He'd cock and fire it all in one motion. "You're all heart, Joseph. I suppose you wanting to look after your own hide has nothing to do with it?"

Joseph still showed no sign of alarm. "I'm not ready to die, but I'm old, and it wouldn't be much of a loss."

"Just supposing I buy into all this rot, how you figuring to save me from all this temptation?"

A big smile came over Joseph's face. "I wrote out a confession for aiding and abetting a criminal. I told the whole story, my part in it, and what I hoped to achieve."

Amos's stomach fell like a boulder off a cliff. The gun he had been tentatively aiming fell back into his lap. He looked at Joseph's broad grin. The old man loved to do this to him. "I thought you said you weren't going to tell."

"I did agree to that, but if I'm no longer alive, then I figure that releases me from the pledge. The confession is in the bank vault and I left instructions to open it only in the event of my death."

Amos sat on the edge of his seat. "But you're blind."

"Thank you for the reminder, but it was you who confirmed that I could still write well enough for someone to read it. I appreciate the help, and the tip."

"Tip?"

"Yes, I wrote it using a ruler to keep the lines straight and to keep myself from writing words on top of each other."

Amos slid the gun back into the holster. Joseph heard the sound, and knew it for what it was. He smiled.

Amos felt ridiculous. He might as well have written the thing for him. "But you're an old man; what if you die of natural causes?"

"Then you may be assured I won't be turning you in, and with luck you may have a day or so before the folks at the bank remember to open my letter. If I were you, though, I wouldn't take the time to attend my funeral."

"Oh yeah, a lot of good it'd do me to run. If I turn over that money, I won't even have enough left to get me out of town."

"Well, maybe you are right. Maybe you don't have any choice right now."

Amos slammed the door on the way out of the sheriff's office, and walked slowly back to his hotel room. Safely behind a closed door, he eased himself down on the bed and began to stare at the ceiling. He crossed his arms on his forehead.

He realized the old man was right. He had always been the guy who could pull the wool over anybody's eyes, and here he was at the mercy of an old blind man. And there didn't seem to be a thing he could do about it.

Amos nodded off. It was almost dusk when a loud voice woke him up. Someone in the hall was ordering the desk clerk to open rooms. "I shouldn't be doing this, sir."

The voice was a low growl, ominous. "You just shut up and don't make me hurt you."

Amos slipped under the bed just as the key hit the lock and the door opened. He looked over at his holster hanging on the chair-back across the room. *That was dumb.*

"Who stays here?"

Backlit in the doorway, Amos could just make out the unmistakable form of Leroy Prescott.

"Preacher by the name of Amos Taylor."

"Preacher, eh? What does the guy look like?"

The wiry little man, who supported his drinking habit by swamping out the hotel rooms and the saloon, stood so that he was between the big man and a view under the bed. Amos knew he hadn't positioned himself that way by accident. "Old man, gray hair and beard, don't see too good."

"No, that's not him either."

The door closed and Amos eased out from under the bed. That had been close. He didn't know why the swamper had shielded him or given the man that off-the-wall description, but Amos made a mental note to make it worth his while.

The next day, Amos rented a buggy and hitched Biscuit-eater to it. As Joseph had demanded, he picked up the old man to take him to where his stuff was buried.

Once they arrived at the spot outside town, Amos got down

and started emptying the hole. He had a plan; he'd just give Joseph a fist full of the money and tell him that's all of it. After all, there was one job the old man didn't even know about.

Amos picked up a handful of the money and started to get up to give it to Joseph. A hand on his shoulder stopped him. The old man knelt beside him and said, "You overlooked a little money there in the bottom."

"So I did; how'd you know? It ain't like you saw it."

"I don't know, but I'm sure it was just an oversight." Joseph knelt to remove the money, then felt the clothes. "What are these? Must be your outlaw clothes." Joseph picked up the clothes, cleaned out the hole, then stood up. "You better fill that in so some horse doesn't step in it and break a leg."

If Amos wasn't sick before he went, the sight of all that money getting away from him was going to make him that way. He saw Mexico flying away like a giant bird.

When they got back to town, Joseph told the sheriff a tale about a man who had found the money and come to turn it in. The sheriff took the clothes over to the Wells Fargo office and established the fact that they were the ones worn by the masked man.

The sheriff immediately sent Lightfoot out to track the man Joseph had told him about, and the Indian turned despondent when the horse's tracks didn't tell him what he wanted to know. Lightfoot then became dead sure the man was a ghost, only playing tricks on them. When he returned he was highly agitated, speaking with exaggerated gestures.

"Do you not see?" Lightfoot said. "The money is the key. Ghosts have no use for money so the spirits returned it. He toys with us. I track him no more."

As soon as he heard it, Amos thought that part to be funny,

nearly worth the money he'd had to give up. Almost as quickly as the thought came into his head, he knew it wasn't true. Nothing would make him feel good about losing that money. That left him with nothing but what he'd gotten from the collection plate. *That ain't gonna do it, so it's time to figure a way out of this mess.*

Eleven

*A*mos woke up with Joseph on his mind. *So that old bird thinks he's got me boxed in, huh? He puts his little confession over in the bank vault, and I'm supposed to roll over and do every weird thing he thinks up for me to do? He doesn't know me very well.*

That left Amos with only one chance he could see. He had to fool that old black man, to make him think he'd gotten religion. Somehow he had to convince Joseph that he had gotten a message straight from God to go to Mexico and do missionary work, or something equally ridiculous.

It wouldn't be easy. At times Joseph seemed to be able to see right into his head. That scared him more than anything.

It was clear that needed to be the plan, but how did he start? He decided he needed to get a Bible. Before he could fool Joseph at all, he had to be able to talk the lingo.

Suddenly there were three sharp raps on the door. Amos answered it to find Joseph standing there in the hall. The old man had a Bible in his hands. A shiver ran through Amos, and he got a prickly feeling on the back of his neck. "I wish you'd quit that."

"Quit what?"

"Reading my mind. Don't tell me you can't do it, either. It wasn't five minutes ago that I decided I needed to get me a Bible, and here you are. This is getting plumb scary." The lack of color in Amos's face testified that he wasn't kidding; he was completely unnerved.

Joseph smiled. He couldn't see Amos's sallow complexion, but he could hear the subtle difference in his voice. He knew what it meant. He enjoyed keeping Amos off balance. "All of a sudden it popped into my head that I needed to bring you a Bible. I knew it had to be this one."

Uninvited, Joseph walked into the room, felt with his cane until he found the bed, and seated himself.

Amos closed the door and turned to face him. "God told you, I suppose."

"I didn't say that, though it wouldn't surprise me to find He'd placed the thought in my mind. He does that more than we know."

Amos looked at his feet and shook his head. "I guess He floats into your room on a white cloud to give you the word."

Joseph chuckled, "I never said any such thing. I've never heard God's voice, never seen a burning bush, nor heard a proclamation from the sky. God speaks to me through thoughts He places in my head or through feelings He puts in my heart. Still, I know when it is He who has put them there."

Amos plopped into the chair. The motion caused it to swing back. The holster hanging on it swung back also, and the gun butt caught him on the elbow. He grimaced and let out an oath as his whole arm went dead. He glanced at the old man. Joseph gave no sign of hearing.

Amos rubbed his elbow gingerly as he said, "I don't know what you're talking about with burning bushes, voices in clouds, and all that bull." His exasperation showed in his voice as he tried to make the feeling come back. He made an effort to compose himself. *This guy is gonna drive me nuts yet.*

"No, I know you don't know what I'm talking about, but

read in this and you will." Joseph showed him a very old, worn Bible.

"Well, I can see why you're ready to give that away; it's used up. Not that you can read it any more anyway."

Joseph cradled the book in his arms. "You don't understand. Other than the clothes on my back, this is the only thing I own. I learned my letters from it, back before my eyes failed me. It was my mother's, and her mother's before her. They both had to hide it because slaves weren't supposed to know how to read anything, much less own a Bible. It is the most precious thing I own. I would rather cut off my right arm than give it to someone like you."

Amos shook his arm, the tingling about gone. "Yet here you are doing that very thing? You're right, I don't get it."

"God has apparently decided you are worth saving. He has something for you to do and has ordained me to deliver you to Him."

Amos resolved that would never happen, that he'd have himself put away before he got as crazy as Joseph. Then he remembered the plan and curbed his tongue.

"You don't believe me, I know," the old man said. "It doesn't matter. He commands, and I serve. Since you are such an unbeliever, I have to use my strongest weapon, and this is it." He still held the Bible firmly in his grasp. "Before I give it to you, I have to tell you about it."

The frustration gnawed at Amos as he wondered how much of this he was going to have to put up with. Now he was not only faced with reading a book written in words that didn't even make sense, but he had to get the whole spiel from Joseph before he'd get the book. With an effort he resigned himself; listening to the old fool was better than listening to a judge saying he was guilty as charged.

Joseph motioned for Amos to sit with him. "This is not just a book. It's pure, concentrated faith. I told you who owned it. This book was in those ladies' powerful hands as they prayed sons and husbands out of sin and into grace."

Joseph held the book out in front of him in both hands. He looked at it as if he could see it. "It's been read over loved ones, and that faith has spilled over on this book in a mother's tears. It has the names of generations recorded in it, with the love that can be felt only for a newborn child recorded in each line. By some names you'll see the word 'deceased,' and it is nearly always close to illegible, as the hand that recorded it was infirm, either from age or from the throes of sorrow."

Rubbing the cover lovingly, he said, "I've seen this book in the hands of my own mother and father as they knelt by my sister's side and prayed for her as she died. When we ran from slavery, my mother only had two hands, so she grabbed up my brother with one and this Bible with the other. That kind of faith is so solid that it's tangible. It has seeped into the pages of this book until you can feel it, right through the cover. You can resist me, but you can't resist what's in this book."

He handed it slowly to Amos. Amos felt a shiver go up his back and the hair on his neck stand up. He told himself it was just his imagination acting up.

Tears glistened in Joseph's sightless old eyes. *This is costing him, costing him a lot,* Amos found himself thinking.

"Thanks," Amos said. "I'm sorry. I didn't know what it meant to you or I wouldn't have made light of it. I'll just need it for a little while. I'll take good care of it and I'll get it back to you."

Joseph stood and shook his head vigorously. "No, I don't want it back in dishonor. If you're ready to give it to me and don't understand, then I've failed and I don't deserve it. If you respond to God's bidding, then it will be a powerful tool in your hands, and I want it to stay that way."

Amos shook his head. Joseph had been pulling him into his net and he had been falling for it. He had to get hold of himself. *What's the matter with me? I feel sorry for the old man, and he up and spouts this wild stuff again. I know what he's up to. Not only does he read minds, I bet he can place thoughts there too. Maybe he's some kind of witch. I gotta get away from this nut as soon as possible, before he makes me crazy too.*

Twelve

Amos lay on the bed trying to decipher some of Joseph's writings. He wasn't having much luck because his mind kept straying to ... he looked up, hearing soft footsteps on the carpet outside. Someone had stopped outside his door.

Judy stood in front of the door to Amos's room, mustering the nerve to knock.

Amos pulled the door open, causing her to gasp, hand poised in midair. He had been sitting there thinking of her, and there she was. "Thought I heard someone stop outside my door."

"I need to talk to you."

Amos stepped out and closed the door behind him. "We'd best go down to the dining room. It wouldn't look right for you to come into my room." The words were hardly out of his mouth before he wondered where they had come from. Since when did he care what people thought?

Shaking his head, he took her elbow and guided her toward the stairs. "No, I suppose it wouldn't," she admitted. "I guess the dining room would be all right. The matter is rather confidential."

"Don't worry," he said softly. "We'll get off to the side where we won't be overheard."

There were few people in the dining room and the pair had

little trouble distancing themselves from everyone else. Nothing was said until they were seated with a cup of coffee for Amos and a cup of tea for Judy. Amos waited for her to broach the subject.

She looked into the bottom of her cup for some time before she said, "Reverend, I need some counseling. I can't get a man out of my mind."

Galloping horseflies, is she going to confess her sins to me? Amos had no idea if listening to confession was part of this job. If it was, he wondered what he was supposed to do when she did it. That Spanish priest at that little mission where he watered his horse had sprinkled water, or waved his necklace, or done something. Was that what he was supposed to do?

"I'm listening," he racked his brain for a clue.

She sipped at the cup with little interest. "I don't want you to get the wrong idea. It's not like I've actually done anything; it's just that I can't seem to get a man out of my mind no matter how hard I try."

He relaxed. *Is that all it is?* "I see. That doesn't sound like much of a problem to me; we all get people in our heads now and then that we can't help but remember."

She lost interest in even pretending to drink the tea as she clasped her hands on the table in front of her. "This is different; it's someone I shouldn't be thinking about at all. I'm fixated on a man who is evil, an outlaw."

Amos felt his temper rise suddenly, unexpectedly, as he thought about an outlaw bothering a sweet little dumpling like Judy. He wanted to say, "You tell me who it is and I'll see he don't walk without a limp for years." Instead, he said, "Well, of course that's different. Is it somebody I might know?"

"Of course not, though you might have made his acquaintance if you had come along a little earlier the other day."

He slid forward in his chair, arm on the table. He looked as if he were about to take flight. "The other day? You mean at the holdup?"

She looked around quickly. Several people were looking their way. "Please keep your voice down."

He glanced around furtively, then again relaxed back into the chair. At least his body relaxed. His eyes told a different story, like an animal seeing a way to escape. He purposely took the edge off his voice. "I'm sorry. Are we talking about the holdup?"

"Yes." Her hands dropped from the table, into her lap. She looked at them as if they weren't connected to her, as if she wondered what they were doing.

It allowed him to study her face. She was beautiful. "So this outlaw is ..."

"The man who held up the stage."

It was his turn to sip at his cup without seeming to care. His mind raced. Here he thought she wasn't interested in him at all, but it was only because he had a competitor. Himself.

He tried to study her eyes, but she wouldn't look at him. "I see, and you can't get this masked man out of your mind?"

"I don't seem to be able to." She reached across to put a hand on his and made brief eye contact. "Parson, is that a sin?"

"Thinking about someone a sin? If we had to account for everything we thought about, we'd be in serious trouble, wouldn't we?"

Her features knitted into an expression of concern. "But I thought God knew all our thoughts, and that we *were* account-able for them."

Yeah, like some God knows what's going on in my head, but I better play the game. "Well, of course, I didn't mean it like that. I meant God knows we're human, and I figure He makes allowances for that."

She looked down again, embarrassed to be talking about this with a man, even if he was a minister. "Of course He does. I should have counted on His forgiveness."

Whatever that meant. Still, if she was happy with that answer, he'd leave well enough alone. There had to be some way he could take advantage of the situation though. "Yes, we should always count on His forgiveness. Now, tell me about this masked man. What is it about him that's getting you so stirred up?" He wanted to make sure he did more of whatever his rival had done, only did it as himself.

"I think it was the way he looked at me. His eyes communicated so much; they told me I had nothing to fear, they told me he desired me." Her hand went to her mouth as her cheeks flushed red. "Oh, I shouldn't have said that, not to a man of the cloth."

"Never fear, I'm a man before I'm a preacher. So he talked to you with his eyes?" That completely fascinated him; he didn't know he could do that.

She looked up at him without raising her head. "Yes, just as you can. Sometimes your eyes remind me of his. They inspire trust."

Whoa, I didn't think of that. Here he had been working hard to make just the kind of eye contact she was talking about, and it had turned back on him. He realized that could be big trouble; he'd better get things shut off quickly before she went too far down that trail. "Well, I'm enjoying our talk, but I'm supposed to go meet some folks. I hope I've been of some help." He stood and offered his hand.

She stood and took it, slightly confused by the abrupt

change. She had embarrassed him by talking of such things. Joseph had been right; she shouldn't have come to him.

He held on to her hand a bit too long, and she finally had to withdraw it as she said, "I think you have. Thank you." She made a hasty retreat.

He watched her go, then remembered he needed to go through Joseph's scribblings to find something for a sermon. Reluctantly he headed back to his room.

He began by lying on the bed reading the Bible aloud, beginning with Genesis 1:1: "In the beginning God created the heavens and the earth."

Amos told himself it wasn't possible to go back any further than that. He smirked as he realized he had never given any thought as to where this old earth came from. It had just always been here. He didn't think he could swallow the idea of a God who could simply wave a hand and make everything about him out of nothing. But he resigned himself to the fact that he needed to be able to convince Joseph that he *did* believe it, every screwy word.

Amos read for a couple of hours as he nibbled on some fried potato skins he'd wheedled the cook downstairs into making for him.

Adam and Eve, Cain and Abel, Noah and the flood; Amos snorted, "This thing is a storybook." He lowered it and began to think out loud. "How come nobody told me about all this? I could do some great shows with this stuff, and that's all this preaching business is, a show."

It did look a lot safer to him than sticking up a stage, and though the money wasn't all that good, living expenses were very cheap. He realized a guy could probably do all right in this business. He looked up at the ceiling as he considered it. If he got a really good performance put together and took it to the big city, those collection plates would probably overflow.

Amos put the Bible aside. To be ready on Sunday, he had to find a little hell-fire and damnation. He pulled out Joseph's papers and found a sermon labeled "The Road to Hell." *That sounds like just the ticket.*

Joseph had the Bible passages written out, but something about actually finding them in the book made them somehow feel different. Amos decided that from now on he'd look them all up. It'd be good practice.

He hefted the Bible, amazed by its weight, and pictured himself using it. In his mind's eye, he saw himself standing up in front of a crowd waving it around as he preached. It would be great theater. It'd also be very convincing.

He opened the Bible to look for the first quotation in the sermon. "All right, Revelation 20:13-15," he mumbled aloud. "Where's the index? Whoa, look at this, there's a book of Amos. This book can't be all bad. I have to read that one when I get through with this one.

"Here it is, almost at the end of the thing. Let's see, 'And the sea gave up the dead which were in it; and death and hell delivered up the dead which were in them: and they were judged every man according to their works. And death and hell were cast into the lake of fire. This is the second death. And whosoever was not found written in the book of life was cast into the lake of fire.'

"Lake of fire? That has to be what Bigelow talked about. This story is a lot more powerful than the story about a big boat some guy knocked together, or a big fish spitting somebody out. Can't imagine anybody who'd believe that could really happen. Sure hope I can keep a straight face as I do this stuff."

Thirteen

*I*t was Sunday, and the hour of the service had arrived. The strains of the music died out, jarring the wandering attention of Amos back to the business at hand. Mrs. McAfee called on Deacon Bigelow to do the opening prayer.

Amos calculated that meant he had another ten minutes to get ready.

He was wrong. Bigelow must have been licking his lips over what he anticipated to be a good dose of hell-fire and damnation. Amos saw Bigelow glance at several in the congregation as he prayed for God to use the preacher to reach lost souls he knew were present.

Something about that image gave Amos a shiver. He didn't believe in this God they were all so fired up about, but the idea of God—or anybody else—using him like some kind of tool was not something that set well in his mind.

He strode to the front and stood there for a moment or so before saying, "Close your eyes." He watched as they did as he said. He looked down the pews. Men and women were sitting quietly, eyes closed.

"Now I want you to picture a bonfire, a big one. It's burned down ... it's a bed of coals ... red hot ... flames lick and flicker here and there ... nothing in this world is any hotter than that, is it?

"Keep your eyes closed. Look at the red-hot coals. See that fire clearly.

"Can you make it bigger? Can you make it the size of a wagon? Spread it out in your mind. A whole wagon. How hot is it now?

"How about a house? Make it the size of an entire house. Some of you have fought a house fire, or been there when one burned; how hot was it? Are you getting the picture? Do you feel it?

"All right, let's go for the big one, make it even larger ... larger ... until it's the size of a lake."

Amos continued to scan their faces as he talked. *These clowns are doing it.* He decided he could talk them into anything as long as he used the Bible to do it. He could tell by their expressions that those seated in front of him really saw it. Some of them were actually sweating.

He stepped back behind the podium. "You can open your eyes." He looked around. "Some of you really did see it, didn't you? Most of you saw enough to understand. The Book of Revelation says there's going to be a lake of fire. Even as good as that imaginary picture might have been, you know it won't do the real thing justice. A lake of fire, torment beyond belief. But you do believe it, don't you? Let's see the hands if you believe it."

Most of the hands shot up. *What suckers!* Maybe he wouldn't go on the road at all. Where could he find a better group than this one? Where would he find more people this easy to lead?

Amos read the text from the Bible open on the podium. The Bible made a great prop, and he used it to hide his notes as he paced. He picked it up and gave it a pat as he held it out to them. They loved that. He knew how much faith Joseph had in that old book, and he knew most of them felt the same way.

He decided all he had to do was find a passage that said something like what he wanted them to believe, and say, "It's true because it says so right here," and they'd buy it. He now knew that anything written in this book was unquestionably true as far as they were concerned. This old book would be the key to the mint.

Amos paced the floor, bounced his voice off the livery stable clear at the end of the street, and made the Devil jump out at the congregation from every corner of the room. Demons peeked out from under the seats while the Devil himself stalked the aisles. He loved this subject. There was a hell all right, and he'd brought it right into the room with them.

He ended the sermon standing all the way at the back of the room. It got very quiet. "Everlasting torment! Is there no escape?"

Amos let the question hang in the air. Not more than a few seconds, but it seemed so much longer, the perfect stage effect.

Then he began to read: "John 3:16 says, 'For God so loved the world, that he gave his only begotten Son, that whosoever believeth in him should not perish, but have everlasting life.'"

He closed the Bible with a snap. "There's the door, people. Jesus died for you. He stands ready to receive you right now. I'm going to ask Brother Bigelow and Brother Witherspoon to stand at the front. If you are ready to receive Jesus as your Savior, I want you to go to them. Get on your knees and unburden your heart. I can't save you. Brother Bigelow and Brother Witherspoon can't save you. Only Jesus can save you, but these men can tell you how to get it done. Go to them now, as Sister Valentine plays. I'm going to go out by myself and pray you through."

Amos walked out as the music began behind him. Bigelow's powerful voice rang out as he said, "Won't you do it today? He's waiting. He's waiting for you right now."

Joseph was right; this *was* better. He'd let Bigelow and Witherspoon shear the sheep. They believed in what they were doing. They could be more convincing.

Really? Do I really believe that? Amos didn't really believe anyone could be more convincing than he had been in that show he had just put on. He owned those people.

"It *was* good, you know."

Amos jumped like a cat whose tail had been stepped on. "Joseph. Where did you come from?"

"I've been listening. I've heard some fine preachers, but I never heard better. God has truly given you a gift."

It was me, you goose. I was the one who knew how to reach these people. I'm the one who had the fine voice and knew how to use it, how to make their sheep minds work on themselves, and how to tie their emotions in knots to separate them from their sheep money.

Amos couldn't say that. As badly as he wanted to take the credit, he had to make Joseph think he was really beginning to believe. He said it aloud, sure that he sounded quite sincere. "Yes, I think I'm finally beginning to believe."

The old man was patient. "No, you aren't. You're trying to fool me into thinking you have, but you haven't. Still, whether you believe or not, God *is* using you. There are people in there being saved, and your words made it happen. Foolish, deceitful intentions, but the words were good, and they are doing their job."

The more Joseph treated him this way, the more exasperated Amos became. "What do I have to do to make you see I'm coming around?"

Joseph dismissed the comment with the wave of a hand. "Don't try. When it really happens, and I have no doubt that it will, you won't have to tell me. In fact, you couldn't hide it from me if you wanted to.

"But I will tell you this," he continued. "I do know there can be no belief without understanding, and understanding won't come if you try to just read the Bible and figure it out for yourself. We all had to have spiritual guides to help us get where we needed to go. Since you can't admit what you do know and don't know to anybody else, your choice of spiritual guides is pretty limited."

So he'd have to let Joseph teach him before the old man would believe he was getting it? He decided he could live with that. He had to get a handle on this stuff before he could use it effectively anyway. He had to be able to answer the suckers' questions to be able to pull it off.

"I have changed, you'll see," he told the old man. "I'm even having thoughts of getting a tent and taking this show on the road."

"It wouldn't be a show, it'd be a tent revival, and I think that's a fine idea."

"You do? I didn't think ..."

"God has already made it clear to me that your talent is not to stay put and pastor a church, but to travel the country to convert people to Him and then move on."

There Amos had been trying to figure a way to get around to selling Joseph on the idea only to find that Joseph was already thinking that very way.

"I'll be there to help you, of course."

"What?" Amos put his hand on his forehead, pushing his hat back on his head with the motion. "Now wait, I didn't ask ..."

"You won't be rid of me until God says it is time."

"I can't be looking after no blind man."

"You won't be, and you know it. I'll cook, work up your sermons, and keep you from making major errors in the way you treat people, while you claim to preach the Gospel."

Amos had thought the road show to be the perfect way to get rid of Joseph, but now he couldn't help but wonder if he'd ever be free of him. "And be there to turn me in if I get out of line, I suppose?"

"That hasn't changed. Only now I have proof in the form of the money we turned in. I added that to my note at the bank, along with information about how you defrauded these people pretending to be a preacher."

"So now I'm looking at more than three to five."

"I'd say so."

"So I still have no choice but to do as you say."

"None."

"When are we going to do this?"

"We have a tent to acquire, and you have a lot of work to do before you are able to take the message out to people."

"But you think the show I did today should stay in?"

"It should become a central part of the performance, Amos. Let's just hope God continues to use you to do it that well."

Yeah. Like your God has any say in the matter.

Fourteen

Amos relaxed on the bed in his room. He wasn't really sleeping, though he had dozed off a time or two. A knock on the door brought him back. He answered it to find Clem Sullivan standing there. Clem had a small ranch north of town. A slim man, he bordered on looking like a scarecrow. His face was gaunt, and he wore bib overalls with a plaid shirt. He looked distraught.

He held his straw hat in his hands. "Preacher, I'm sorry to bother you, but I need a little help."

Amos had a bad feeling about this. "What can I do for you?"

"It's the missus." He indicated a direction with his thumb over his shoulder. "She's going to leave me and go back East. Going to move in with her mother."

"What brought this on?" Amos said, as if he really cared. He was only making conversation until he could figure how to get rid of the man.

The farmer got a sour look on his face. "She says I'm a really rotten husband and she's tired of putting up with it."

"I'm really sorry, Clem, but why tell me?" The advice he wanted to give the farmer was to go downstairs, get wobble-kneed, and tell his troubles to the bartender as a man is supposed to do. He sighed. That wouldn't work.

The man looked perplexed. "A preacher is supposed to

know all about how a good marriage should work. Phyllis agreed to come with me to talk to you about it."

"I've never even been married; how could I advise you?"

Clem's attitude rose to border on outright anger. "What's that got to do with it? You're supposed to be able to tell us the religious way to save our marriage. You saying you can't do that?"

"I didn't say that." Amos stepped into the hallway and closed the door behind him. "Let's go talk to her. Phyllis, did you say?"

"Yes sir, and I best warn you, she's got her back up a considerable amount."

They headed down to the parlor. As they made their way down the stairs Amos considered his options. This could be really bad for him. If he did a bad job of it, the women might run him out of town. If he got Clem in a bad way, the men might do it instead. If he didn't do anything at all everyone would surely start wondering about what kind of preacher it was that couldn't advise people on marriage problems. He had a lot to lose here and so far he didn't see any way to come out a winner.

He walked into the parlor and didn't need to have Phyllis, a homely woman, pointed out to him. Her face was drawn up as if she had been sucking on sour pickles. She had on a very plain traveling suit, and a couple of worn bags sat on the floor beside her.

She looked up as they came in. "Preacher, I'm sorry that old fool bothered you with this. It's a complete waste of time. The stagecoach is due in here in an hour or so, and I'm going to be on it when it leaves."

"How about if we sit down here for a bit?" Amos sat down

next to her on the settee and Clem took a seat facing them. The air crackled with tension.

Clem wrung his hands anxiously and said, "Quote her some Scripture, Preacher, something that'll make her see how wrong this is."

Scripture? I can't quote Scripture unless Joseph has written it out for me. He looked to the floor and considered what he could do. It dawned on him that his first sermon had something that might work. He didn't remember the name of the passage, but he'd have to run with it. "Clem, I'm not sure it's her that's wrong here." That got a surprised look from both of them.

He continued. "Were you in church when I preached about love?"

Phyllis drew herself up indignantly. "We've been there every service since you came."

"That's good. I won't have to go into it again, but I need you to think back to it. Whether it's religion, family, business, no matter what it is, the most important thing is love."

Indignation began to border on resentment. "Well, I didn't say I didn't love the old goat, but I don't like him very much anymore."

"You're dead right there; the two things aren't the same, are they?" Amos felt like he had found a chink in the armor; now to see if he could do something with it. "Clem, do you still love her?"

"Of course I do, Preacher, what a silly question. Would I be here trying to get her to stay if I didn't love her?"

"Yes, he would," she said. "He can't do without the cleaning and cooking and sewing and laundry. He doesn't need a wife, he needs a servant."

"That true, Clem?"

"Of course not." Clem's expression said he was the wronged husband, misunderstood and betrayed.

"When's the last time you told her you love her?"

The expression melted into confusion. "I don't know. I ain't much for words, Preacher, but she knows."

"How's she supposed to know if you don't tell her?"

Clem looked down and grimaced.

Phyllis looked smug. Amos looked over at her. "Did you tell him you were unhappy?"

The smugness disappeared. She had thought him to be on her side. Now she wasn't sure where he was going. "I most certainly did."

"Did you tell him why, or did you just nag at him on things in general?"

She gave Amos a hard look and said, "Hummmph, I'll have you know I don't nag."

"Seems to me she just rags on me, Preacher; how am I supposed to know what she's really mad at?"

The two launched into recriminations of each other, voices rising, fingers pointing. Amos listened, and understanding dawned on him. He didn't need Joseph for this one.

"Are you hearing yourselves?" They looked at him quizzically. "Both of you are saying 'I need this,' and 'you do this and that.' You have any idea how wrong that is? That's not how love works."

He stood up. He needed to get into a preaching mode. He needed to induce a little guilt. "You say you love each other, but I have my doubts. Two people who really love each other would be saying just the opposite. They'd be saying 'I know you need this,' and 'I need to do that.' You get what I'm saying?"

They shook their heads no.

"When two people really care for each other they don't

worry about their own needs, they worry about the needs of the person they love. If they are doing that, and the other person is doing the same, each person's own needs are met as well. People instinctively do that during courtship, but if we aren't careful, we can get away from it. Is that any clearer?"

Clem wrestled with the idea in his head. "Maybe. You saying that if I spend all my time trying to make her happy, my own happiness is going to take care of itself?"

"You're on the right track, Clem, but you haven't quite got it. Phyllis, you have to do your part too. One person can't make a marriage. If you're doing everything you can do to make Clem happy, without worrying about your own needs, and if he is doing the same, you are both going to find more happiness than you could ever imagine. But if one of you is trying hard to do that and the other isn't, it just won't work. It makes a really bad deal."

They both nodded.

"Any time you find yourself pointing fingers, and pointing out where the other person is falling short, it should be a sign to you that you're locked in the 'me mode,' and being really selfish. If you'll look at that hand you're pointing with, you'll see one finger pointing at the other person and a whole bunch of them pointing back at you."

Clem moved over to the seat Amos had vacated. "It *is* all my fault, dumpling. I'm sorry; I really didn't think it was. I've been an old fool."

She took his hand. "No, it isn't all your fault. I've been so busy trying to figure out all of your shortcomings that I haven't seen my own."

Amos smiled. "I'm going to leave you two to talk this out. I think you're on the right track now. Just remember, when you find yourself thinking about what you need instead of what you need to do to make the other one happy, you are the one who's in the wrong."

He paused at the door and looked back. They were holding hands and looking into each other's eyes, both talking at once. *Well I'll be. I think I actually did it. Does that beat all or what? Wish I could solve my own problem as easy. How does a guy compete with himself for a girl? I need something that will get her mind off the masked man—something.*

Fifteen

Amos slipped through the twilight, wearing old clothes and a floppy old hat he had bought under the pretense that he needed some "clothes to work in." As he came up behind the little house, he could hear Judy singing softly in the garden. He pulled the bandanna up over his nose and slipped up behind her on cat feet.

Judy straightened up and put her hands on her hips to survey what she had achieved. Amos closed the gap, pinned her arms to her side with one arm, and closed the other hand over her mouth.

"Mmmmmmppphhh."

"Easy girl, I'm just trying to make sure you don't cry out. Wouldn't do anything but stir up a bunch of trouble." He released his grip just enough that she could catch sight of him over her shoulder, but he maintained the hand over her mouth.

She caught her breath as she saw the masked face, those mesmerizing eyes. *Oh, it's him. All of the dreams and thoughts, and now he's here; it's coming true.*

He enjoyed it as he held her close, soft and warm against him. "I came to see you. If I take my hand off your mouth, will you scream?"

She shook her head no.

He released the grip on her mouth but held her fast in his

grasp with her back to him. They stood that way in the fragrant shadows, suspended in time.

"Me? Why would you come to see me?" She trembled at the romance of being wrapped in his arms.

He spoke very softly, a whisper, not wanting her to recognize the voice. "Ever since we met at the holdup I can't get you out of my mind."

Judy's breath was coming in short gasps. "Really? I find it hard to forget you as well."

"I came for you."

Her tone changed. "What do you mean?" She expected this to be where she would receive the pledge of undying love, where he would offer to give it all up for her, where he would renounce his outlaw ways for the sake of love. This was exactly the way she had pictured it in her dreams, only ... only not with him hidden behind her.

"Leave with me. I'll take you places you can only imagine."

"I couldn't do that; I don't even know your name. Or for that matter, what you even look like. Pull down your bandanna." She began to struggle, trying to turn and see him.

"Not a chance."

This wasn't going the way she had expected. "Yet you expect me to go with you? You have some nerve."

"I know you're attracted to me. I can tell. Leave with me, and you'll get to know me soon enough."

Judy tried to scream then, but the hand closed it off, trapping the sound in her throat. "This is not what you want to do," he said. "I can take you places you've never seen. I can pleasure you in ways you've never imagined, and you have a body built for pleasure." The touch she had first thought pleasant began to feel coarse, uninvited. His hand moved as if he were trying to ...

It was too much. She kicked him in the shins, and when his grip loosened her scream pierced the shadows and echoed off the barn. The masked man disappeared into the night. "Unless I miss my guess," he muttered, "that ought to divert her thinking a little." He scurried down the dark alleyway.

Uncle John burst through the door with his shotgun at the ready. "What is it?"

Judy trembled. "The man who robbed the stage, he was here."

"Here? What'd he want?"

"He wanted me to go with him. He said disgusting things. *He touched me.*" She crossed her arms and hugged herself.

"Are you serious? I told you no good would come of you having romantic notions about him. You get back in the house while I go get the sheriff."

John waddled off, trying to get his dangling suspenders up over his shoulders. Judy stared at where the man had stood. How could she have been so wrong? He came for her as if she were a common trollop. He actually believed all he had to do was ask, and she would run away with him. He couldn't have cared for her. *I've never had anyone lay their hands on me like that. How disgusting.*

The next morning Joseph heard Amos across the street and called out to him. "Massa Amos, could I trouble you for a minute?"

Amos followed him inside the building, and as soon as the door closed the old man said, "That was a nice thing you did last night."

"Me? I stayed in my room."

"So you don't know anything about a masked man scaring the life out of Judy Valentine?"

It was a shame the old man couldn't see the look of feigned innocence Amos affected. He would have enjoyed it. "Me? Not a thing. That's terrible."

"And I suppose you wouldn't know she had a crush on this masked man?"

"How would I know that?" More to the point he wondered how the old coot happened to know it. Joseph seemed to know everything about everybody.

Joseph walked across the room, oblivious to the dark with the door closed. "Deny it all you want, you know she was hung up on somebody that was no good for her, and you went over and made a play you knew would bring her to her senses. It was a nice thing to do, though I think you went too far."

"I'm sure whoever did it felt he needed to go far enough to make sure she had a change of heart. She's an unspoiled little dumpling. I bet he didn't go as far as she felt he did." Amos headed over to light a lamp, but tripped over a chair in the darkened room. "Ouch."

"Are you all right?"

"I just don't get around in a dark room as well as you do."

"I suppose not. For your sake I hope you're right about it not going as far as she thought." Joseph stuck a match, turned up the wick in a lantern and lit it. He waited to feel the heat so he knew it was working.

Amos rubbed his stinging shin. "I hope it doesn't get whoever did it into trouble."

Joseph blew out the match and let the globe down on the lantern. "You don't have to worry about that. John came over and got the sheriff. They rousted Lightfoot out of bed, but he wouldn't even come with them. He said he's already tried to track that ghost all he is going to. I can probably track better than the sheriff can so you know how well he did without Lightfoot. They combed the place half the night, but they didn't find anything. Only bad thing is you've got it all stirred up again. They thought the bandit had gone out of the territory."

"Not that I know what you're talking about, but I have a feeling we're not going to see him any more."

Sixteen

As he passed the corner of the building, a voice came from the shadows. "Amos?"

"Fargo? I told you not to talk to me like this." Ford Fargo looked like what he was, a furtive little man who had acted as Amos's sideman in a number of dodges. To merely be seen talking to the little man might raise questions in the good people's minds.

Fargo hissed, "Just lean back against the wall and listen. I'm outta sight back here."

"This better be important." Amos leaned back against the wall and crossed his arms as if watching the street.

"You consider your life important?"

"I'm listening."

"The Prescott brothers have a reward poster out on you. It says three thousand dollars, dead or alive. Word being passed around is they want it to be dead."

"Why?"

"You know why; you ran a game on them."

"No, I mean why are they saying they want me dead?"

"I got their mousy little desk clerk drunk. His guess is the Prescott boys claimed a lot more money is missing from the bank than you took, and I figure they took advantage of the robbery to squirrel it away themselves. They don't want you walking into court and telling that."

"It figures. To begin with, I did the old railroad right-of-way dodge on them; I didn't rob the bank."

"Oh, I see. If that's the case it'd be a sure thing Prescott wouldn't want it known somebody took him on something like that. He'd be the type that couldn't handle people thinking he'd been made to look a fool."

"How about you stay over there and keep an eye on him. I'll make it worthwhile for you."

"All right, I better get out of here now."

"Hey, one more thing, Fargo."

"What's that?"

"Three thousand is a lot of money. How come you didn't give me up?"

"We've both done some pretty shaky things over the years, Amos, but I'd never turn on a partner."

"I appreciate that, Fargo, and thanks for the warning."

Amos tried pretending he wasn't interested in Judy, but she did intrigue him. There was no getting around it. He'd been asked over to eat by nearly everybody in church except her, so when the dinner invitation finally came, he was as happy as a kitten in the milk shed.

Her aunt and uncle weren't home, so to be proper, Judy invited her friend Marcie. The girls had spent the whole afternoon in the kitchen before he arrived, and the smell that washed over him as Judy opened the front door immediately made his mouth water.

"Hello, Parson."

"Miss Judy." He looked past her at the fresh scrubbed face peeking out of the kitchen. "Miss Marcie."

"Oh, please," Judy said, "putting that Miss on it is so formal sounding. We've known each other long enough."

"Same here," the tall blonde said, wiping her hands on her apron. Marcie was a perfect example of hardy ranch stock, yet because of her family's wealth, she'd obviously seen her share of pampering as well. Firm muscle rounded out her trim figure and enhanced her shapely curves, and her hazel green eyes were captivating.

Amos shook himself free of their spell and turned his attention back to Judy. "You still don't call me Amos."

They looked at each other. Judy said, "We'll try. I've never called a preacher by his first name. You may have to be patient with us."

Amos lifted his nose gently into the air. "I'd say ham, definitely apple pie, fresh baked bread, and a few delicious scents I can't quite place."

Marcie laughed. "What an educated nose. You didn't miss anything but the green beans and sweet potatoes."

"Ah, sweet potatoes, so that's what the cinnamon and butter smell is."

"I stand corrected. I don't suppose you smell the green beans now that I've mentioned they're there."

"I don't know what green beans smell like, but I know what they taste like and I can hardly wait. Is that ice in the drinks?"

"Yes, the restaurant ships it packed in sawdust from San Antonio during the cold months. A lot of people like uncle John get some too, and when we have a freeze we add to it. He buries it back into the wall of the root cellar and if we're frugal it generally lasts all summer."

"Where do they get the ice in San Antonio?"

"Three different places make it; the first one came in 1860."

"I didn't realize." He tried a sip, cold and refreshing. "I've had hot tea, but iced is quite a treat."

They made a little small talk and then settled around the table. Amos rattled off the boarding house prayer, now refined a little by Joseph to be more appropriate for a minister.

The food fully lived up to its promise, and the company was as delightful as he knew it would be.

Amos wiped his mouth with his napkin. "This food is fantastic."

"Judy did most of it. She's a great cook. I barely got here in time to help her finish up."

Judy looked pleased and embarrassed at the same time. She changed the subject. "We have a dual purpose for inviting you. I mean, we wanted to do our duty, but we also have something we wanted to ask you, too."

Amos felt his heart sag. "Duty? This invite was only a church duty?"

"Well, not entirely." She returned to her subject, obviously not going to be drawn into that discussion. "Marcie is engaged to the foreman on her daddy's ranch."

"Delbert Fisher, as I recall?"

Marcie brightened up. "Yes, isn't he wonderful?"

"He's a nice young man. I'd say the word 'wonderful' hadn't come to me."

She giggled. "No, I'm sure it didn't."

Judy continued. "Well, they've set the date, and they'd like you to perform the ceremony."

A wedding? Amos was sure he could find out how to conduct it, but would it be legal? He was sure it wouldn't be. Joseph would bust a gut.

Marcie frowned. "Is something wrong? You don't want to do it?"

"Oh no, it's not that. There's nothing that would please me more, but you know I just moved to this state and I'm not sure my license to conduct weddings is good here."

"Oh, I hadn't thought about that."

"How about if we do it like this? How about if I do the ceremony, and the judge hitches you as man and wife? Then we'd be sure."

She perked up. "That'd be fine. Even more impressive."

"I thought you'd like it."

Amos rubbed his clammy palms together. Another close call, but he had handled it nicely. Looking at Judy, he found her appraising him with a very thoughtful look. He swallowed hard as he wondered what was going though her mind, whether he had gotten her suspicious again.

Marcie pulled her into a discussion of wedding plans, and it got him off the hook.

Dang I'm good, Amos chuckled silently.

Seventeen

They were sitting in the sheriff's office sipping Joseph's strong coffee when the law officer broached the subject. Sheriff Wilson sat with his feet on his desk, a cup of coffee cradled on his chest. "Parson, people are beginning to wonder about you."

Amos felt a lump come into his throat. "Oh, really?" His voice sounded weak to him, and he took a sip of the vile fluid to settle it down. *Is this it? Does he know?*

The sheriff didn't seem to notice. "All this time you spend with old Joseph. I mean, well, you two are together constantly."

Whew, is that all this is? "Sheriff, a preacher is color-blind, surely you know that."

Sheriff Wilson gestured that point aside with his free hand, nearly spilling his coffee in the process. "Oh, it ain't that; I mean I don't treat Joseph no different than I treat anybody else. But you two are together every day. Folks wonder about that."

Amos leaned forward in his chair, a dark look on his face. "Sheriff, you better not be suggesting there's something going on between us of a …"

The sentence trailed off into the air. Wilson looked at him curiously. Their eyes remained locked, then it dawned on him. He became flustered. His feet came down with a thud. "*Oh no, not that!* Honest, Preacher, I wasn't suggesting anything between you. I mean, I know both you and Joseph ... really ... I know nothing funny was going on." Wilson was so embarrassed he looked as if he were about to explode.

"Well, then what, Sheriff?"

"Nobody thought that kind of thing at all, just wondered why you'd want to spend so much time with an old black man. It ain't like you've got a lot in common."

"More than you know, Sheriff. You said yourself that Joseph is kind of a chaplain here at the jail. He knows the whole Bible by memory. He'd probably be preaching himself if there was a black church here for him to work with."

"I see, so you two ..." The color in Wilson's face and neck began to fade. He sat back in his chair.

"He listens to my sermons and tells me what he thinks. He's a good audience to practice them on, the closest thing to having another minister in town to get together with."

"Well, that makes sense. I admit I hadn't thought of it like that."

"What do you suppose I ought to do about these people who are wondering, Sheriff?"

The big man came to his feet, filled with a sudden resolve. "I think you'll find in a day or so they won't be."

"Yes, I know you are a man who's closely listened to."

"Has to do with respect." The sheriff pulled himself up to his full height. "Not so much for me, of course, but for the badge." He looked down and gave it a quick shine with his shirtsleeve. "Comes with the territory."

"You're being modest, but I understand. Can I ask you something else?"

"Fire away."

"It's just not right that one of the most religious people in town isn't welcome at church."

The big man came around and sat down on the edge of the desk. "You talking about Joseph?"

"Of course." Amos swallowed involuntarily. He found it intimidating to look up at him like that.

Wilson glowered at him. "Nobody has ever said he can't come to church."

Amos got up to keep the sheriff from looking down on him. He pretended he wanted to warm his coffee. "No, and maybe he can't see the looks he gets when he's tried it, but he can feel it. He can hear it in the voices. You think God only intends white people to go to church?"

"Certainly not, but those people generally prefer to go to their own churches."

"Need I remind you?" Amos took the pot off the stove and poured a little. It looked awful.

"No, you don't have to say it. I know there aren't any other churches for him to go to. Give me a little time; I'll work on it. You're right; it ain't proper, but you know there's a lot of years' worth of thinking a certain way that's got to be overcome to have a black man sitting right there in church."

"You saying people will be against it?"

"Not really; everybody likes old Joseph. It's just gonna have to be approached right."

"I'm sure you can do that, Sheriff."

The sheriff paused on the way to the door. "Sure don't know how you can drink seconds of that stuff. Joseph makes terrible coffee." He pulled his hat down to shade his eyes and went out the door.

Amos got up to follow the sheriff out and had just opened

the door when he heard Joseph say, "I'm mighty grateful for that."

"Huh?"

"I heard. You didn't have to do that, but it'd sure be a comfort to be able to go to church."

"You've got it coming. Besides, I'd like to have you there."

"Maybe you are making some progress after all."

Judy sat on her front porch. She looked up to see Amos approaching down the dusty street. It came unbidden to her mind that he really was a nice looking man. She couldn't believe she was so stupid as to get hung up on an absolute scoundrel and pay no attention at all to Amos, right under her nose. She wondered if he had any interest in her.

He stopped in front of the house and tipped his hat. "Afternoon, Miss Judy."

"Hello, Reverend, care for a glass of cold lemonade?"

Amos thought what he'd really like was a beer, but he said, "Why thank you, I'd like that."

He opened the gate in the white picket fence and ambled to the porch. He was alert to see if his little stunt had actually done any good.

"Well, sit yourself down and I'll pour some up."

He took a seat, and she returned almost immediately. She obviously already had it prepared.

He closed his eyes and took a long pull on it. The cold liquid flowed down his throat, at once sweet, yet tart from the bite of the lemon. It finally cut the taste of Joseph's coffee for the first time all afternoon. "My," he wiped his lips. "That's mighty refreshing."

"Glad you like it."

They exchanged a little small talk before she finally said, "I just can't figure you out."

"Figure me out? I don't understand."

"I heard about you interceding for Joseph, trying to get the church to accept him. That's wonderful."

He found it amazing she had heard that news already. "You don't think it's something I should be doing?"

"It's *exactly* what a minister should be doing. Only I don't know, there are times ..."

Eighteen

Amos couldn't believe what he was hearing. He had taken drastic steps to take the masked man out of the picture, yet Judy still seemed suspicious. "Is there a problem? Have I been doing something wrong?"

She avoided looking at him. "No, nothing I can put a finger on. You've been every inch the gentleman, and everything a minister should be. It's just, I don't know, sometimes I get this feeling ... call it intuition. I can't seem to shake it, and there's absolutely no reason for it."

"I don't get it." Amos pulled up on the edge of his seat, moving closer to her.

She gave him a little half smile, glanced up quickly then immediately back down. "No, I'm sure you don't. I'm just being silly. You know how women are."

He studied her face intently. "I don't have much experience with women, but maybe I understand better than you think."

She gave him "the look" again, as if she were measuring him for something. He was getting tired of this routine, but still he knew he had to be careful. He knew women's intuition was nothing to take lightly. He just wished he could put it to rest once and for all.

The calculating look lasted but a few moments before she

broke it off. He worded his response carefully. "Judy, I know I'm cut from a different kind of cloth. That's why I've roamed around in the West instead of staying in one place at some big church. I'm still looking for answers, still trying to firm up my religious beliefs."

"The sheriff says that's why you spend so much time with Joseph."

Amos sat back in his chair and took a sip of lemonade. The change in his posture seemed to relax her a little as well. "I certainly wouldn't want to say the sheriff is a busybody, but he certainly does get around. Yes, Joseph knows lots about the Bible and is very sure about his beliefs. I enjoy talking religion with him, and he's a good man to practice sermons on."

"I guess that's it. I suppose I was only picking up on that uncertainty."

Amos held up a hand. "Now I didn't say uncertainty. I wouldn't want that to get spread around."

Her forehead furrowed. "You said you were searching; doesn't that mean uncertain?"

"I'm not uncertain about my religion, just how well I might understand it. I think we should always question our understanding and seek to know better what the Bible has to teach us." It even felt like he used Joseph's voice as he fed the old man's words to her. As usual, the mention of the Bible seemed to erase all doubt.

She began to worry the hem of her apron in her hands. "I feel so embarrassed. Here I thought something might be the matter, and you were only trying to challenge and strengthen your own faith. You were just doing something all of us should be doing, and I tried to judge you for it. I'm ashamed."

"Don't be. You sensed something to be wrong and didn't

understand. You were honest about it and we dealt with it. You have nothing to be ashamed about."

If Amos didn't find a way to divert her attention, he was going to be living in constant fear that she'd put him and the masked man together. He had thought that little stunt in her garden would make the problem go away, but he saw now he couldn't take that for granted.

Amos steered Judy to less dangerous subjects and talked quietly as Billy Bob ran up. Eight years old, towheaded, all boy and a yard wide, he was constantly into everything. Not only that, but he was always at hand when anybody needed someone to run an errand, as he was doing right now.

"Reverend," he yelled at the front gate, then again as he ran up to the porch.

"I can hear you fine, son, there's no need to shout."

But Billy Bob continued to talk so loudly that everyone on that side of town surely must have heard every word. "It's the widow, Widow Simpson. She's dying. She said come quick."

Dying? Amos's palms got sweaty, and he didn't know what to do or say. He should take Joseph with him, but even as he thought it, he knew it wouldn't work. The old woman would never want Joseph in there since she was sure to be in her bedclothes. He'd simply have to play it the way the cards fell.

"Lead the way, son; I'm right with you."

Amos had to half-walk, half-run to keep up with the spry youngster who led him to a small whitewashed house on the edge of town. He gave the boy a nickel and sent him off to play, wanting no witnesses on hand.

He went into the house to find a frail, white-haired lady lying in bed, clutching her Bible to her breast. She had on a high-necked, frilly, print nightgown. She had little color in her face and her eyes were closed. When he saw her, he feared he was too late. She slowly opened her eyes and gave him a weak smile. "Parson, thank you for coming."

"Hello, Mrs. Simpson. What's this I hear?"

"Would you sit with me a bit? I'm afraid my old ticker is giving out on me."

He moved to sit on the edge of the bed, taking her hand. "Hadn't I better get the doctor?"

"No, I've seen the doctor. We've spent more time together than I did with my late husband in his latter years. If Walter was awake, he was fishing. That's how he wanted to spend his last days, and he did. In fact, that's where we found him, sitting on the bank with a pole in his hand. He had a smile on his face, and Parson, would you believe it? He had a fish on the line. We turned Walter's last fish loose for him."

"I'm sorry."

"Don't be. He lived a mighty fine life, and I have as well. I have no regrets. I'm just in need of a little spiritual comfort here in my final hours."

He couldn't stand it. He couldn't let this woman die thinking she was getting something he couldn't give her. Amos was rotten and not fooling himself about it in the least, but he still couldn't take this on his conscience. It would probably mean he'd have to take his chances, probably have to go on the run, but this little old lady deserved to know the truth. He paused and took a deep breath. She *had* to know.

Amos turned toward her and covered her small bony hand with his other hand. It felt like a small covering of brittle skin over a skeleton. "Mrs. Simpson, let me go get Joseph for you."

"Oh, I couldn't. I'm not a bigot, mind you, and I know Joseph is a fine man, but a lifetime of thinking a certain way can't be just brushed aside."

Amos had to make her see. "But you don't get it. You need somebody right now, and I'm not it."

"You're right, I don't understand. I thought this is part of what you do."

He couldn't return her gaze. He released her hand to lean forward. He folded his hands with his elbows on his knees. "I've fooled this whole town, but I can't fool you. Not now, not like this. I'm not a preacher, Mrs. Simpson."

"But I've heard you."

"I'm only a guy who's good at telling people what they want to hear."

"I see."

"Do you?" He turned toward her again. "Then let me get Joseph. He may be blind, but he knows what's in that Bible backwards and forwards."

Her eyes sparked and she pushed herself more upright in the bed. Amos put a couple of pillows behind her to make it less of an effort. "You think I need someone to tell me what's in here? I can quote this book as good as anybody."

Her eyes flashed again, and the color returned to her face and neck. "It was my primer. When I was a girl, it was the only thing we had to read, so I practiced my reading in it. It's been my constant companion and my guide. I don't need him or you to tell me about the Bible."

Amos began to pat her hand. "Settle down, settle down. I didn't mean to get you so excited."

She stayed upright in the bed, but the momentary anger left her eyes.

"If it wasn't for that, then why did you send for me?"

"Preacher, I'm ninety-seven years old. I was beginning to think God had forgotten He'd left me here. I just needed someone with me to help pray me over to the other side."

"And all you got was me." His head drooped.

She smiled. "I don't think so. I think you sell yourself short. You have a good heart. If you didn't you could have just let me go without a word, but you couldn't do it, could you?"

Amos just shook his head.

"You're fighting Him, aren't you? You preach about Him but you fight Him."

"Fighting who?" He finally met her eyes. They were as penetrating as he knew they were going to be.

"Jesus. Who clsc could I mean?"

"I'm not fighting anyone. I just read sermons Joseph writes and give the people a good show."

"Rubbish."

Amos got up and began to pace the room. "Look, you don't need to get yourself so worked up right now. It can't be good for you."

The frail little lady disappeared and in her place sat a diminutive ball of fire, suddenly and unexpectedly filled with purpose. "Are you kidding me? One last chance to witness for Jesus before I go meet Him face to face? Young man, you're giving me the greatest gift I could possibly receive."

"I don't get it. I'm supposed to be here to help you in your last hours, and all you can think about is helping me?"

"That's what Christians do."

She closed her eyes, and again Amos thought she was gone, but then he realized she was only gathering up a little more strength. Her breath was labored, but other than that she didn't appear to be in pain.

"Are you all right?"

Her eyes snapped open. "No, I'm not all right; I'm dying." She saw him jerk back and softened her tone. "But if you mean am I in any pain, I'm not, to any amount that matters."

He patted her hand gently with his other hand, as he continued to hold it. It was a calming, placating gesture. It didn't appear to work. "So you're trying to make a few last points on the ledger before you go up there?"

"You really aren't a preacher, are you? We can't earn our way into heaven."

"This stuff gets me so confused. I'm all right when I simply read it and give it out like lines in a play. But when I start trying to understand ..."

"Listen to Joseph. He can make it clear for you." She smiled and put her hand on his before finishing the sentence. "Only don't wait too late, and quit fighting it. God's working on you now, but it's possible for your heart to harden, and you can no longer hear."

She asked if he'd pray with her, only she voiced the prayer. She didn't pray for herself, she prayed for him. For herself she simply asked that God's will be done.

They sat and talked quietly about her life for a number of hours. Mrs. Simpson was teasing when she said God had forgotten her. He never would, but about two in the morning, He did call her home.

Joseph helped Amos prepare what he would say, but as they wrote the words the old man kept giving him questioning glances as he added things from the hours he'd spent with the woman before her death.

"She really got to you," he said.

"I never met anybody like her. And I need to tell that to the people gathered at the gravesite."

Joseph's voice was gentle. "They knew her very, very well.

They've had many years to learn about her. You've had only a night."

"I didn't say I would be telling them anything new. The need is in me. I really *need* to say it to them."

"I understand."

Later, Amos looked over to the group that had assembled in the cemetery. Everyone in town appeared to be there for the burial. They gathered around the pine coffin, hats off and heads down. Nobody talked.

As they stood on this lonely little rise above town, it struck Amos as a lonely place, no trees and no vegetation of any kind. A plot with a fence around it and an archway for a gate, with flowers here and there adorning graves as the only bright spots.

Amos thought about it as he and Joseph walked toward the waiting people. The old lady didn't expose him after all. She took his secret to the grave with her. What a break for him. Yet it made him uneasy.

"God finally called Mrs. Simpson home last night," he began. "I had the tremendous privilege of being with her in her final hours. She was a remarkable woman. She told me that Jesus had gone to prepare a place for us and that as long as He's had to work on her place, it must really be something."

Smiles broke out all over the group.

"She also told me what she wanted me to say to you. Joseph and I worked really hard on the words to read over her." He looked at the notes inside his Bible. "But I'm not going to need them."

Amos stuffed the notes in his pocket. He was going to wing it. "She said burial services are for the living. By the time we're doing this, she expected to already be there with the

Lord. There's no doubt in my mind, and I know none in yours either, that she is there just as she said.

"Mrs. Simpson was present every time the church doors opened, but just being in church is no guarantee. The worst sinner in town could be right there, and we might never know it." *And that is exactly where the worst sinner is*, he thought.

"But she was there with her heart right, and as full of faith as it would be possible for one person to be. I envy her faith. I envy her life. She told me nobody could ever have had a better life than she had. She said she had never been mistreated, never been hungry, never been sick, and that the Lord had blessed her every day of her life."

Amos shook his head. "It may have not looked that way to us. She had a neat little house, but it wasn't much. She always had to make do to make ends meet, but it was enough. What we saw as barely getting by, she saw as having her needs met and being taken care of. She saw it as *being blessed every single day of her life.*"

Amos held up the Bible. "Do you realize what an amazing statement that is? That's as powerful as anything written in here and more powerful than any sermon I've ever preached."

He looked at those assembled. "I don't think I can say anything to improve on that. Brother Bigelow, I don't think Mrs. Simpson needs us to intercede on her behalf in the slightest, but will you try? I think I've said all I'm going to be able to say."

As Bigelow began to pray, Amos retreated a couple of steps, turned his back and hung his head. *Amos, you're getting soft.*

Nineteen

Way too close, Amos thought. *I actually confessed.* It caused him to realize it would only be a matter of time before the whole thing blew up in his face. When that time came, he knew he would have to make tracks, and make them fast.

He needed to get some running money. In case of an emergency he had to have getaway money squirreled away, and the loss of that holdup money really had him in a bind. Another holdup was out of the question. Joseph seemed to be able to see right through those. He decided the best bet was to run another quick game in some neighboring town where he wasn't known.

To explain his absence, Amos told the people around town that he intended to ride around to some of the ranches. Then he slipped out and headed for Single Tree, a little railroad town a good way down the line.

As he rode, he pondered a strategy to replenish the funds. Maybe a pigeon drop? Or maybe run the old saddle lottery? That was always good for some money. Cowboys generally considered anybody down to selling his saddle to be in big trouble, and they'd cough up equally big money. Yes, that was the ticket, the old saddle game.

As soon as Amos hit town, he went to the saddler's shop. The little man was just closing the door as Amos rode up. He stopped, and a small look of resignation came over his face. But hungry for business, he immediately opened back up. "What can I do you for, stranger?"

"I need to see about a used saddle."

The man peered over the top of his spectacles, looking past Amos to eye his horse. "What's wrong with the one you have?"

"Nothing. This one is for a friend. A gift, but I can't afford to give him a new one."

"Wish somebody thought enough of me to buy me something as good as a saddle. Let me show you what I have."

He showed Amos several saddles. Amos settled for a Texas rig that was in decent shape but that had obviously seen a lot of hard work.

"Somebody get hard up and leave this with you?" He couldn't afford to have some local yahoo recognize it.

"No, I've had that old thing so long I don't even remember where I got it. No, wait a minute; I do too, now that I think on it. It was a wagon train that came through, years back. Guy decided to go home and sold off near everything he had."

Perfect, nobody would remember it. They haggled a little, and Amos got it cheaper than he really thought he would. He also bought a pair of well-used chaps and two pair of old spurs.

Now he had to try to make sure this funny little man wouldn't actually be in the saloon when he made his play. Amos handed over the money and said, "Sorry to be keeping you from your supper."

"The missus will be keeping it warm for me."

"You don't stop off for a bracer on the way home?"

He handed back the change. "Heavens no, she'd nail my hide to the barn door if I ever came home with liquor on my breath."

Amos gave thanks for a good temperate woman. "Well, tell her I'm sorry I kept you."

"It'll be fine," he held up the money Amos had just given him, "when she sees it was business."

Amos led Biscuit-eater down to the livery stable. No one was around, and the sign hastily painted on an old board read, "Pick you out a stall, hay's in the trough, feedbag and oats in the bin. We can settle up in the morning."

Excellent. There would be no liveryman who knew anything for Amos to worry about. He calculated this dodge was going to go slicker than axle grease on a two-dollar mirror. Still, as a precaution, Amos left Biscuit-eater saddled with the cinch loosened in case he had to leave town in a hurry.

Twenty

Anybody who walked into a saloon lugging a saddle and some leather chaps was sure to attract attention. Amos tossed the saddle on the bar and hollered for a beer. He let the cool liquid trickle down his throat.

He relaxed for a few moments, well aware that every eye in the room was on him. Then he leaned back against the bar on both elbows, hooked a heel on the rail, and in a loud voice said, "I guess you rannies know what it means to toss my saddle on the bar. It's for sale."

"Hard times, cowboy?" the bartender asked in a sympathetic tone.

Amos put on his practiced hangdog look and spoke back over his shoulder. "The worst. I'm up against it, and that's a natural fact."

"I reckon so. A cowboy that gets ready to sell his saddle is generally pretty much down as far as he can go."

An old man sitting at a front table spoke up. "Son, you don't have to sell your saddle. There's plenty here that'll stand you to a drink or a meal."

As if answering the question, the bartender pushed the money back at him. "I ain't taking drink money from a cowboy trying to sell his saddle."

A redhead over in the corner said, "Ain't no riding jobs

around here, cowboy, but if you go to riding the grub-line, all the ranches will feed you."

"Thanks, Red, but that ain't the whole story. Maybe I ought to tell you how things really are."

Amos looked out over the crowd. If he didn't have their full attention before, he had it now. It was time to lay it on. "It's my mother."

Amos knew there was only one thing more powerful than a cowboy having to sell his saddle, and that was motherhood. "She's dying of the consumption."

A soft gasp whispered through the room, and Amos hadn't even started to lay it on them thick yet. He was already seeing this was going to be worth a mint.

"I've already sold my horse," he lied, "but it still didn't give me the price of the fare home."

"Where's home, son?" the old timer asked softly.

"Mama's still in the old country. That means I have to get back over to Europe, and boat rides cost plenty of money." Amos opened the saddlebags. "The saddle is on the bar. It's served me well. My chaps are up for sale too, as are these spurs."

He had split up the two pairs of spurs that he'd bought to produce a mismatched set that was much more likely to produce sympathy. "And there's my rope. That's everything I own but the clothes on my back, and my mama's old Bible." Amos sat Joseph's Bible next to the saddle.

The old-timer said, "Nobody's going to buy your mama's Bible, son. Put it away. Ain't nobody here that cold. Let's see how this works out, and if'n it don't do the job, I'll pass my hat personal-like to make up the difference."

A buzz circled the room, a sort of low grumble like some small animals in the underbrush growling quietly at one other.

"None of this stuff is worth much, but it's all I got. I don't have any idea how to go about selling it. Anybody ever been an auctioneer?"

Nobody volunteered, as he knew would happen, and he really didn't want the gear auctioned anyway. That'd produce one top bidder on each item, and though the money per item might be good, it'd leave too many suckers out. Amos was about to suggest a lottery when the piano player said, "I seen them do a lottery once at a place I used to work up in the gold country."

Even better for somebody else to bring it up. "How's that work?" he said naively.

The young piano player perked up. Even though he performed nightly, it was background noise and generally nobody paid any more attention to him than they did to the faded mural on the wall. The attention made him seem to grow taller right there in front of their eyes.

"Well, this cowboy would put his items up as a prize. Everybody that wanted in would put up some sort of money, as I remember it was five bucks on that one. Once they put up their money, they would get to write their name on a piece of paper and put it in a hat. Then names were drawn for the stuff."

Amos was figuring a buck a head, so this was terrific. He resolved to use somebody to front for him in the future on a dodge like this. "That's good for me," he said quietly. Amos had been doing a quick head count in the room. Thanks to the railroad track-hands being in town, there were over seventy people in there.

The redhead said, "If we want to improve our odds, can we buy in more'n once?"

Bless your heart, cowboy. I didn't even think of that one. This takes sheep shearing to a whole new level.

They got up the money and there was hooting and hollering as names were drawn. You'd think they were vying for the crown jewels instead of an old used-up saddle and some worn-out gear.

Quite a few must have gotten in several times, because Amos had $545 in his kick when he said he was heading over to the train station to buy a ticket. Actually, what he had in mind involved getting out of town as quickly as possible, before the saddler or the livery stable owner blew the whistle on him.

As a matter of fact, he knew it would get downright interesting around there when the proud new owner of that saddle went over to sell it back to the saddler tomorrow, as he was bound to do. It didn't pay for a fellow to hang around after running a saddle lottery.

Rushing back to the stable completely intent on escape, he failed to notice the grinning man who blocked his path. Amos looked up to find Sam McDonald standing directly in front of him. Sam was Marcie's dad. "Preacher," he said, "whatcha doing over here dressed like that?"

"Uhhhhhhhh ..." It was getting harder and harder to think fast. "I'm ashamed to say I'm hiding."

"Hiding? What do you have to hide from?"

"My job. I put on these old clothes so I could relax a couple of days and not be called on to do the usual things preachers have to do."

"I reckon I understand that. Most folks on a ranch sure enjoy getting away from them cows for a couple of days."

"There, you see. Is that what you're doing?"

"More or less. I came over here to get Marcie's wedding present. You see that little Palomino over there at the hitching post?"

"Mighty fine looking horse."

"I think she'll be pleased. You going to be here a while, or are you headed back? I'd enjoy riding with you."

"Actually, I was on my way out of town right now." But Amos also wanted McDonald out of town before the thing blew up. McDonald would know right where to point any-body ready to come after him. "But I sure would like to have the company."

"Why not? I planned to head out in the morning, but my gear is still together. I can leave now."

McDonald stopped at the hotel, paid his bill, grabbed his saddlebags, and came back out. "You weren't kidding," Amos said. "Don't take long for you to get your stuff together."

Amos stepped up on Biscuit-eater and they headed out of town. The pair rode in silence for a while before Sam said, "Sorry I ain't been able to get acquainted with you before this. We tend to just stay out at the ranch and tend to things."

"My fault, I oughta been out there before now."

McDonald gave Amos a long, appraising look. "You know, you ain't like no preacher I ever met before."

Here we go again. "In what way?" *Seems to always be some-body looking crossways at me.*

"Well, I never heard me no better preacher, gotta say that, and you've sure enough got it all together when you're up there in front of folks. But I don't know, when you aren't up there behind that pulpit, you seem like a different guy."

"How so?"

"I don't know, you never quote from the Bible or talk to people about spiritual stuff unless you're actually preaching. And the way you talk, durned if you don't sound like a differ-ent guy just chewing the fat."

"I guess that's a failing of mine, Sam. I don't shoot from the hip very well. I have to have time to work up what I'm going to say. I do know it sounds different after I get it all writ out and just start giving it."

"That a fact? I thought you preachers always had a mouthful of words, and all you had to do was just spit them words out like a mouthful of horseshoe nails."

"Everybody thinks that. Preaching is harder work than folks think. A sermon takes a powerful lot of figuring." *Maybe not for me, but Joseph sure sweats a bucketful over them.*

"Ain't that a kick in the pants? You learn something new every day. I never figured on preaching like it was a real job or something. I mean like actual work. Aw, I'm messing this up something terrible. I don't mean that like it sounds. I just mean, I thought it was something that came plumb natural, not something that took so much effort."

"Don't let it bother you, Sam. I know what you mean."

Twenty-One

Amos did want to make his move on Judy. He admitted that now. Besides that, there was no way he could risk the word getting around if he decided to sport one of the local working girls, so that option was clearly out.

But how was a guy posing as a preacher supposed to go about it? How would she react? Amos didn't have any experience with nice girls, and he sure didn't know what might be expected of him as a parson. Still, he calculated that dinner should be safe, and the dining room at the hotel would be the most acceptable place in town.

Amos was used to women who could go with anybody they pleased, wherever they pleased, and if it ended up in a guy's room with a bottle and a warm bed, it was nobody's business but their own.

It occurred to him that maybe that was what he still needed to be doing. What business did he have messing around with a nice girl anyway? He had already found out that a preacher lives in a glass bowl, always watched and always judged. Of all the things that made this dodge a sweet deal, this constant scrutiny was a real pain.

Well, I've always been good at reading people, figuring out what they're thinking, how they're reacting, and making the necessary adjustments. I can do this.

Amos weighed these thoughts as he approached Judy's house but as he stepped up to knock on the door, an even bigger question nagged at him. Why was he working so hard to get with this girl under these circumstances? There *had* to be easier targets. He *knew* he wasn't looking for a lasting commitment.

Amos shined his shoes on the back of his pant leg before he knocked. John Daniels answered the door.

"Evening, Parson," John said, stepping aside and making room for Amos to enter. "Helen, the minister is here. You want to see if Judy is ready?"

He asked Amos to sit down. *Danged if I don't feel like a schoolboy waiting in the parlor under some father's watchful eye.* It turned out Amos wasn't the only one who was thinking that way.

"This feel as funny to you as it does to me?" John asked as he tapped his pipe out into the spittoon by his chair.

"I beg your pardon?"

"I don't know," he said. He turned to refill the bowl of the pipe with tobacco from a sack of rough-cut. "It's sort of like being back in the days when the cowboys around here used to come to court my Ellie."

"Strange that you should say that. It had just crossed my mind, too. You know, it takes me back a few years to when I was a youngster coming to call on a girl."

John finally got the pipe packed, set a Black Diamond match to it, and popped out his cheeks as he sucked the flame down into the tobacco. He completed the ritual, and seemingly satisfied with the results, blew out a long, lingering cloud of smoke that drifted slowly across the room.

"Let's see, where was I? Oh yes. Somehow it doesn't seem right for a growed man to be sitting here with his hat in his hand like a wet-behind-the-ears kid. But I reckon preachers have different rules to play by. Sorta have to go that extra mile to show nothing is going on, eh?"

"I guess so. I'll tell you the truth, John, I haven't courted anyone since I became a preacher." *That's the absolute truth, too.* "I'm charting new territory here. Listen, if I don't do what's expected of me, you'll let me know, won't you?"

"Sure I will, Parson, only we don't know what the right way to do it is either. We ain't had no preacher around to see how things work. I'd say you're taking steps to make sure everybody knows it's being done right and proper. I reckon most folks are watching real close, but I ain't heard nobody say nothing bad."

"I'm glad to hear it."

John laughed.

"I say something funny?"

"No, all of a sudden I got this feeling I ought to ask you what your intentions are."

Amos laughed too. Then he asked himself, *What are my intentions? Why did that question bother me? John was only kidding, right?*

"Good evening, Parson," a silken voice said.

John and Amos both got to their feet quickly. "Miss Judy, my goodness but you look lovely." Amos wondered if the nervousness that he was feeling was as obvious as it felt like it was.

She wore a high-necked, light-gray dress with a row of brass buttons up the front that stretched from the hemline to the neck. Small wonder it took her so long to get ready. It had buttons on the sleeves too, but they only came about three-quarters of the way down to her wrists. She had on white gloves and a little white hat with some sort of net attached to it on the sides.

"Thank you, sir."

"If we're going to walk out together, don't you think it's time you finally called me Amos?"

"Yes, Amos, you've asked me to do that several times. It's a bit awkward for me, but I'll try."

The walk to the hotel dining room was pleasant in the early evening air. Somewhere in the trees in the square, a mockingbird sang its young to sleep in the dusk.

They found the dining room more crowded than usual, but they asked for a table over to the side. Everyone in the room seemed to be watching them as they entered, though Amos thought it could have been his imagination. The buzz in the room subsided as they made their way through the crowd, then took on a higher pitch after they had passed by, somewhat like a beehive that had been disturbed.

"I'd say we're the topic of discussion tonight," Judy said.

Amos held out her chair for her. "You noticed that too?"

"How could I not notice?"

"You want to leave?" he hesitated before he took his own seat.

"No, sit down," she impatiently waved toward the chair. "I don't mind if you don't. It's rather fun being the center of interest for a change."

"For a change? I'd think you would be used to being the center of interest."

"What a sweet thing to say." She unfolded her napkin and put it in her lap. Amos did the same.

The light in the room had been subdued for the dinner crowd, the hotel doing its best to create a bit of elegance in a rustic setting. Crisp white tablecloths with blue linen napkins and flickering candles helped set the mood.

In stark contrast, the pair knew that down the street the

Trail's End Restaurant would be buzzing with loud talk and the clatter of plates being tossed at customers. Across the railroad tracks that served as the deadline between uptown and the lower end, cowboys would already be drunk and raising a ruckus in the dingy saloons. Small wonder decent towns-people wanted this little oasis of civility in the midst of it all.

The waiter came and lit the candles on the table, then handed them each a menu.

Amos smiled at him. "What do you recommend?"

"We have some very nice quail this evening that the chef prepares in a rather delectable garlic and butter sauce. We have new potatoes on the side and a fresh garden salad."

"Oh, that sounds lovely," Judy said.

"Then that's what we'll have," Amos replied as they handed the menus back.

"Shall I bring you some wine, sir?"

Amos thought about how good that would taste, but just before he replied in the negative, Judy said, "Are preachers allowed to have wine? I'm afraid I don't know. But then, Jesus and the disciples drank wine with most of their meals, didn't they?"

How convenient; that opened the door. He was going to have to look up more of this stuff in the Bible. "Yes, it is allowed as long as it is in moderation." He turned to the waiter to add two glasses of red wine to the order.

The waiter returned shortly and said, "The owner sent this bottle of fine champagne over instead of the wine, with his compliments. He is very pleased to have you in attendance this evening."

"Please give him our thanks."

"This is turning out to be an extraordinary outing." Judy favored him with a shy smile.

They sat in an awkward silence for a few minutes, noise-lessly sipping the champagne. She broke the silence. "I heard what you said to Uncle John."

"About what?"

She held the glass at eye-level in both hands, looking coyly over the top of it. "About not courting since you became a preacher and being unsure of how to go about it."

"And what did you think about that?"

"It's flattering. And it's really nice that you want to make sure everything appears quite proper. Before we came into the restaurant, I would have said you're making too much of it."

She looked around suddenly to catch a number of people sneaking a look. She glanced away quickly, as did they. A slow smile stole its way to the corners of her mouth. "See that? I suppose you didn't overstate it at all, and I don't think it's just me that is the center of attention."

"Perhaps you're right."

Later, she took his arm as they left. They strolled in the warm evening air, in no hurry to get back to the house. As they finally stopped at the door Amos swung her gently around and kissed her. Her lips were soft and warm, the kiss escalated, then ...

"*Reverend!* I'm not that kind of girl."

He took a step back, seeing the shock on her face. "I'm sorry. It was the evening." He swept a hand up to the stars. "Quite romantic."

She clasped her hands in front of her and looked down. "Yes, it was as much my fault as yours. Perhaps it was the champagne. Our old sin nature is never far away, is it?" Her breath was coming fast, her bosom rising and falling.

Old sin nature? Amos didn't know what that was, but it

sounded like something he could identify with. "No, I suppose not. I'm sorry if I offended you. I'm afraid I got caught up in the mood of the evening."

Her eyes came up. In the scant light they were soft and inviting. But now he knew better than to act on how it might appear. "It isn't that I didn't want you to kiss me. I did," she confessed. "But it isn't proper. We must be strong, Amos. We must pray for strength to resist temptation."

"Yes, we will. Take my hand and we'll voice a silent prayer." They closed their eyes and bowed their heads. *Preachers must be made outta iron,* Amos thought. *How in the world is a fella supposed to get anywhere with a girl when he has to play by this kind of rules?*

Twenty-Two

Amos slowed it down, determined to get it right. He planned a picnic, with a basket especially prepared by the cook at the hotel: the usual fried chicken, corn on the cob, and beans. There were plates, napkins, and utensils; the cook had left nothing to chance.

As he put the basket in the buggy, Amos supposed the cook wanted him to have his full attention on Judy. A lot of the town seemed to have the same thing in mind. They needn't worry; his attention could hardly be anywhere else.

Amos picked up Judy to head out of town in the sparkling surrey he had rented from the livery stable, pulled by a pair of matched blacks that were the hostler's pride and joy. He had been totally surprised to arrive and find them hitched to the rig.

"Looks like we've got ourselves a nice day for a picnic," Amos said, as the couple headed out of town.

"Yes, Amos, I'd say it's a perfect day."

Judy had on a crisp white blouse and a gray skirt, with a perky little flat straw hat secured with a hatpin on top of her head.

"That's nice. It's the first time you've used my first name and sounded comfortable saying it."

The countryside around Quiet Valley was all cattle ranches and open range, gentle rolling hills, green from a decent amount of rainfall for a change. There was a lot of foliage for sure, but not a lot of large trees. What trees there were tended to be mesquite, which could take the appearance of either a tree or a bush.

The pair made small talk as they drove along, until they came to a small pond surrounded by shady trees, primarily elms and cottonwoods. Amos unhitched the team and set them out to graze as Judy spread the red-checked tablecloth and laid out the picnic.

Judy removed her hat to let her hair down. She shook her head to let the long brown tresses fall free about her shoulders, sat down, and arranged her skirt about her.

"That's pretty; I didn't realize your hair was so long."

She gave him a shy smile. "I suppose I do keep it up most of the time."

"You should let it down more often."

She handed him a plate, and Amos said a very brief prayer over the food before he stretched out on his side of the tablecloth, propped up on one elbow, and began to gnaw on a chicken leg.

This was something new for him, relaxing with someone and being genuinely at ease without scheming and manipulating or trying to make something happen. He rather liked it. He put it into words; "I guess you're the easiest person to be with that I've ever met, actually, in my whole life."

"Why, Amos, what a nice thing to say. I enjoy your company as well."

"I suppose I'm a bit surprised you agreed to ride out without a chaperone."

"We've demonstrated our intentions clearly enough. We've shown people that nothing improper is going on. People expect us to be alone at some point."

"So that's how it's done. I wasn't sure." Amos wiped the grease off his fingers on a napkin, then took a drink of lemonade.

"You're an unusual man, Amos. A strange mix of very worldly and very naive, all at the same time."

You don't know the half of it, he thought as he reached for another piece of chicken.

"There are times I feel I know you so well," she continued, "and times I feel I don't know you at all."

Amos didn't feel the usual need to be on his guard that usually came with people asking personal questions, the hallmark of a man with too many secrets. "What would you like to know?"

"Just more about you. Who are your people? What do you like or dislike?" She took a dainty bite of chicken, barely a nibble.

"My people are from Missouri. My father dealt in livestock." *Stealing them mostly, wouldn't you like to know that?* Amos hated to lie to her. Technically he wasn't lying, merely choosing what to withhold from her, but the result felt the same. A little of the ambivalence toward the questioning disappeared.

He became more wary as he answered. "I'm afraid I didn't know my mother; she died in childbirth. I was raised by an uncle on a farm, and I'd have to admit I couldn't get out of there quickly enough."

She took time to swallow. "Raised by an uncle? Why not by your father?" If she noticed a change in his demeanor or tone of voice she gave no sign of it.

"He was gone a lot." *Mostly in jail or hiding out trying not to go to jail.*

"And what caused you to go into the ministry?"

That was a tough one. He couldn't say it was a good way to hide. What *did* cause people to do this foolishness? What would Joseph say? Then he had it. "I confess I didn't really want to, but the Lord put it on me to do."

The look on her face as she nodded told him he had guessed right. She blotted her lips with the linen napkin. "I see; so it was not so much something you wanted to do as much as something you felt you had to do?"

"Exactly." To be specific, he *had* to do it or Joseph would have made sure he got put in jail.

They ate for a while, then suddenly she looked up as if she had been sitting there thinking about it, and said, "Amos, what is it we're doing?"

The abrupt question caught him off guard and in the process of taking a bite of a chicken leg. It stayed poised in front of his mouth as he responded. "I take it the answer you're looking for is not that we're having a picnic?"

"No, silly, what are we doing as a couple? Are we becoming friends, or are we headed somewhere more serious?"

Amos stuck a finger in his collar and pulled on it. "Uhhhh, well, that's an interesting question. I suppose ... I mean I hadn't thought about it, but I surely do enjoy being with you, and I guess ..."

She smiled. "Never mind, Amos; you're turning as red as a tomato." She patted him on the arm. "I think it's a bit early to have this discussion. We'll talk about it later."

"If you say so." *How about much later? I better be careful here; this lady is starting to think about building a nest.*

Joseph and Amos sat down by the creek where Amos practiced his sermons, but Amos couldn't get his mind on what he was doing. The sun shone warmly on their faces, yet the gentle breeze cooled and relaxed them. That could have been the reason Amos wasn't practicing, but he had much more on his mind than simply woolgathering.

His voice was plaintive, his eyes asked for help. "She turned on me, Joseph. There we were having a nice relaxing picnic and all of a sudden she got serious."

"Methinks thou doth protest too much." He had a *huge* grin on his face.

"Methinks? What part of the Book is that from?"

"It's not from the Bible. It's a paraphrase of a quote from an old English writer, William Shakespeare."

His forehead furrowed, "What's a paraphrase?"

"You might say reworded. He was actually talking about a lady thinking too much."

"You've been reading old English writers?"

"I told you I got to read a lot while I still had the sight to do it. You should read more."

"I'm reading more already than I ever have in my entire life, trying to make some kind of sense out of the Bible. Still, I gotta say, that thing you just said sounds funny enough to be from there. What does it mean?"

"In a nutshell, it means you wouldn't be setting up such a fuss if you weren't more interested than you let on."

"You're as crazy as she is. The last thing I need is somebody around all the time poking her nose into my business. I'm only interested in a little female companionship. After all, it ain't like I can go see the girls across the tracks and still keep up this preacher front."

"That's true enough."

They sat in silence for a few minutes before Joseph changed the subject. "So, have you come up with more questions you want to ask? We can't neglect your religious education."

"I've got lots of questions. You believe prayer is answered?"

"With all of my heart."

"How do you know? Do you hear voices or something?"

"There have been those God has spoken to directly, or who have had angels bring a message to them. It would require less faith if it were that straightforward for all of us."

"You gonna give me the 'hear it in your head or feel it in your heart' stuff again?"

"Yes, that's most of it, but a major part of it is the results. Did we get what we prayed for?"

"Old man Tucker prayed for rain to save his crop, and he didn't get it; does that mean his prayer wasn't answered?"

"No, sometimes the answer to prayer is no, hard as that may be to accept. However, it's also true that a lot of people don't recognize answers to prayer because they didn't get what they asked for. They don't take time to realize that they got what they needed."

"Tucker didn't get rain."

"But he didn't lose his farm."

"Only because the railroad put in that spur and bought the right-of-way from him."

"Which gave him what he needed."

"But God didn't do it; the railroad company did."

"You think so? God works in mysterious ways."

Twenty-Three

*J*udy swept out the room that served as the church. She wore a full-length white apron, and her hair was caught up in a kerchief knotted in the front. Clouds of dust hung in the air as she paused to wipe her forehead.

She looked to see Amos come in the front door and bestowed a smile on him. He returned the smile and then stopped. He screwed up his face in a terrible contortion, catching and recatching his breath, until the threatened sneeze broke forth with awesome power.

He pulled the bandanna from his pocket as he sneezed again and again. Finally he got his sneezing under control and tried to catch his breath, holding the bandanna in place lest he be mistaken about the attack being over.

Judy shook her head as she watched him fight the onslaught, knowing full well that she had caused it. She started to apologize when it dawned on her what she was looking at. Those eyes looking over the top of the bandanna. It wasn't Amos, it was … it was … her vision blurred, and she felt darkness encroaching upon her. Her knees gave way, and she felt herself falling.

She awoke to find Amos looking down at her. "I can see you've been working way too hard. You must have gotten overheated."

"*Take your hands off me.*" Judy scrambled to her feet.

"What's the matter?"

"You pig."

"What? What are you ...?"

"That bandanna over your nose; I know who you are. I can't believe I never saw it before." She turned and ran from the room, leaving Amos standing there stunned.

Tears ran down Judy's face as she ran all the way to the sheriff's office. Joseph could hear her sobbing as she ran in.

"Here now, Miss Judy, what's all this?" He went to her, guided by the sound of the muffled sobs.

"Joseph, where's the sheriff?"

"He's over in Three Forks. What's the matter?"

"I know who the masked man is."

He took her by the arm and guided her to a chair. "You'd best sit down, Miss Judy. You're plumb winded."

She spun from his grasp and turned to face him. "Joseph, it's Amos. The masked man is Amos."

"Yes, I know."

"*What?* You know?"

"I've known almost from the beginning."

Judy dropped into the chair like a sack of flour. "Joseph, I just don't understand. I told you how I felt about him, yet you ..." Her hands fluttered like young birds learning to fly. They seemed to be moving of their own accord.

He stood where she could see his face, his hand on her shoulder. He could feel the suppressed sobs still racking her body. "I tried to discourage you without giving it away, remember?"

"Why? Why didn't you just tell me?"

"It's a long story."

"I have to know, Joseph. Why are you protecting him?"

"All right, how about if I tell you over a cup of tea?"

She nodded, wiping her eyes and nose with a handkerchief as Joseph made her a cup of tea. He returned, poured himself some coffee, and went through the entire story. He spared her no details. When he finished, he simply sat and waited. He knew it'd take a while for her to process the information.

Finally, she said, "Do you expect me to go along with this?"

"I can't tell you what to do. I can only tell you what the Lord is requiring of me."

"If I tell the sheriff, won't you get into trouble too?"

"You don't worry about that. You just do what you feel is necessary."

"Oh, Joseph, what am I to do? I'm so confused."

The fat's in the fire now, Amos thought as he watched Judy run straight to the sheriff's office. He didn't know why the sheriff hadn't come for him already, but he decided he'd better get his carcass out of there while he still had the chance.

He grabbed the sock that hid his money and stuffed it into his saddlebags. With the proceeds from the collection plate added, he had more than six hundred dollars, over a year's pay for a forty-dollars-a-month cowhand.

It wasn't enough. He couldn't run on that pitiful amount. As he threw his gear on Biscuit-eater, he wondered what on earth he was going to do. He needed money to buy silence, and enough money to put space between Quiet Valley and someplace far enough away to be safe. He couldn't afford to have to stop early and try to raise another stake.

But he had no choice. He reached under the horse for the cinch strap, kneed the animal to make him expel the air he was holding so the cinch wouldn't be so tight, and jerked it taut. He quickly worked the buckle, then led the animal to the back door of the stable.

A voice stopped him. "I thought you might be getting ready to run."

Amos spun, his gun covering the old man. "Joseph, you knot-head, I nearly shot you."

"That's the benefit of being blind. If I ever get shot, I'll never see it coming."

Amos looked past the old man, gun still at the ready. "The sheriff's not with you?"

"He's out of town. I think you need to know that Judy is not going to tell him. Not now anyway."

He holstered his gun and turned to the horse, gathering the reins and putting a foot in the stirrup. "Terrific. That should buy me some time." Amos stepped up into the saddle.

"No, it won't. Our deal still stands. If you run, I'll be the one who tells him." Amos again drew and cocked the pistol, but Joseph added, "and if you use that thing, my letter will do it."

Amos cursed him. "You don't leave a man any choices." He let the hammer down on the weapon.

"It's not me who doesn't leave any choices, but I don't have to go into that again."

Amos stepped back down. "So, I just wait and see? It's like living with a loaded gun to my head." He looked at the weapon in his hand. *Maybe that's it. Maybe it's not him I ought to be thinking of using this on. That's one way out of this mess he couldn't do anything about.*

Twenty-Four

Amos was sure he needed to pull another job. Whatever he did, he'd have to do it fast. It'd just be a matter of time before Judy's conscience started bothering her, and when that happened, he'd have to high-tail it out of there. If he had to chance running, he'd need a serious road stake.

I need something that ... that ... oh, wait, I've got it. Yeah, that's it. Smiling, Amos went up to his hotel room, washed up, and put on his Sunday suit. Time to get back into the part.

Cleaned up better than a newborn calf whose mama has just got through licking him down, Amos went to the stable and got Biscuit-eater. Clearly glad to be free of his stall for a while, the big horse wanted to stretch out, tossing his head to get more slack in the reins.

It was a long ride out to a big ranch over in the next county. The name on the gate proclaimed it to be the Box R, now headed by an old lady by the name of Splendora Cole. Her husband had been dead for several years.

Splendora could be classified as elderly. Who knew what her actual age might be? Her hair fell in tresses, too raven black to be natural, and the powder and rouge on her face still hinted at the profession she had been engaged in before her husband decided to make an honest woman out of her.

Splendora carried a lot of guilt about her earlier vocation.

Amos had called on her before, and this time he hoped to make that guilt work for him.

He dismounted outside the huge ranch house that would have been more at home on Nob Hill in San Francisco than sitting alone out on a flat Texas prairie. He wiped his boots on the back of his pant legs and used a handkerchief to flick the dust from his hat and shoulders.

A Chinese cook answered the door. "Nobody home," he said in a high nasal voice.

Amos stuck a foot in the door "Whey Fong, you tell Mrs. Cole the parson is here to see her."

"Missy not taking visitors, no home."

The little man winced and pulled his shoulders up until his neck nearly disappeared as a shrill voice cut through the air. "Whey Fong, you oriental doorstop, you turn the preacher away from the door and I'll use my scissors to cut that pigtail off. I'll use it for a tassel on this curtain pull."

The Oriental scuttered off, making a noise like a pig caught under a gate. The pigtail was more than ornamental for the little man and figured into his plans for the hereafter in a big way. Splendora knew this and used it on him like a weapon.

She sashayed toward the door, patting the curls on her neck into place. "Parson, come on in. You are so naughty coming to call on a woman without giving her time to prepare."

"Yes, ma'am, I know, only it's not practical to send word with you living out so far. But I knew you'd be presentable no matter when I called. I know a lady of your quality is always quite together before she shows herself downstairs. Lovely actually."

She smiled and swatted a hand at him, "How you *do* go on. Come in, Parson."

She turned, and Amos followed her in. She held herself very erect, partially because of the high stiff collar she wore. The heavy skirt made a soft, swishing sound as they walked down the polished hardwood floors of the hall. She was a big-boned woman, but not fat; nature had merely been generous in endowing her with a good frame and the soft curves to round it out.

"I'll have Fong make us some punch." She looked toward the head poking around the doorjamb off to the side. "You hear that, you oriental doorstop?"

The head disappeared and the muted sound of a sing-song language Amos had never heard before drifted back.

"That would be very nice after such a long and mighty dry ride."

She led him into a sitting room furnished with expensive furniture in shades of red and burgundy. A breakfront side-board loaded with expensive-looking china and various trinkets stood against the wall. They were obviously just for show or they would have been in the dining room. The room and its furnishings fairly screamed, "Look at me, I'm wealthy."

"What brings you out this way, Parson? Nobody rides thirty miles for a social call." She settled into a plush chair as she motioned for him to take the twin facing it.

"God sent me out here, ma'am," he intoned rather piously as he dropped his hat on the floor by the chair.

"How intriguing. Would God mind if you had a bit of cake while you explained?"

"Cake is one of God's best creations."

"But I divert you from your mission." She picked up a fan and used it in a delicate motion.

"A pleasant diversion, Mrs. Cole."

Fong came in with a silver tea service, but it held punch

instead of tea. Small squares of cake lined a serving plate. Fong served individual portions as he muttered quietly under his breath. He reminded Amos of a parrot he had once seen in the lobby of a Denver hotel; the bird had talked to itself in tiny musical tones all the time.

Amos shook his head as he watched the little man leave. "He'd drive me nuts."

"Fong is a dear," replied Mrs. Cole. She held the cup precariously in one hand as she made a dismissive wave with the other. "Besides, I don't understand what he says half the time."

"Is it just the two of you living in this big house?"

"No, there's my housekeeper, Marsha, and there are a lot of hands who live on the place, but they don't take meals with me. Well, perhaps the foreman occasionally."

"Of course."

"So tell me, what can I do for you?"

Amos cleared his throat as he sat up a bit straighter. He leaned forward and affected a look of intense sincerity. "It's my ministry, Mrs. Cole. God has told me He wants me to take my message on the road, to go out and reach the people wherever I might find them."

"What a wonderful goal. How can I help?" She snapped the fan shut and closed both hands around it.

"In order to do as God has told me to do, I need a wagon, a tent, and a portable pump organ."

"I see." He saw her smile become insincere and knew from long experience that she was framing a refusal in her mind.

"I know how devout you are, Mrs. Cole." Amos scooted forward to the front of the chair as he set his cup on the side table. "I hesitate to do this, but may I be brutally honest?"

"Well, I don't know ..." She snapped the fan open and

began fanning furiously. An expression approaching fear crossed her features.

He didn't wait for her to finish the thought. "I know about your past—"

She started to say something, but Amos held up a hand. "Don't fret yourself, ma'am; your secret will go to the grave with me. I only mention it because I know you'd like to atone for your past life. God keeps records of our donations in heaven, you know. Providing the funding to start this soul-saving effort will look mighty good on your record when it comes time to try and get in that gate."

"But I thought we couldn't earn salvation. I thought that ..."

"No, ma'am, don't get me wrong," Amos interrupted politely. "It's just your chance for a little good publicity up there where it'll do you the most good. And think of all those poor souls that'll be reached because of you."

"I suppose it is a good cause."

"Of course it is."

"What do you think it would cost?"

His gut told him she would name a better figure than he would, so he took a chance on it. "God never sets a price on a person's faith, ma'am. How much atonement do you need? What is heaven worth to you?"

The old Splendora came back for just a moment. "Since you are dead set on taking my lurid past to the grave with you, I must confess that I'm not sure the sum total of my late husband's estate could atone for all of my many sins," she laughed. "But I think five thousand dollars might buy me a little peace of mind."

Five thousand dollars? I was right; I'd have never tried for that much. "A magnificent gesture, ma'am. It will put the ministry on the road without having to pinch pennies."

"I can afford it, and it's only right." She moved to her desk and wrote out a bank draft. "Just present this to Jed down at the Quiet Valley Bank he'll take care of everything."

"Jed? Does it have to be that bank?"

"No, any of the area banks will honor it. Is there a problem?"

"I just don't want the folks in Quiet Valley to know I'm planning on leaving so early. They're rather attached to me over there. They want me to stay and be a regular pastor to them. But I know I have to take my message to those who haven't heard it."

"Of course, I understand."

They visited for a good while. As Amos left, he had just stepped into the saddle when she said, "By the way, Preacher, don't think I don't know what I'm getting for my money."

"Ma'am?"

"I know I can't buy my way into heaven, but I figure helping advance the spread of God's Word can't hurt any when I have to stand up there before Him and explain myself."

Twenty-Five

Amos met Judy on the boardwalk as he left the livery stable. He couldn't understand how she could look so cold and have such fire in her eyes at the same time. He stopped a couple of paces away. "Are you speaking to me again?"

"I suppose." She folded her arms across her chest.

"I know you're mad. I know you're disappointed."

"You don't know the half of it. I'm furious." Her eyes remained down, darting up occasionally to send hot little blasts. "I can't believe you put your hands all over me."

"Did I? What did I touch? Or did I just make a move, and you reacted? Didn't you read more into it than was there?"

"You were about to do it."

"No, I wasn't. You were too close to finding out the truth. I would never be disrespectful to you. I knew what you'd do, but if you hadn't reacted exactly as I expected, I would have stopped short of touching you any way I shouldn't have. I just needed to do something that would spook you, make you hate the masked man."

"You accomplished that well enough; now I hate both of you."

"Hate is a pretty strong word."

"I don't think it's strong enough. You're just lucky I can't turn you in without implicating Joseph, or you'd be behind bars now. You deceived me, deceived this whole town."

"I didn't intend to. I just planned on a simple disguise until things settled down from the robbery, then I intended to ride on. I didn't know I'd be asked to actually act like a preacher. I sure didn't know I was going to meet someone as wonderful as you."

"Don't try your silver-tongue ways on me. The blinders are off. I see you for what you are, and I don't like what I see."

As she stalked into the jail, Sheriff Wilson said, "Well, good morning, Judy, what can I do for you?"

She murmured "Good morning" in a sullen voice as she stomped straight through the office. Joseph stood at the stove in the back. She stopped, looked at him for a moment, then disappeared through the back door.

"Oh my," Joseph said. He set the pans of food off the heat and followed her. A prisoner heard the clatter and complained, but Joseph said, "Hush now, I got business to tend to."

As Joseph pulled off his apron, the sheriff stuck his head in and said, "What's the matter with Judy? She nearly took my head off."

"It's a personal thing, Sheriff. She didn't mean anything by it. She just needs somebody to talk to."

"Well, I do know she finds it comforting to talk to you. There's folks that'd think a white woman being that friendly with a black man wouldn't be appropriate, but I know better. Harrrumph, guess I'd better keep my nose out of things that don't involve me."

Joseph smiled behind the big man's back as he heard him snatch his hat off the rack and rush out the front door as if a brush fire were licking at his coattails. The sheriff could face down a desperate man with a gun, could probably take on a grizzly bear with his bare hands, but an angry woman was another subject entirely. He didn't know what the sheriff would do if one actually started crying on him. Start crying with her, probably.

Joseph stepped out the back door to find Judy pacing the yard. She was muttering to herself and had her arms folded to hold herself closely. She was primed to explode and he didn't intend to be the one to light the fuse. Not if he could help it.

"Miss Judy, I swear I can smell smoke coming out of your ears."

She stopped and glared at him. "That wouldn't surprise me in the least."

His voice was soft, gentle. "Let me guess. You've talked to Amos?"

"I have."

"And it didn't go well?" He motioned for her to sit down. She ignored him. "Come on, take a seat over here. I can't sit while you're standing, and my old legs don't hold me up as good as they used to."

She dropped onto the bench with a pronounced air of resignation. He smiled. "Whenever you're ready."

"He denied that he touched me."

"Didn't I say back when we talked that you may have gotten scared and thought the whole thing to be more than it was? You need to be real clear on this. Did he or didn't he?"

"He tried anyway." She snapped out the words, biting off the end of them.

"Is that true, or did he intentionally make a move to scare you?"

"Whose side are you on?" It was a good thing he couldn't

see the anger on her face. Then again, he didn't have to see it to know it was there.

He spoke in gentle, placating, quiet words designed to take the heat from her anger. "Yours, Miss Judy, all the way. That's why I want to make sure you are absolutely clear on things. You are a little excited, after all."

"No, I'm not excited, I'm mad. Extremely mad."

"It doesn't take eyes to see that. What I'm wondering about is *why* you're so mad. Are you just mad at him in general, or are you mad about something specific he might have done? I'm afraid I don't think we're talking about the real issue. Be honest with me, and with yourself, and we can get somewhere with all this."

Her shoulders slumped as she let out a long sigh. "Be honest with myself? That's not easy."

"I know."

They sat quietly for several minutes, staring off into space. Both had their hands clasped in their laps. Finally, she said, "All right, so he really didn't actually do anything. I can't see it makes any difference. He deceived me."

"No secret there, Miss Judy. He deceived the whole town, and in that he had my help."

"Yes, that's what has kept me quiet."

He hesitated before saying what he knew must be said. "Is it all that's kept you quiet?"

"Of course." The brief flare-up subsided. Joseph waited it out. "Oh, you know it isn't. Just hours before this happened I was starting to dream of a future with him."

"So your feelings are all confused? Is that what you're saying?"

"That's it exactly. I suppose I'm mad because I hate him and love him all at the same time. I don't know what to think.

I mean, he's done terrible things, but he's so considerate, so polite. I'm so mad I could spit, but at the same time, oh, I just don't know."

"You didn't see it coming. Outlaws should wear a sign, or at least cuss, spit tobacco, scratch themselves, and belch. Maybe not ever take a bath."

"You're teasing me." A smile toyed with the corners of her mouth. He heard it in her voice.

"Yes, a little. I don't think he's an outlaw. I think he's a young man with a good heart in spite of himself. He's made a lot of bad choices, I admit, but I don't think it's too late for him. And as to why he's polite, he's been impersonating a preacher. Would you believe him in that role if he had been any other way?"

"Of course not."

"There you have it." He paused, his words hanging in the air. "You have feelings for him, but you don't know what to make of him?"

"Yes. Oh, Joseph, you obviously see something in him; tell me what you see."

"It's not what I see in him, but what I believe God sees in him. He's a scoundrel, sure enough, but under all that roguish exterior is something good, something worth keeping. I do know he has a powerful gift for preaching."

"Yes, I know you feel that way, and I've certainly seen the gift. Do you think you'll win him over?"

"To be truthful, no. I've been able to reach him with a lot, more than he knows. I've been able to make him stay and to actually use his gift. I've been able to get him to read the Bible, although he does it for the wrong reasons. But the very fact that I've had to use so much pressure to do these things, I really believe, makes me the last person in the world who could ever win him over. He's too stubborn. He wouldn't allow me that victory if he were standing at the gates of hell and could see the flames inside."

"Well, if that's the case, then who ...?"

"I think we both know the answer to that one."

"You mean?"

"Yes, little lady, if you can forgive him enough to become God's instrument, I think he'd follow you right into those Pearly Gates. I don't think he knows it yet, and certainly wouldn't admit it even to himself, but he would."

"Oh my. Now I really don't know what to think."

Twenty-Six

*S*unday came, and no description could do justice to the look on Joseph's face as he sat on the front row in the service. He had to be happier than anybody had ever seen him.

His clear, booming baritone gave a depth to the singing that had never been there before. People smiled at each other as they watched him belt out the old familiar hymns. This was no token welcome; they were genuinely glad to have him there. It hadn't been easy for some of them, and the town had been buzzing with the discussion for weeks, but finally the right of it had prevailed.

Judy was at her usual place at the piano, but she was very reserved. She hadn't even spoken to Amos that morning.

Amos was so wrapped up in worrying about Judy that he didn't even notice when Brother Bigelow finished the opening prayer and called on him. "Brother Amos ... *Brother Amos.*"

"Huh, oh I'm sorry, I was meditating before I began." He walked to the pulpit and opened the Bible. He had finally gotten around to reading in the Book of Amos. The idea of a book of the Bible with *his* name on it appealed to him, and he really wanted to make use of it. The problem was that Joseph had never written anything from it.

Amos looked out over the congregation. It was time he showed Joseph that he wasn't as dependent on him as he thought. After all, he was a smart guy. Amos made up his mind that it was time the old man found out that he was the one who understood how to work these people, how to play their emotions like a fiddle.

"Turn in your Bibles to the Book of Amos." Joseph's head snapped up, confusion on his face. That was not in the sermon they had worked on together.

Again Amos looked out over the crowd. "Yes, I know it sounds a little funny for me to refer to that book, but I've always enjoyed having a biblical name. My mother was very religious, so naming me for one of the disciples was the natural thing for her to do."

Joseph squirmed in his seat, shaking his head. *Disciples*, he thought. *I don't know where this is going, but I have a bad feeling about it.*

Amos couldn't help but notice Joseph squirm, but he misinterpreted it, thinking the old man couldn't stand the thought of his branching out on his own.

"Now I'll admit it's not the easiest book to read," he continued, "what with all that old language, and full of the names of people who are long dead, but fortunately years of study have prepared me to do it."

Amos reasoned that if they liked that hell-fire stuff last time, they were going to love it this time. "Look at chapter 2 verses 1 through 3: 'Thus saith the LORD; For three transgressions of Moab, and for four, I will not turn away the punishment thereof; because he burned the bones of the king of Edom into lime:

"'But I will send a fire upon Moab, and it shall devour the palaces of Kerioth: and Moab shall die with tumult, with shouting, and with the sound of the trumpet:

"'And I will cut off the judge from the midst thereof, and will slay all the princes thereof with him, saith the LORD.'"

Amos snapped the book shut and looked directly into the faces in front of him. *I've got them now.* The expressions on those faces were those of shock and confusion. *Now to nail it home.*

"I know you don't know who these people are, but it doesn't matter. This is God talking. This is God passing out punishment on those who oppose Him."

The vision of the fiery pit stirred them deeply last time. How about a vision of a looming, powerful God who punishes those who challenge Him? This is my best yet.

Amos thundered ... he prowled the aisle ... he painted a picture that showed the congregation the divine retribution hanging over their heads if they failed to do what God wanted them to do. He took that dreadful theme all the way through to the bitter end and then again turned the altar call over to Brother Bigelow, saying he was going outside to pray.

Leaning back against a tree in smug satisfaction, he looked up and saw Joseph come out. "Over here," he called out.

The old man headed toward Amos, yelling at him while he was still halfway across the yard, "Have you lost your mind?"

"You better quiet down; somebody is going to hear you. You're just sore that I was able to write a sermon without you."

"I sure wouldn't have written that one." There was a tone in his voice that had never been there before, and the look of disgust on his face was obvious. He wasn't kidding; he really was mad.

"Really? And what was wrong with it?"

It took an effort for Joseph to restrain his volume. "Other than the fact that you named Amos as one of the disciples?"

"So?"

"He wasn't a disciple; he was a prophet."

"What's the difference?"

"I don't have time to explain it to you before they come asking you the same question."

"Why would they ask?"

"They're asking right now. When you left, they didn't have an altar call. They gathered up front and started trying to figure out what in the world was going on."

Amos felt his stomach tighten, and his voice sounded strained as he answered, "I don't understand."

"I know you don't, or you'd have never said the things you said in there. My guess is that you've let the cat out of the bag. I've seen you talk your way out of a lot of things, but I don't know a thing to suggest as a way to talk yourself out of this one."

"So I got a name wrong. You watch; I'll smooth it over."

"It's not just *a* name. You said it was one of the twelve."

"Twelve what?"

"My point exactly." Then he pointed. "What's that I hear over there?"

"People beginning to come out of the service. I better get over there and do the hand-shaking bit."

"I wouldn't if I were you."

"Maybe you're right. The glances they're shooting over this way are like war arrows."

Joseph just shook his head. "Amos, I think you've done it now."

Twenty-Seven

When the crowd came out of the service, they looked more like a lynch mob than a church congregation. Amos was puzzled. He went over to the Turners' house for Sunday dinner, as per the invitation, but the curtains were all drawn, and nobody answered the door.

Amos walked back downtown. As he progressed down the boardwalk, people suddenly crossed the street or turned around and went the other way to avoid him. He realized that Joseph was right; he had really done it this time. This was going to take a heap of smoothing over.

Amos went into the Trail's End Restaurant for lunch. Spuds Horton waited on him personally. Spuds was an ex-army cook, balding, and pot-bellied. He had a stub of a cigar in his mouth and wiped his hands on the towel he wore as an apron as he approached the table. He wasn't a church-going man, so he had no idea that anything was going on.

"Well, howdy, Amos," he said jovially. "Unusual to see you not booked for a meal on a Sunday." Amos managed a weak smile. Spuds took his order.

Later, as he served Amos his meal, Spuds leaned over and said quietly, "What's going on, Preacher? I don't think I've ever seen anybody so pointedly ignored in my whole life."

"It's a long story, Spuds."

"Well, it'll have to keep then. I'm busier than a one-armed paperhanger here."

Amos focused his attention on his meal. The tension in the room was so thick it could be cut with a crosscut saw. People ate quickly and filed out. Amos soon had the place pretty much to himself, except for a few folks who were blissfully unaware that anything was happening.

Spuds came over, again wiping his hands on the towel, a long-established habit. "Well, Preacher, you sure know how to clear out a room. You were going to tell me what ... uh-oh."

Amos followed his gaze to see a delegation come in the front door. Spuds disappeared as if he had never been there. Amos used his napkin to wipe his mouth and then steeled himself for the approaching confrontation.

The crowd pulled up in a solid front. Brother Bigelow apparently would be the spokesman. He looked like he had clouded up and was about to rain all over the place. Those with him didn't look any happier.

"We want to know what that was all about," he growled menacingly.

"What do you mean?"

"A man of the cloth who says Amos was one of the disciples? Unthinkable."

"I was just testing. You people claim to be Bible-readers; I wanted to see if that was true."

"That won't wash, Preacher, if in fact you are a preacher."

Witherspoon then jumped into the fray. "And what was that sermon all about? That wasn't a picture of God; that was ... was ... I don't know, some sort of ... actually, I don't know what it was."

"You don't think God can be vengeful?"

"Most certainly, but even-handed, and then only when it's

justified. God never punishes His flock just to show His power."

"That's what I heard in there, all right," Bigelow said. "It was disgusting. You used Scripture to make your point, all right, but the picture you painted with it was ridiculous."

"And how about Joseph?" Witherspoon said. "What's his part in this? He always listens to your sermons, I hear."

"He didn't hear this one. He was over there in a flash after church asking me some of the same questions you are."

Bigelow didn't look satisfied with the answer, but he let it go. "There's something really, really wrong here, and I intend to get to the bottom of it."

They spun on their heels as if they were hitched in tandem and marched out in righteous anger. Amos got the impression they were actually giving off sparks as they stomped out of the room.

Spuds peeked around the corner, then eased back out. "Tarnation, Preacher, I hear tell it ain't uncommon to step on people's toes a little in a sermon, but you must have come down on them uncommon hard. Them folks are plumb upset."

"They are that, Spuds. They are that."

Twenty-Eight

The next morning the hotel clerk informed Amos he would have to move out because his room was needed. Funny thing, there weren't many other guests. It looked as if he'd be sleeping in the stable come nightfall.

Amos tried to make a few calls around town to members of the congregation, but nobody seemed to be at home. He wondered if he had already been tried and convicted on the basis of a single sermon, or if he'd get a chance to redeem himself at the next service.

It wasn't as if he could just run out, which would be his usual response when a game he was running went sour. No, Joseph had him locked in. If he ran for it, he'd be in jail before the day was out. Joseph had promised that would happen, and there was no doubt he was a man of his word.

Amos had never had to stand and fight when things went astray like this, and he didn't like it.

Maybe it was best just to put the issue squarely on the table. He turned in at the bank. Bigelow couldn't hide; the bank was open for business.

The banker looked up, and an expression came over his face as if he had just bitten into something very distasteful. "You've got some nerve coming in here." He didn't get up, and he didn't offer Amos a chair.

"That's just it, Jed ..."

He shot Amos a hot look. "That's Mr. Bigelow to you."

Amos wilted under his glare. "All right, Mr. Bigelow. What kind of Christian is it who condemns a man on the basis of one sermon, and without letting him at least have the chance to explain?"

The banker pushed back in his chair, to put the maximum distance between them. "It's the kind of Christian who has had his faith mocked and has been dealt with falsely."

"But surely this much flap over a simple slip of the tongue ..."

Bigelow came swiftly to his feet, leaning on the desk with his left hand and shaking a finger in Amos's face with his right. "That's just it, you scoundrel. That was no simple slip of the tongue. Calling Amos one of the disciples is something no man of God would ever do, not ever. And that sermon you piled on top of it made it absolutely clear."

"I was just a bit overzealous."

"Overzealousness had nothing to do with it." He waved a hand at Amos in a dismissive gesture and sat back down. He picked up a paper from his desk and began to study it. "I don't think you really are a preacher," he said without looking up. "Most of us don't. If you are, you are no preacher any of us wants to listen to."

"So I don't get a chance to square things next Sunday?"

"Go ahead; nobody will be there to listen."

"Surely everybody deserves a second chance."

Bigelow finally looked up. His eyes were hard, uncompromising. "If you really were a preacher, you'd know that a Christian can forgive almost anything except someone who mocks God. There are no second chances for that with us."

"But ..."

The banker turned his attention back to his paperwork. "I've said all I intend to say, *Mister* Taylor. Now if you'll excuse me, I am most busy." His tone made it clear the former title of Reverend was permanently gone as far as he was concerned.

Amos walked out of the bank, turning to go down the walk. People disappeared in front of him like magic. He remembered what he had read in the Bible about the people who had leprosy. He felt as if he should be shouting, *"Unclean ... unclean."*

"I think I've gotten to the bottom of this," a voice said behind him. He turned to see the sheriff striding toward him. His face was dark, foreboding, and his eyes fixed Amos in their glare as he approached. Amos was *not* surprised to see him.

The sheriff stopped, his face uncomfortably close to Amos's nose. "Funny thing, Taylor, it never occurred to me to pay any attention to the tracks your horse makes until you got folks so riled up. Set me to thinking."

The lawman inched even closer. "When I went to look, those tracks were mighty familiar, and I ought to know, I've followed them all over the place for months. Made me feel mighty foolish that you've been right under my nose all along, and I couldn't see it. Sorta feel like you've rubbed my nose in it the whole time."

The sheriff spun Amos around roughly as he snapped a pair of manacles on his wrists. "I think it best we change your accommodations a mite while we sort all of this out."

The magic disappearing act reversed itself. As the sheriff propelled Amos roughly down the boardwalk, people came from everywhere, to gather in twos and threes, heads together, whispering and pointing. A small town loved nothing better than something juicy to talk about and they knew this would fuel the gossip for weeks to come.

Yet it was no longer simply a matter of speculation and gossip. People now knew they had been deceived, and they weren't happy about it. Angry voices followed Amos, striking like rocks thrown at his back. The most shocked face in the crowd was a very pretty one, marked by tears slowly coursing down her cheeks. Judy's decision had now been made even harder, if not impossible.

Twenty-Nine

I guess you're going to get to find out about these beans for yourself now," Joseph said. He slipped a tin plate through the bars. "It certainly won't be as good as all the food those ladies have been plying you with."

"That's for sure."

Amos sat down on the bunk. His "new accommodations," as the sheriff called them, were pretty sparse. The jail was the pride of the little town, red brick with bars set solidly in the thick walls, and a cement floor. It was an even more imposing structure than the courthouse, which was a two-story wooden structure on the square.

The brick and steel made it a cold, imposing place. Even in the warmth of summer it felt damp and depressing. Amos looked through the bars at Joseph. "They still looking cross-ways at you about this?"

"I suppose the jury is still out on that one. They're meeting on it tonight. They told me I should be there."

"Joseph, I'm sorry I got you into this. You've really stuck your neck out for me, and there ain't no way you deserve any part of what I have coming. I know you don't believe me, but ..."

"You're wrong there, Amos. I do believe you this time. I can hear it in your voice." He reached over to pick up his old

Bible and pushed it through the bars. "I brought this from the church. I thought you might like to continue to read in it."

Amos pulled back as if the old Bible were hot. "Reading that thing is what got me into this mess."

He continued to hold it out. "No, trying to use what you read in here incorrectly is what got you into this mess. I told you we all need a spiritual guide when we first start trying to understand. I believe what you can find in here is the only thing that can get you *out* of what you've gotten yourself into."

Amos took the book but said, "Even your God can't get me out of this one."

Joseph sat down in a chair outside Amos's cell. "You're wrong there. Nothing is beyond the power of God."

They sat and looked at the floor together, though only one could see it. Amos ignored the plate of food on his lap. "So if you prayed for Him to get me out of this, you figure He might do it?"

Joseph nodded gently, "He might, but that's the wrong kind of prayer. I will simply pray that His will be done. He might feel you need to be disciplined to help you learn your lesson. If He does, then that's what would be best for you."

"I figured you'd say something like that." Amos set the book beside him on the bunk. "Well, I have to do something to pass the time. I might get around to reading some more."

Amos sat and stared at the food without eating. "There is one thing I do want to know."

"What's that?"

"I just don't understand. I preached a hell-fire and damnation sermon before, and everybody was tickled to death. This last one had to be every bit as scary, and exciting, but this time everybody got all stirred up like somebody had kicked over an ant bed. I don't get the difference; isn't the goal to make people fear God?"

"It's a good thing to respect God's power. He can get angry, and just like a father down here on earth, He will punish His children if they disobey. But fear of God isn't sufficient for salvation. You know Satan fears God, but that fear doesn't help him at all."

"So what are you trying to say, Joseph? You always talk around things."

Joseph got up to pace the floor. "No, I don't. It's just not as simple as you want it to be. God can visit difficulties on His children, give discipline when it's called for. He knows how to get angry, and He knows how to get our attention. But some things just happen to everyone, like that tornado that happened last year over in the next county. It just happened."

"You gotta chew it finer, Joseph. I'm not following."

The old man stopped and rubbed his chin as he studied on what he needed to say. "God doesn't promise bad things won't happen to His children, but He does help us get through things and comfort us when things do go bad for us."

Joseph put his fingertips to his forehead. "Look at it like this, if you had a child playing on a swing, and you saw the rope was frayed, you'd have the chance to protect her. But if the rope broke before you got there, and she fell and scraped her arm, you'd kiss it and offer her comfort. You wouldn't have intended for the child to get hurt, but it would have happened anyway, and you would respond with love and concern. I think it's the same way with God and His children."

"So people got mad because ..."

"Because you portrayed Him as a mean God, always watching for us to make a mistake so He can heap judgment on us, punishing people for no particular reason just to show

His power. There are lots of illustrations in the Bible where God found it necessary to demonstrate His power, but never without reason. He is a just God above all else."

"I see."

"Do you?"

Amos's head dropped. "No, not really. I guess I thought I had a free pass on that railroad. You said God was using me, and that I was doing a lot of good. I figured that meant He'd take care of me, whether I believed or not."

"You had the answer right at your fingertips."

Puzzlement filled Amos's eyes as he looked up. He didn't feel like he'd had *any* answers in his hands, not recently anyway. "I did? When?"

"When you were looking for something to use over in the book of Amos, you should have looked further over, in chapter 5, where the prophet Amos makes it clear that unacceptable or insincere worship is worse than no worship at all."

"So even if I'm doing good ..."

Joseph held the bars in both hands as if he looked through them at the distraught man. "God can be pleased something good is happening, even if done for the wrong reasons, and be displeased about the motives of the one doing it."

A pain situated itself in the middle of Amos's forehead, threatening to spread to a full headache. It was so hard to try to *really* understand instead of just going through the motions. "So when you said you were helping me because God was being served even if I wasn't doing it for the right reasons, it meant what?"

"It meant it was the right thing for *me* to do."

The pain intensified. "But you're saying that didn't make it the right thing for me to do?"

"Now you're getting it."

"You're right. I wish I'd found that passage and used it instead of the one I settled on."

Joseph turned to walk away. Amos said, "How about letting me out of here?"

Joseph chuckled, "We both know the only safe place for you now is inside that cell."

Thirty

*E*veryone met at the school/church. They were still angry. Joseph couldn't see the looks directed at him, but he could hear the anger in their voices.

Sheriff Wilson put Amos over at the side and warned him to keep his mouth shut or get thrown back in jail. Amos vowed to keep quiet, as he didn't want to take a chance on missing this meeting.

The sheriff moved up to hold down the pulpit. His voice was not unkind as he called Joseph down to the front. The silence in the room was almost tangible as Joseph slowly made his way to where the sheriff stood.

"Joseph," the sheriff said as he put his hand on the old man's shoulder. "I don't want you to be nervous about all of this." He looked up to send a glare at those assembled, a challenge as strong as an elephant's trumpet.

"I've never known a finer, more upstanding man," he said as he looked at the crowd. Then his voice softened, and he turned to Joseph, "But I figure you know something about all of this, and I reckon it's time for you to tell us."

"Yassah, Sheriff, reckon I knows all of it, and I believe it's time." He turned unseeing eyes toward Amos. "Massa Amos, it's all out now. Does you release me from my pledge? It won't serve no use for me to be quiet."

The con man glanced nervously at the sheriff who said, "Answer the man."

"You do what you have to do, Joseph; nothing you say can make it any worse for me."

Joseph turned his head toward the crowd. "Massa Bigelow, did you bring that envelope I done asked for, sah?"

"I did." The banker handed the document to a young boy to deliver to the sheriff.

"Sah, can I ask how long you've had that letter?" Joseph said.

The banker frowned. "You know very well how long; you gave it to me."

"I'se sorry, Massa Bigelow, I meant to ask if you would tell everybody how long it is you've had it."

"Oh, well, for about three months now."

"Sah, wouldn't that be almost from the day that Massa Amos Taylor got to town?"

"Why, I suppose so." He nodded. "Yes, the time would be about right."

"Thank you, Massa Bigelow, sah. Sheriff, I 'spect it'd help if you read this to everyone first, then I'll say my piece."

Wilson opened it to look at the paper inside. "Did you write this?"

"Yassah."

"How ..."

"Yassah, Sheriff, I know, but I can writes some right now to show you how I can do it if you like."

"Ain't necessary. If you say you writ it, that's good enough for me." The sheriff looked embarrassed as he fished a little pair of half-glasses out of his pocket, but he offered no apology. He cleared his throat and began to read. The whole story was there in exact detail. The proof against Amos, and his complicity in the whole affair, was spelled out in meticulous detail.

As the sheriff finished reading, a voice in the back yelled at Joseph, "You knew he was skinning us, and you kept quiet? You ought to be in jail with him."

"Mr. Duval," Judy said sharply. "There isn't a more godly man alive than Joseph, and he doesn't deserve to be talked about that way. He said in his letter that he went along with that charade because he knew God wanted him to do so."

The man pulled off his hat. "I don't mean to be taking issue with you, ma'am, but it still don't set right with me."

"If anybody has a Bible here," Joseph said, "you might turn to Acts 9:15. There's a story there about how Saul done come under conviction, and this feller named Ananias complained that Saul was a sinner and not worthy to be healed."

He paused while some people looked it up. He could tell by the paper rustling when they had all found the passage.

"You have it?" Joseph fought straying a little from his affected Southern dialect. It was hard to do and still make his case. "You see there where the good Lord done told him, 'The man is my chosen vessel to bear My name.' I reckon Massa Amos ain't worthy to do what God wants him to do, any more than them folks thought Paul was, but I'm dead sure God done chose him, and it ain't up to me to second-guess God."

"God was sure right about Saul, or Paul," Edgar Duval said. He grinned as he looked around. "It always has confused me for Paul to change his name partway through things. I like to have never figured out the Bible wasn't talking about two separate people."

Then he remembered what he was fussing about, and the anger returned to his voice as he continued. "But we ain't talking about Paul here; he's one of the most important figures in the Bible. We're talking about this snake. Joseph, you say God chose him? How can you be so sure?"

"Yassah, it ain't my place to lecture nobody, but that's just the point. Paul wasn't one of the most important men in the Bible when God chose him. In fact, he was not only a non-believer, he was persecuting them Christians."

Joseph took several steps toward the man. "I mean, it's hard for me to figure, Massa Edgar, but how does any of us know when God speaks to us? We hears it up in our heads, or in our hearts, and it comes on us that it's real. I knows I'm an old fool, but I'm very sure."

The sheriff walked over to put his hand on the old man's shoulder, but when he spoke he looked at the crowd. "I don't know if people believe you or not, Joseph, but I know *you* believe it. I'm just as sure you acted out of faith, and out of a belief that you were right."

"Thank you, sah." Joseph said. "I remembers reading about when Paul was in prison, people told him there was a bunch of folks out preaching for the wrong reasons, and he said it was okay, that it didn't matter what the reasons was, they was getting the Lord's work done. I hear tell that several people sitting here right now came to the Lord because of the words God put in Massa Amos's mouth. I got to wonder if it means they weren't really saved if he wasn't sincere. Anybody feel like they ain't really a Christian 'cause it was him what spoke the words?"

"That's a good question," Sheriff Wilson said as he removed his hand and took a step toward those gathered. "Anybody feel like that?"

There was silence for several moments. Then Bill Dance spoke up. "I reckon I would have made my peace with the Lord whether Amos brung me to it or not."

The sheriff walked over to him. "You saying you'd have got it done with or without Amos?"

"Sure I would have." The sheriff continued to look him square in the eye, measuring, calculating.

Dance broke it off first and looked down. "Aw, I reckon not. The Devil had a good solid hold on me. Whether he played games with us or was serious, it was Amos what put the fear of God in me."

"This is preposterous," Bigelow shouted as he jumped to his feet, pointing an accusing finger at Amos. "The man is an outlaw and a brigand. I can't believe we're even talking about this."

"I don't mean to be disrespectful, Massa Bigelow," Joseph said quietly, turning in the direction of the banker's voice. "But didn't I hear you say he was the finest preacher you'd ever heard after he done give that lake of fire sermon?"

"I did, but that was back when I thought ..."

"So if he really had been a preacher, he'd be the finest one you ever heard?"

"Don't be insolent," Bigelow barked. "And don't try to put words in my mouth."

"No, sah, I'd never presume to put words in anybody's mouth, particularly a fine, upstanding gentleman like you. I knows my place, I do. It just seems that we either believes what's in that book, or we don't. I believes it to be God's truth, every word of it. So I figures that if there's a problem with it, the problem's gotta be in our own thinking, not with what's written down."

"Well, sure ... of course every word in the Bible is true. It's ridiculous to think otherwise," Bigelow muttered as he slowly sat down.

"Yassah, yassah, so I reckon that if it was written to carry the message down through the ages, it means the story recorded about Paul and Ananias is there for a reason. 'Spect the reason has to be one like what we're talking about right now."

Bigelow was obviously confused, torn between being a strong church deacon believing implicitly in the truth of the Word, and being an upstanding citizen demanding justice. He finally said quietly, "I see what you're saying, Joseph, and it makes a lot of sense. I for one can't fault you for what you've done. I can't speak for anybody else, but you've given me a lot to think about. I honestly can't say I buy it. The man is a scoundrel. He has a talent, misdirected as it may be, I'll give you that, but—"

"You is a good man, Massa Bigelow. Don't think I ain't had me no misgivings, and lots of them, helping him like I done. The Lord has had to work on me mighty hard to keep my feet to the fire. Maybe you folks figures I'm crazy, but I still think there's a powerful tool locked up in that man over there, and I ain't giving up on him. Not until God tells me to."

Judy stood up again and said, "Joseph wasn't the only one who knew."

"Hush, Miss Judy," Joseph whispered.

"If she's got something to say, she needs to say it." The sheriff looked at her in a sympathetic manner. "Do you?"

"I found out the other day who Amos really was, but I've kept my mouth shut." She briefly went through the story of the sneezing attack and the recognition. "I should have said something."

"So why didn't you?"

"It certainly wasn't for him," she retorted, sending a fiery look toward Amos. "I didn't want to get Joseph in trouble."

"Miss Valentine, you can't go around doing stuff like that; it can get you caught up in it with them," Sheriff Wilson said.

"However, since you haven't known but a day or so, I can't see how that affects anything, so I reckon there won't be any charges brought."

"I just wanted to make it clear that I kept quiet to support Joseph because I believed him. I know he feels God gave him instructions to do as he has done. I don't see the same thing in Amos that Joseph does, but I respect Joseph's determination to do what he's been trying to do."

"Be that as it may," the sheriff said, "it's a matter for the law now. Amos has to stand trial and answer for his crimes. Unless something happens to make me see things differently, I don't plan on bringing any charges against Joseph."

He looked over at Amos. "You got anything to add to this?"

"You mean I can talk?"

"If you've a mind to."

Amos stood up, restraints clinking. He kept his hands clasped. "Everything I just heard is the truth. I've skimmed this town from day one, but Joseph is not at fault. He has my best interest as well as the best interest of the town at heart, and always has. He really does believe I'm worth saving."

He paused halfway to his seat, then added, "I don't know why."

Thirty-One

How could you?" Judy's face was again tear-stained. "I believed in you." She looked at Amos through the bars, holding them as if she were about to climb them.

He sat on the cot, keeping his distance. "At least you're talking to me again. You have to believe I didn't mean to hurt you." It was hard for him to meet her eyes.

She leaned her forehead against the cold steel. "How am I supposed to believe that? How am I supposed to believe a word that comes out of your mouth? Every word you've said since you came to town has been a lie."

"You weren't a lie, Judy. I do care for you. I tried not to. I told myself it wasn't the smart play, but I couldn't help it." He got up to go to her and closed his hands over hers on the bars.

She jerked back. Her rich chocolate-brown eyes pinned Amos to the wall right through the bars like a Comanche war lance. "I didn't know you felt like that."

Amos scratched his head. "That's not surprising. I didn't know I felt like that either until it just now spilled out of my mouth."

She leaned back against the cool brick wall, as much space between her and him standing at the bars as the confined space would allow. "I don't know what to think. You have me so confused. I should hate you for how you've lied to me but ..."

Amos reached through the bars, holding up a hand as if to stop the flow of words from her pretty lips. "You should hate me. I don't blame you. I hate me for what I've done to you. If I could undo it, I would."

She nodded. The tears flowed again, then she lowered her eyes as she turned and left the cellblock.

Amos looked small and forlorn in the tiny cell. "I'm pretty well done in as far as Judy is concerned."

Joseph nodded. "She's a pretty unhappy girl, I'll give you that. She just needs some time to figure out what she thinks."

"No, she knows what she thinks. She thinks I'm lower than a snake's belly."

Joseph smiled; this was a new Amos here in front of him. The confident manner was gone. "I don't believe that's it at all. Aren't you the same guy who was just in here saying she was talking home and hearth?"

"That seems like a lifetime ago."

"You knocked her down a mite; she'll need to get over it."

"I can't see how she'll ever get over it."

Joseph turned and disappeared back into the other room. Noises came out as he busied himself. His voice came from out of the darkness, "Well, for right now you have other things to think about. The circuit judge will be here in a couple of days."

"There's a scary thought," Amos said, his head coming up. "I've never had to go to court before. Do I get a lawyer?"

Joseph came back in with a tin tray and stooped to slide it

under the cell's door. Scrambled eggs, toast, coffee. Amos could tell by the smell of the coffee that he didn't want to be in any hurry to drink it.

Joseph retreated to get himself some of the scrambled eggs folded into a tortilla and came back with it in one hand and a tin cup of the obnoxious fluid in his other hand. "You know there aren't any lawyers who live here. The sheriff will act as prosecutor."

"So there won't be anybody to speak for me?" Amos mumbled around a mouthful of eggs.

"How about Mr. Bigelow or Mr. Witherspoon?"

Amos washed the bite down. The coffee tasted much worse than he'd anticipated. A shudder ran through him so hard it caused him to slosh out some of the vile fluid. "I'm not sure how they feel about me. How about you, Joseph, would you stand up for me?"

"A black man in a white court? You think that'd help you? Besides, I don't think they're all that sure I'm not part of this myself."

"All the more reason for you to help me answer the charges. And to tell you the truth, ain't nobody else I trust."

Joseph took a sip from his cup and didn't appear to notice the taste of its contents at all. Amos wondered if they were drinking from the same pot. After all, Joseph *had* said that it was his job to punish the prisoners with his food.

"I'll give it a shot, if that's what you want," Joseph said. "I suppose I thought you didn't have much use for me, after the way I held your feet to the fire."

"No, you're a good man, Joseph. I have a lot of trouble swallowing all that faith stuff—nearly as much trouble as I have swallowing this coffee. I trust you though, and I believe everything you've done has been with the best of intentions."

The days passed quickly. The school/church had been transformed to become a courtroom. Judge Leland Keaton had seen to it that it was set up to use the teacher's desk as a bench, and twelve straight-backed chairs were arranged to his left to seat the jury. There was a witness chair next to the desk, and two tables were positioned in front of it for the defendant and the prosecution.

Judge Keaton was a spare man, with such a pale complexion that the black robe made him look more like a vampire than an officer of the court. He had fine, girlish hands and solid white hair that he combed back into a mane.

Amos thought the man to be genuinely spooky. It even occurred to him that the judge should see about getting some stage makeup before he went out in public.

School had been let out for the duration of the trial. To say the normal inhabitants of the building had wholeheartedly approved this decision would be an understatement of the greatest possible magnitude.

Sheriff Wilson sat at one table, Amos at the other. The sheriff stood, and Judge Keaton recognized him: "Judge, begging your pardon, but we got no lawyers around here. I reckon it falls to me to act as the prosecutor in this case."

The judge nodded, then pointed at the lawman with the handle of his gavel, his elbow on the desk. "Yes, that's the usual procedure in such a situation. Have you performed in this capacity before?"

"Yes, Your Honor, several times, but nothing very important, like murder or such."

"Very well, Sheriff Wilson, the state recognizes your credentials as prosecutor."

He turned his attention to Amos, swiveling the gavel like a pointer in his direction. Amos felt as if as if the eyes of the whole world had suddenly been focused on him. He was used to attention, normally thrived on it, but this was different. "And you, Mr. ..." The judge looked down to flip through some pages on his desk. Finding what he wanted, he looked back up, and continued. "... Mr. Taylor, are you not represented by counsel?"

Amos stood up. "As the sheriff said, Your Honor, there aren't any lawyers around here. If possible I'd like Joseph Washington to speak for me."

A murmur ruffled through the room as the judge looked out over the crowd. "Very well, is Mr. Washington present?"

Joseph moved forward. The judge looked over his glasses at him as he approached. "Yes? Is there something you wanted?"

"You called me up here."

"*You* are Mr. Washington?" He looked at Amos, amazement on his face. "Is this the man you are referring to?"

"Yes, Your Honor."

"This is most irregular. In all my years on the bench I have never ..." He pushed back in his chair, seemingly unable to continue. Then he noticed. "Wait a minute, are you ... Sheriff, is this man blind?"

"Yes, Your Honor, near half his life."

He leaned back and threw up his hands. "This is preposterous, I cannot allow ..."

Amos cleared his throat, then spoke up. "Don't my wishes count in this matter, Judge?"

"But the man is black."

Amos wished he could jump up and yell, "Oh my gosh, Joseph, you're black." But he was afraid the judge wouldn't find that funny. Or he could tell him that Joseph was the one who was blind, that Amos could see him fine. No, that probably wouldn't work either.

Amos fought back these impulses and said, "Your Honor, I know most of his race ain't got much schooling these days, not that it's their fault. But I'm sure that's why you're making such a point of it. However, Joseph was very well-read while he had his sight, and now he's probably better educated than most folks hereabouts. I don't mind telling you, he's a lot smarter than I am."

The judge flushed to the point that his face almost took on some color. "Well, of course I didn't intend my comments to be racial in nature."

"I knew you didn't, Judge. Now the fact is that I trust Joseph more than I've ever trusted anyone in my life, and I'm prepared to put my fate in his hands. If I'm willing to do that, I don't see why the court should have a problem with it."

"Sheriff, does the prosecution object?"

"Your Honor, as I seem to be having to repeat a lot here lately, Joseph Washington works at the jail, and is as fine a man as I've ever come to know."

The judge busied himself with the paperwork on his desk. "Very well, I find this rather unsettling, but Mr. Washington may be seated as counsel for the defense. I fear in so doing, we have already established grounds for having the verdict in this case overturned."

He looked up from the documents. "Sheriff, the man I just accepted as the counsel for the defense was also under scrutiny as an accomplice?"

Wilson half rose from his chair. "He was, Your Honor. We had a meeting, and the whole town talked with him about it. After all the dust cleared, we figured he hadn't really done nothing wrong." He sat back, then added, "Unless you say otherwise, of course."

"If the town is satisfied, I suppose I am. What about this Miss Valentine?"

"Same thing, Judge. We looked at it, and figured she didn't do nuthin' but get confused for a couple of days and not report it when she should."

"The town doesn't want her indicted either?"

"No, Your Honor."

"Very well, I see no difference in such an occurrence and a grand jury returning a 'no bill.' We will restrict our activity to the defendant. Most unusual town."

"Yes, Your Honor."

The remainder of the day was consumed in the selection of the jury. It came as no surprise to anyone to see Jed Bigelow named as the foreman of the jury. Seated with Jed were three cowboys from outlying ranches. Amos thought that was good because they weren't members of the congregation. Neither was Spuds Horton, who was also chosen.

John Daniels was named to the panel. He and Sam McDonald were both church members, but Amos felt pretty good about his relationship with them. The remainder of the jury included five sour holier-than-thou faces. Six and six. He at least had a fighting chance, if not being a church member actually meant anything.

He'd like to have seen a few of the ladies on the panel, but of course being unable to vote, none of them were on the list of potential jurors. Still, it could have been worse.

Thirty-Two

The jury looked as solemn as, well, a jury. They were taking this case quite seriously, as was Sheriff Wilson. Dressed in his Sunday-go-to-meeting suit, he had even polished his boots to a high gloss.

The judge cleared his throat to speak. Amos was sure he was a fine fellow, but his spooky appearance gave him cold chills.

Judge Keaton said, "Sheriff, are you prepared to present the charges?"

"I am, Your Honor." The big man stood to walk out from behind the table. He held a law book in his hand. "The defendant is charged with two counts of robbery and with fraud." He tossed the law book on the table. "I couldn't find no statute in here on impersonating a minister. I sure enough tried to."

"No, I never heard of one either," the judge said. "Though I've thought on occasion that there should perhaps be one."

The sheriff nodded. "Lot of snaky things done in the name of religion all right." He returned to his chair.

"I object," Joseph said, rising.

The judge sighed, as if resigning himself to having to deal with this affront to the dignity of his court. "What's the basis of your objection, counselor?"

"Your Honor, this dialogue is certain to prejudice the jury against my client."

"Prejudice? I'm beginning to think you're more educated than you appear, counselor. Very well, the jury will disregard that last exchange."

"Right," Amos said sarcastically, "as if a jury could *unhear* something they've already heard."

"The defendant will hold his tongue," the judge said, banging his gavel. "That's why you have counsel, Mr. Taylor."

"Yes, Your Honor."

Amos leaned over to Joseph and whispered. "You do know you are slipping out of your role in public?"

Joseph looked deadly serious. "I see no way to do this without it. I fear, for better or worse, the citizens are about to see me in a different light."

"They may hang us both, for different reasons."

"They may indeed."

The judge finished making some notations on the papers in front of him. "Very well, and how does the defendant respond to the charges?"

Joseph stood up. "Guilty, Your Honor, with mitigating circumstances."

"Guilty?" Keaton transferred his attention from the paperwork to Joseph, puzzlement in his eyes from both the statement and from the change in the old man's demeanor. "Then why are we bothering with a trial?"

Joseph came out from behind the table and came closer to the bench. "The defendant admits to the charges, but we feel the circumstances may weigh heavily in the determination of punishment."

"Normally the punishment phase is the province of the bench, Mr. Washington."

"I'm aware of that, Your Honor, but with all due respect, the bench is not in a position to judge the unusual circumstances involved in this case. I believe the defendant is within his rights to ask to be judged by his peers, is he not?"

"He is, unless I woke up in some foreign country this morning. Very well, Mr. Washington, you shall have your jury trial. Sheriff, you may present your case."

Wilson stood at his table. "Yes, Your Honor."

"Bring your witnesses, but first, let me say this; Sheriff Wilson, you may think my comments prejudicial, as Mr. Washington did earlier. Please allow me to tell you, the jury, and the spectators assembled here a bit about frontier justice."

He sat forward in his chair, put both elbows on the desk, and formed a steeple with his hands. "You see, normally in a trial it is in very poor taste for the bench to say anything that might affect either side of a case other than making a ruling on a point of law. However, out here in the West, where experienced personnel often do not exist to adequately serve the needs of both the prosecution and the defense, the bench often has to intercede on *both* sides to ensure that justice is done. I would say that is the situation here."

The judge then looked directly at Amos. "Mr. Taylor, you may have been poorly advised to plead guilty on the basis of the evidence that appears to be arrayed against you. Be that as it may, the plea is entered, and we must proceed."

He sat back in his chair. "Let's get on with it, Sheriff."

The sheriff called his first witness, John Lightfoot. He had dressed up for the trial in his best coat, a red blanket fabric jacket with some fancy beadwork on the front. He wore a headband with beadwork to match.

Lightfoot walked to the witness chair. After the swearing

in, the sheriff came up to face him. "Mr. Lightfoot, you have a reputation as a tracker?"

Lightfoot lifted his chin high. "I am the best there is. I say this not as a boast, for when a thing is true, it is true, whether it sounds boastful or not."

Wilson turned to the judge. "Your Honor, it is well known that John Lightfoot is the best tracker around."

The judge sat cradling his head with his right hand, looking out under the palm. He released his forehead long enough to give a desultory wave of his hand. "The court recognizes Mr. Lightfoot's abilities."

Wilson approached. "Mr. Lightfoot, can you tell us what you found when you searched for tracks at the site of the two robberies?"

"I thought it to be the tracks of a ghost. They came, they went, they made no sense." He made a sign as if he brushed dust off a table, but he carried it further, out to arm's length. It was as if he were watching the tracks disappear from in front of his eyes all over again. "You were there, you saw."

"Yes, but it ain't me that's testifying. The court has to hear what *you* have to say, not me."

"It is so? Then I tell." Lightfoot's attention returned to the court. "It was only later, when the sheriff had me check the tracks of the horse of the preacher, that everything fell into place. I had not thought to check the tracks of our own animals."

The sheriff said, "You are saying it was definitely his horse that was at each robbery?"

"It was. The tracks left no doubt."

"No more questions. I pass the witness." Sheriff Wilson returned to his seat. He gave a smug look at Amos as he passed the defense table.

Joseph stood, "No questions, Your Honor."

The judge gave a big sigh. "Bad as I hate to do this, I must. What the defense counsel means to say is that he is willing to stipulate that his client's horse was at the scene. Mr. Lightfoot, can you prove it was Mr. Taylor who rode that horse?"

"Judge, I object," Wilson said.

"The basis for your objection?"

"You are making the defense's case for them."

"I just got through explaining all that. In the case an obvious point is not made which I feel would have been made by experienced counsel, I am obligated to see that justice is served. Objection overruled." He slammed down his gavel. "Mr. Lightfoot, you are directed to answer."

The tracker looked up at the bench. "There are no tracks of people at the scene, Your Honor, only the horse."

"Very well, Mr. Lightfoot, you may step down."

I might have misjudged the judge, Amos thought. *He might look like some kind of bloodsucker, but he helped me a bunch then.*

"The prosecution calls Miss Judy Valentine."

The judge swiveled to survey the crowd; the tone of his voice became more solicitous when Judy rose. "Come forward and be sworn in, Miss Valentine."

Every eye in the room followed her to the seat next to the bench. She raised her hand and took the oath. The sheriff said, "Miss Valentine, we've already heard about how you came to recognize the defendant, and why you withheld that information at first. Isn't it true that the defendant physically attacked you?"

Judy frowned; she hadn't anticipated this line of questioning. "I thought he had."

"I'm sorry," the judge leaned forward. "You're going to have to speak up. I can't hear you."

She squirmed in her chair, sitting up straighter and visibly composing herself. "I said I thought he had."

The judge interrupted again. "Does that mean he didn't attack you?"

Sheriff Wilson scowled, obviously resenting the interference of the judge.

"He slipped up behind me and scared me. I thought he had done more than he did, but I have come to understand it was my imagination amplifying the whole thing."

The sheriff responded quickly, eager to get the judge out of the exchange. He looked confused. "Why would he do that?"

Amos jumped to his feet. "Your Honor, there's no point in embarrassing her. I've admitted the entire thing."

The gavel came down hard. "Sit down, Mr. Taylor. I've warned you to speak through your counsel. The witness will answer."

Judy turned bright red. "I suppose I had something of a crush on the masked man. He was trying to put a stop to that without giving himself away."

Consternation was clear in the judge's voice. "A crush on the masked man? Does that mean you had a crush on the defendant? He *was* the masked man, after all."

She turned a hard look on the judge. Her words were crisp and measured. "It *isn't* the same thing."

"Very well, this is getting us nowhere. You have questions of this witness, Mr. Washington?"

"No, Your Honor." Joseph felt the judge was doing fine without him, and the more he could get him to do it, the better it'd be for Amos.

"Call your next witness, Sheriff."

"I call Joseph Washington to the stand."

"Wait ... wait," the judge motioned for an individual in the front row to come forward. There was a brief whispered conversation and the man left. He returned promptly with some headache powders and a glass of water. The judge washed down the powders with one great gulp.

He sat there for a few moments with his eyes closed, his head resting against the back of the chair. "All right, I've had a moment or two to think on this, and when I tell you it pains me to do so, you may take that as a literal statement."

He composed himself. "There are all kinds of legalities involved in a man's lawyer testifying against him. Still, given the peculiar circumstances, and the fact that I am trying with all my might to turn this charade into some sort of a legitimate trial, I am going to allow him to step out of his role for a moment. Mr. Washington, you may be sworn in as a witness."

He sat back in his chair, then apparently had a second thought on the subject. "Oh, and in return, the bench shall itself represent the witness in the cross-examination."

The sheriff looked puzzled. "Ain't that kinda strange, Your Honor?"

"It most certainly is." The judge looked worn.

Wilson stood at his table, holding up a letter so the judge could see it. "May it please the court, I'd like to put this here letter into evidence."

Keaton held out a hand for the letter. "What's the nature of the letter?"

"It's an account written by Mr. Washington telling all about Amos Taylor committing two robberies, and how he made him give back the money."

The judge's mouth hung open. "The counsel for the defense wrote a letter implicating his client?"

"Well, Your Honor, he *did* do it before he was the counsel."

Keaton closed his eyes, slowly shaking his head. He

opened them and made impatient little gestures until Wilson placed the letter in his hand. His mouth hung open as he read. "Astounding, he stands identified by a blind man?"

Joseph was sworn in, and the sheriff came forward. "Joseph, did you write this document?"

"I did."

"If necessary, can you prove you are capable of writing it?"

"I can."

The sheriff turned to the bench. "Your Honor, since the witness is blind, may I read the document?"

Keaton answered him with a fluttering gesture of his hand.

Sheriff Wilson read it in its entirety, then turned to Joseph and said, "Are those your words?"

"Yes, they are."

"Pass the witness." The sheriff returned to his chair.

"Very well," the judge said. "I shall now step out of the bench for a moment."

He got up, but before he could come around the table the sheriff said, "Is that legal?"

"Yes, there is ample precedent for this procedure." He walked over to the witness. "Joseph, this document says you were able to determine that Mr. Taylor committed the robberies and that he took you to the place where the proceeds from them were buried, whereupon said proceeds were then dug up and turned in to the sheriff. Is that an accurate account?"

"Yes sir."

He turned his back to walk several steps, looking at the letter. He raised his head and turned. "Mr. Washington, if I presented you with that money, could you identify it?"

"I got down and pulled the money out of the hole myself. I made sure we got all of it."

"That's not the point, Mr. Washington. Could you identify any money I might show you as being that particular money?"

"No sir."

"I thought not." He took a couple of steps to stand looking at the jury, making eye contact with first one and then another as he spoke. "Could you identify the clothes that were said to be with the money?"

"No, Your Honor."

He spun suddenly, closing the gap between Joseph and himself as he spoke. "So basically you only have the word of Mr. Taylor that what you dug up and returned was in fact the money from the robberies?" He seemed to be enjoying being on that side of the bench for a change.

"I suppose so."

"Mr. Washington, can you in fact prove that Mr. Taylor was at either robbery in any manner other than what he has himself told you?"

"No, Your Honor. I hadn't thought about it that way, but I suppose not."

He walked back over to the witness. "Let's turn to the fraud portion. Whose idea was it for Mr. Taylor to start preaching?"

"I suppose originally it would have been the sheriff's."

"*The sheriff's!* Is there any more of that powder?" Judge Keaton got another dose of the powder from his bench and washed it down before returning to the witness.

Keaton sighed heavily and turned back to face Joseph. "Very well, Mr. Washington, let's take another shot at it. Why did the sheriff want him to preach?"

"Mr. Taylor didn't want to do it, but the sheriff gave him no choice. Then after he got Amos started, I made sure he kept going."

Keaton had his left hand on the back of his neck, gesturing with his right. "Why on earth would you do that?"

Joseph said, "Because he's the finest preacher I've ever heard."

"Even though he really isn't one?"

"Even though."

"And even though he really doesn't even have religion?"

"That too."

The judge looked totally exasperated. "Mr. Washington, are you telling me that both you and the sheriff, the prosecutor and the counsel for the defense, coerced the defendant into perpetuating this fraud?"

"I'd have to say the whole town did, Your Honor. We were all mighty hungry for some good preaching."

"Astounding."

Thirty-Three

*T*he judge called a recess, then walked out to sit in the shade of the old elm tree in the schoolyard. Those in attendance milled around talking, occasionally casting a glance at his motionless figure. He sat in that position for more than two hours. The white hair and colorless complexion that had cast fear and conjured visions of an unearthly creature inside the court simply looked old and frail out under the tree.

The leading citizens were waiting for Joseph as he came out. Bigelow was the spokesman as usual. "What is the meaning of that performance in there?"

Joseph ducked his head, "Massa Bigelow, I ..."

"Don't," Bigelow held up a hand to silence him. "You argued that case in there as well as any white man. No, that's not true, what I heard was a better vocabulary than I have myself. What is the purpose of this charade?"

Joseph pulled himself up to his full height, lifting his chin. The Deep South caricature was gone; in its place stood a self-assured man few had gotten to see. "Back East, my education was accepted. The further West I came, the more of a problem it became for me. It was finally easier just to hide it."

"Why didn't you stay back where you were accepted?" The question wasn't asked in an accusing tone, but seemed to indicate a deep need to understand.

"I came hunting some family, but it never worked out. I caught on here and just stayed."

"This feels like as much of a betrayal as what Amos did," Mrs. McAfee said. Her tone was very much accusing in nature.

"Yes, ma'am, I suppose it is, but it was just easier to be what people wanted me to be."

"I suppose the fault is ours." Bigelow seemed to have to force the words out. "I mean, look how much effort it took to get people comfortable with just accepting you in church. If we'd tried that before we all came to like you as a person, that probably wouldn't have happened."

"That's how I saw it."

"So you shouldn't have deceived us, but then we shouldn't have put you in a position where you felt you had to do it."

Witherspoon stepped forward. "I think we best start over." He held out a hand. "Welcome to town, Mr. Washington. We're pleased to have such an educated gentleman in our midst."

Joseph couldn't find the words to respond.

The sheriff went over to see if the judge wanted to let the people go and continue the trial over to the next day. He was rewarded by having a boot thrown at him.

John Daniels walked up to Bigelow and said, "You got any idea why it's the judge out deliberating instead of the jury?"

"I don't have the foggiest idea what's going on," admitted Jed, "and you can take that to my bank."

"Well, it's got to be the strangest jury I ever sat on."

"I'll go along with you there."

Finally, the judge returned, limping on one sock foot, and called court back into session. He put his boot back on.

As they gathered in the courtroom again, Joseph asked the judge, "Is your headache better?"

"Yes, Mr. Washington, it is. Thank you for asking."

He composed himself a minute, then with a visible effort, began to speak. "When I went out to the tree I saw no possible way this case could be reconciled in any manner that would stand up on appeal. I have changed my mind."

He closed his eyes a moment and took a deep breath. The onlookers clearly had the distinct feeling that he did not want to do what he was about to do. That scared Amos.

Keaton let out a sigh and continued. "In order for a case to be overturned, somebody has to appeal it. I think I have arrived at a solution that no one is going to take exception to, therefore, there will be no appeal."

He turned to look at the jury. "Thank you, members of the jury, but you are discharged. There is insufficient evidence to conduct a trial. If we went on the basis of the evidence alone, no one could be convicted of the robberies except the horse, and I don't believe there are any provisions in the law that pertains to the conviction of domestic animals. Don't bother to step down; I don't think it's going to take that long."

The jury shot puzzled looks at each other.

The judge swiveled in his chair and addressed himself to those assembled. "On the fraud charges, I find it impossible to convict a man of such an offense when the entire town made him do it."

He looked from face to face as if expecting some sort of objection. There was none. He continued.

"Yet there is guilt here on the part of the defendant, and everybody knows it. There is even a guilty plea entered; therefore I cannot in good conscience let the defendant off with no punishment."

He stopped for effect and again looked about the room before turning his full attention on Amos. "Mr. Taylor, please stand."

Amos got to his feet, as did Joseph.

"Mr. Taylor, rather than rule on guilt or innocence, I'm simply going to accept your guilty plea, which is why I didn't need the jury."

Amos's mouth fell open.

"However, in light of all of the unusual mitigating circumstances, I'm going to place you on probation and community service. I sentence you to three years as the minister of this local church."

There was an immediate uproar in the room. The judge banged his gavel. "Silence, silence in the court."

He continued to look at the crowd, using his eyes to administer a warning. Then he came back to Amos. "We are all aware that you are not really a minister. Therefore, there are conditions to this probation."

He sorted among the papers on his desk and held up a folded document. "I have prepared a bench warrant for your arrest, and if the conditions of your parole are violated, the sheriff is directed to serve it. That would immediately put you in prison for the remainder of your probation, guilt or innocence not even being a factor."

The room had become quiet again. "The conditions of your parole are as follows: Since you are not an ordained preacher, I release you in the custody of Mr. Jed Bigelow, Mr. Sam Witherspoon, and Mr. Joseph Washington. These three gentlemen are to approve each and every sermon you present, and you will not deviate from what they approve. If you fail to follow their instructions, the probation will be considered to be in default, and you will be apprehended. Is that clear?"

Amos could only nod.

"Very well. Now I wish to add that if at any point these gentlemen determine you really have come to believe what you represent and they feel that their services in this capacity are no longer necessary, they are empowered as the local church deacons to ordain you as a lay preacher. Should that situation occur, I hereby declare that such ordination would immediately supercede the provisions of your probation and release you from the remainder of your sentence. Do you understand this provision and the sentence I am imposing?"

Amos was stunned. His legs threatened to let him down. "I think so. I suppose it's a lot less than I expected when all this started, but a lot more than I thought the way the trial was going."

"Let me be perfectly frank with you, Mr. Taylor. If you were to appeal this case, and get the opportunity for a retrial without the guilty plea entered, there is a substantial chance the case would be thrown out of court. There is also the chance a jury would believe the circumstantial evidence and send you to prison. Whether or not you appeal is up to you."

"I'll have to think about that."

"While you are thinking, consider this: I have reason to believe there are people in this town you care about, and who care about you. An appeal is likely to sever your relations with this community, win or lose. You appear to enjoy it here, and there seems to be the possibility of a future for you here if you could secure it for yourself. I would not take that possibility lightly."

"No sir, I won't, and I know you're right. An appeal is out of the question."

"Very well." He banged his gavel on the desk. "That's my ruling. Court is dismissed."

Amos found Judy sitting on the porch. He stopped, took off his hat and held it in his hand, but made no effort to open the gate.

"Well, don't just stand there, come on in," she said.

"Are you sure you want me to?"

"Why not?"

He studied the toes of his boots. "I don't know where things stand between us right now."

"My feelings about you are still not completely clear, but I'm working on that."

Slowly Amos came down the walk. "I wouldn't blame you if you never wanted to speak to me again."

"Don't be silly. Have some lemonade." This time the pitcher sat on a table between the two chairs.

He sat down cautiously, like a man about to be physically struck. "You've been on my mind all the time; I can't seem to think of anything else."

She poured him a glass and handed it to him. His eyes searched her face, but she was impossible to read as she responded, "You've said that to me before. As I recall, it was a lie."

He grimaced. "No, you know what I was trying to do then, make you quit thinking about the masked man, but the words were true even then."

"I will give you the benefit of a doubt, but I can't forgive you, not yet."

"I thought we had something going." He was still holding the untouched glass of lemonade. He suddenly became aware that his mouth was very dry and took a sip of it.

She cocked her head. "More than that. I had some very strong feelings for you. I suppose I still do."

Hope blazed up in Amos's eyes and he sat forward in his chair. Before he could respond, she held up a hand to prevent it. "But too much has happened. I just can't pretend otherwise. It's as if there is a battle going on inside me right now, and the whole thing is over you."

"Between me and the masked man?"

"In a way. The disguise you used to wear represented the good side that Joseph has been working so hard to bring out. The masked man is the perfect representation of your evil nature. I suppose I'm not sure which one will win out, and if it were to be the good side whether the transition would be permanent or not."

Amos leaned forward, set the glass on the ground, and hid his face in his hands, elbows on his knees. His voice was muffled but understandable. "I ain't ever going to jail again; you can carve that in stone."

"Does that mean you are reforming?"

"That's the only way to make sure I don't ever go back."

She put her hand on his back as he remained hunched over. He could feel her warmth through his shirt. "So what do you plan to do?"

"I really don't know. I have to do this preacher thing 'til they turn me loose of it. Guess I'll see where I am then."

"I think that's where we are now, Amos. Taking it a day at a time."

His head came up. "Are you saying there's still hope for us?"

"Oh, Amos, haven't you preached enough of Joseph's words to know that there is always hope?"

"There's a note in your voice that's never been there before," Joseph observed.

If Joseph could see his downcast expression, he wouldn't have had to ask. "Really? I suppose I am a little down."

"Why?"

"You heard the sentence. I have to keep preaching; only now people are going to be skeptical. I'm sure the dinner invitations will continue to be withheld. The hotel clerk still says he can't provide my room free any more. I've got a little money put back, but I'm not so sure I'm going to see anything in the collection plate for a while, if ever, so I can't afford to pay to stay there."

"This doesn't sound like you."

"I've never let trouble bother me because I always believed in my ability to do whatever I had to do, or go wherever I needed to go, in order to survive. This time is different. I have to stand and fight it through right here. I can't leave, or the law will be all over me. Most of the ways I know to get money in a hurry would put me right back behind bars, and I'm serious when I say I don't want to ever have to do that again."

"So you need a little help. Everybody needs help now and then."

"Not me. I've never needed anybody but myself."

"Well, I'm still here, and the first thing we have to do is get you ready for that sermon Sunday."

Thirty-Four

mos faced the crowd. They looked even more severe than they had at the trial, if that was possible. His heart was pounding like a blacksmith banging on an anvil, and his mouth felt drier than dust in an old saddlebag.

"I stand here morally naked and ashamed," he said. "I figure you probably don't understand, but this is something new for me. I can't remember ever being ashamed of anything I've done in my whole life."

Amos forced himself to look out at his audience, but he could see nothing but stern, serious faces; there was absolutely no positive support coming from them at all. The church gathering looked like a convention of undertakers.

Wait, he thought, *the problem is I'm looking at the wrong place*. There on the front row sat Joseph, a slight smile on his face as he nodded his head gently. Amos looked over toward Judy. There was not as much reaction there as he had hoped for, but he'd take it.

Amos took a deep breath and launched into his presentation. "You see, my mother died in childbirth, and my father run out not long afterwards. I've been on my own from a very young age. I learned to live by my wits and to make my own way in life. I learned to look at other people as opportunities, not to them for help."

He looked around the room for some kind of encouraging response. There was nothing. "I tell you this not to get your sympathy or even as an excuse, but just to help you understand. For me to have to ask someone for help is something I can hardly bring myself to do. I can't tell you how low it makes me feel."

Still nothing. Not even a sign that they had heard what he said. *All right, I'll make do with that.*

"The only reason I'd try to do this again is because the court said I had to. You enjoyed it when I preached before, but you did so because you thought you could look to me for spiritual guidance.

"Things are different now, and you think you can't look to me for guidance, but I'm here to tell you that isn't true. I am only a presenter, a mouthpiece, and the message was written, as were my earlier ones, by that beacon of faith sitting in the front row. It has been approved and made pure as spring water by Brother Bigelow and Brother Witherspoon, and you know you can trust them."

Still nothing. He forged ahead. "Yet even that is just a tiny part of the story. Every word that I've given you, yes, even the sermon that caused everything to blow up in my face, was based on a biblical text. It came right out of the Word of God. I did a bad job of spelling that one out for you, but there was nothing wrong with the text. You can always trust the Word when the interpretation is sound, no matter who the messenger is. And with these three on the job, you know the interpretation will be sound."

Amos opened the old Bible. For the first time, he really did feel comfortable having it in his hands. "Today's text is found in Psalm 51:1 and 2." He began to read: 'Have mercy upon me, O God, according to thy lovingkindness: according unto the multitude of thy tender mercies blot out my transgressions. Wash me thoroughly from mine iniquity, and cleanse me from my sin.'"

He smiled. "Anybody in doubt as to why my little pulpit committee chose this subject? Let me tell you that much of today's message will be my words, but like the judge said in the terms of my probation, I've passed them by my three advisors, and they've been approved. Like I say, you can trust the message even if you don't trust the messenger."

Amos walked around the pulpit and came to face his listeners with no barrier in between. "Let me read that again," and he did.

"This speaks to us today on several levels. The first is the level that Joseph originally wrote this sermon on, the lesson for us all. He said, 'The lesson is that repentant people know in their hearts that inexcusable wrongs can either be judged or forgiven but can never be understood or overlooked.' That's where you are right now. You're judging, and you don't understand." He smiled, and meant it. "I'm hoping you get around to forgiveness."

He stepped back behind the pulpit, suddenly feeling very exposed. He stole another look at Judy; she seemed to have softened somewhat. *Or maybe it's my imagination because I want her to forgive me so much.*

"But before I get too deep into the other levels of forgiveness that I want to discuss, I need to get you to understand that this applies to you as well. Your wrongs don't have to be as bad as what I've done. We're all sinners; we all fall short. I've come to understand that much. Don't get so caught up judging me that you fail to learn from my example. We all need forgiveness."

Amos hung his head. This was so easy before, but not any

more. He took a deep breath. "All right, here goes. Level two is all about me. You gotta know that's why they selected this message for me to give. You know I'm preaching to myself even more than to you.

"You have an advantage; you are all believers. You need forgiveness, and you know how to get it. I'm not going to lie to you any more. I've never been saved, and I've never believed much of what I've been preaching to you about. I still don't know where I am, but I will tell you this: I'm missing something. I've come to realize it. You have it, and I don't. I have come this far; I do believe there is a God."

"Praise the Lord!" Joseph yelled.

"Yes, old friend, maybe there is hope. I admit I don't understand, and there is much I have to learn, but I'm looking for it now. I tried to fool all of you into thinking I believed. I tried to fool Joseph, but I couldn't. He said he'd know when it was real, and now I understand that he will. Most of all, I tried to fool myself. Now I'm going to try to understand. I don't think I can do it without your help, but I'm going to try."

Amos closed the Bible. "Something else I'm going to try. Brother Bigelow, with your permission I want to do the prayer of benediction. Maybe I don't understand who I'm praying to yet, but I know somebody is out there listening, and I sure enough need to make contact."

Bigelow nodded.

Amos bowed his head and grasped the pulpit in both hands. Then Joseph shouted, "Wait!"

Amos looked up as Joseph moved up behind him. The old man put one hand on his back and raised the other in the air. Judy quickly moved to join him and did the same thing, followed by Brothers Bigelow and Witherspoon and three hard-praying ladies from the front row. They all laid their hands on him.

Joseph said, "Let 'er rip, Amos. Anything we got to give you is flowing right on through now."

I can feel it, I really can. It's hard to believe, but a very tangible warmth and power is surging through those hands. I can feel it all the way through my clothes.

"Lord, I've talked to You many times, but it was never real. I guess You know that, since Joseph says You know the content of our hearts. If that's the case, You know this is the real thing and my very first prayer. All I can say is that I know You are real, I know I need help, and I know it has to come from You. I humble myself before You now, God, and I ask You to show me the way. These people will never hear a false word from me again. I'll never profess to believe until I have real understanding, until it is real. I guess that's it. I don't know where to go from here. Amen."

The hands on his back began to pat him. There were shouts of joy. He looked to see people rushing down the aisle toward him. He looked at Joseph. "I don't understand."

"God's moving, boy. You see, we love you much more as a sinner than we ever did as a preacher."

Thirty-Five

*J*udy came up to him after everyone had left. She stopped to face him on the walk in front of the building. "The church really reached out to you today."

Amos held the Bible in both hands in front of him. "They did, didn't they? I don't understand. I thought most of them hated me. I thought they'd never come around."

Her smile was gentle. "That's what makes it clear you don't really understand what Christianity is all about. It's all about forgiveness and love. None of us is worthy of forgiveness, but Jesus gave it to us anyway, because He loves us. No one in the church can do less, and we know it. When you quit playing games, and showed that you realized you were a sinner, people quit hating you and started praying for you."

He shook his head in wonder. "That is absolutely amazing."

"Yes, it never fails to amaze me too."

Amos froze in his tracks. "Wait, you said *we* know it."

"Yes, I did."

He reached to put one hand lightly on her arm, but she didn't look up. "Does that mean you forgive me?"

"It does. But it doesn't mean I've forgotten, and it doesn't mean I can trust you. Being forgiven, and earning trust, are two different things."

"How about if we just start over? You know, begin at scratch?"

"I think that'd be a fine idea."

Several people came out of the hotel dining room as Joseph came down the walk. They all spoke and he stopped to acknowledge them. Witherspoon said, "Have your ears been burning, Joseph?"

"I expect I've been the topic of conversation."

Bigelow put his hand on Joseph's shoulder. "That you have, Joseph, that you have. There's been a lot of soul searching going on around here. Had you asked us, we would have told you there wasn't a bigoted soul in town. But there was more prejudice here than we knew."

"It takes a big man to say that, sir."

"No, it just takes a man who's been forced to look in a harsh mirror. I'll admit, though, there are times I miss the old darky."

"I expect it was rather like having a town pet."

Bigelow couldn't help but laugh. "Yes, God forgive me, it was. I'll bet it was that way for you too. Like we were petting you on the head."

"I didn't mind, and I'm still the same man. People act like a major transformation has taken place. The only thing that has happened is that I'm a little smarter than folks took me for. Is that such a big thing?"

"No, Joseph, it isn't. It's just that people are slow to take to change ... even when it's a good change."

Amos and Joseph worked on his sermons. Amos preached one on the Beatitudes. He loved that part about the meek inheriting the earth, but the main show was yet to come.

Joseph said it. "Easter is coming, Amos. That's going to be the hard one."

"The hard one? I don't get it."

"We tend to lose sight of the real message of Easter, but it's your job to see that we don't miss the point. We've got a lot of work to do."

"The real message?"

"Don't worry, you'll see."

Work they did. They read the Bible day by day, often with the two deacons. This message had to be just right.

Joseph helped Amos get it together, and the pulpit committee approved it, but Amos knew that practice with Joseph down at the creek wouldn't get the job done this time. He had to get his head straight for this one.

Amos saddled Biscuit-eater and headed out of town. His brain spun like a whirlpool with so many thoughts that he paid no attention whatsoever to where he was going. He found himself stopped in front of the cemetery, with no forethought that it had been where he was headed. Yet as soon as he realized where he was, he immediately knew why he was there.

He stepped down, left his hat on the saddle horn, and pulled the old Bible out of the saddlebags. He walked to a nearby field and picked some wildflowers before he went to see Mrs. Simpson.

He laid the flowers up against the simple white cross marking her resting place. Amos got down on one knee and absentmindedly began to pull up some small weeds.

"Mrs. Simpson, I don't know how things work up there where you are, but looking here at this marker makes me feel like I'm talking with you. Maybe you are looking down on me. I just know I wish you were here right now. I barely got to know you, yet in only one night you made it clear you knew me better than I know myself."

He sat down, clasping his knees in his arms. "Joseph seems to be able to read my mind, but you, you read my heart. I wish you were here to read this old ticker right now and tell me what's in there."

Big white fluffy clouds filled the skies above like giant sailing ships. He looked up at them, not really seeing them. "But you're still here, aren't you, inside me? You reached out with more love than anybody has ever shown me. At a time when you should have been concerned with yourself, all you could think about was helping me. I couldn't believe it was true. I didn't think it was possible that anybody would do that.

"You did though. You knew I was fighting God, not listening to what He was trying to tell me. I sure wish you were here now."

Amos wasn't watching, or he would have seen the dust devil coming. A tiny tornado, licking its way across the prairie and through the cemetery where he sat, enveloped him before he knew it was there.

Out of nowhere the dust assaulted his eyes, tousled his hair, and filled his nose. Then poof, it was gone as quickly as it had come. He blew his nose and wiped his eyes, coughing up a little dust.

Then he noticed his Bible. It had blown open. He picked it up. It had fallen open to the book of Romans. He focused watery eyes and began to read at the top of the page, "Romans 10:9-10—That if thou shalt confess with thy mouth the Lord Jesus, and shalt believe in thine heart that God hath raised him from the dead, thou shalt be saved. For with the heart man believeth unto righteousness; and with the mouth confession is made unto salvation."

Amos sat down hard. "Joseph said I'd know if I got a message from God, but it's pretty hard to see this any other way."

Amos felt like he had a weight on his chest. When he and Mrs. Simpson had talked, he had told her she could see into his heart, but he had still missed the point. It wasn't what she could see there that was important, but what she didn't see. She had known immediately, Joseph had known from the beginning, but he was just beginning to see.

"'For with the heart man believeth ...' That's it, isn't it? Mrs. Simpson looked in there and didn't see Jesus. Didn't matter what I told her, she looked and she knew. I couldn't hide it from her.

"And I can't hide it from Joseph. He said he'd know if it was real without my telling him. That's what Mrs. Simpson tried to tell me too. I was just too stupid to see. Yes, I was definitely fighting Him, but no more." He looked down at the marker again. "Mrs. Simpson. Thanks to you, I won't be fighting Him any more."

Thirty-Six

Amos was as ready as he was ever going to be. At least that's what he thought. He looked out over the crowd waiting in anticipation of a strong Easter message. He held the Bible in trembling hands. "For the real meaning of Easter we have to turn our attention away from this happy gathering. We have to turn to the hill of Calvary, an old rugged cross, nail-scarred hands. We have to ... we have to ..."

He began to sob. His shoulders heaved. "I can't do this. I'm not worthy."

He sat down in the front row. Nobody seemed to know what to do. Finally, Brother Bigelow started forward. As he passed by, Amos put out a hand to stop him.

"No." Amos looked up at the banker with eyes brimming over.

Bigelow halted.

"Brother, you know who has to do this."

They looked into each other's eyes. Then Bigelow smiled broadly and nodded. "Yes, you're right."

Amos pressed the Bible into his hands. "Give him this; he'll need it."

The banker stepped over to Joseph. "We need you."

Joseph appeared shocked. "I shouldn't ... I can't."

The banker displayed a gentle, reassuring smile as he

placed the Bible in the old man's hands and covered both hands with his own. "You know what this is?"

"I know every crease in the cover, and it's a comfort to touch it again, but I still can't do it."

"You can, and you will." The banker helped the old man to the pulpit.

"Amos is right," Joseph began timidly. "At Easter we have to turn to Calvary. It is the bedrock of our faith. On it all else rests."

The subject matter began to fill him with confidence. It began to put power into his voice.

"God has always hated sin. Throughout the whole Bible we see testimony of blood sacrifice being offered to God in atonement for sin. In Hebrews 9:22, the Bible says that blood is required for the remission of sins. Finally, God put the issue of blood sacrifice to rest, once and for all. He sent His Son to earth, not only to teach us, not only to serve as a wonderful example to us, but also to die for us and for our sins. Jesus became the ultimate blood sacrifice for the sins of the whole world. He gave His life for us."

Joseph openly wept; tears ran out of his sightless eyes and down his cheeks. He let them fall. Most of the congregation joined him.

Amos felt his heart swell with pride. He knew Joseph had wanted to do this his entire life, and now he was not only able to preach, but was able to preach on the greatest subject of all. Amos had a lump in his throat the size of an apple.

Joseph's voice began to soar. He held his hands palm up to the heavens. "If that were all of it, it would be miracle enough in itself, but it doesn't end there. Three days later, Christ arose. He conquered death, for Himself, and by so doing for us all. Glorious!"

"Amen!" several shouted.

"Preach it, brother!" the austere Mr. Bigelow found himself yelling.

Amos looked at the old man and smiled as he saw him transformed before his eyes. His white hair and beard appeared to glow in the light streaming through the windows.

He returned to a normal speaking voice. "Turn, if you feel the need, to John 3:16. It is undoubtedly the best-known passage in the Bible, and with good reason: 'For God so loved the world, that he gave his only begotten Son, that whosoever believeth in him should not perish, but have everlasting life.' There it is, brothers and sisters, the corner-stone of our faith. Either we believe that, or we believe nothing at all. Jesus conquered death, not only for Himself but for us all."

Joseph's rich baritone carried out over the crowd as he took the volume up another notch or two. "He gave everything, and what does He ask in return? Look again at Romans 10:9 which says that if you confess with your mouth, 'Jesus is Lord,' and believe in your heart that God raised Him from the dead, you will be saved. It's just as simple as that. Look on down the page in verse 13; 'For whosoever shall call upon the name of the Lord shall be saved.'

"Does that verse say that only good people are going to be saved? Does it say that only people who have lived right, and never had a misstep, will be saved? I believe the word is 'whosoever.' And that means anyone. *Anyone.*"

He paused for effect. "If you don't believe that, look what else happened on the hill at Calvary. Jesus wasn't there alone; two thieves hung there beside Him. One of them called out to Him, and Jesus said to him in Luke 23:43, 'Verily I say unto thee, Today shalt thou be with me in paradise.' I don't know about you, but that pretty much says to me that the door to salvation is open to anyone."

Joseph moved around the pulpit and stopped in front of it. "I can't think of any better way to celebrate our Savior's resurrection than by offering His invitation for Him. This hand I hold out now is not my hand, but the hand of Jesus. According to Revelation 3:20, He stands and knocks on the door of your heart, and all you have to do is open that door and let Him in."

Joseph felt a strong young hand take his, and he caught his breath. "Please tell me this is Amos."

"Yes, Joseph, it is. I'm ready. I don't think I understand it all yet, but I believe I was purchased from my sin, and I'm ready to study and learn the rest."

Joseph grabbed the outstretched hand with both of his and pulled it to his chest as if it were a canteen of water in the middle of the desert. "Amos, we live our lives, and we never learn all of it. I think that's part of what troubles you so. God is too big for our tiny human brain to understand. We can understand a lot, and we keep trying to learn more, but it finally comes down to faith. When all is said and done, we have to accept on faith whether we fully understand or not. Amos, some answers we simply aren't going to have until we get face-to-face with our Savior in heaven."

"Well then, count me in, Joseph, because that's one trip I want to make."

Thirty-Seven

*J*oseph was still floating as high as an eagle when he came to sit with Judy and Amos under the elm tree in the yard. The church crowd had dissipated. He lifted his arms to the sky and shouted, "What a wonderful day! I could die right now and be a happy man." His face beamed.

Judy smiled, "Because Amos finally got saved?"

The old man clapped his hands together. "I can't believe the Lord let me be the instrument for that. I didn't think I'd be allowed to do it."

"Would you two quit talking about me as if I weren't here?" Amos said.

"Sorry, I'm just bubbling over with the Spirit. I never thought I'd get the chance to preach either." He reached out to locate Amos's hand. "You gave me that."

Amos took his hand, rose and helped him find a seat. "No, I didn't. When I fell on my face, you were there to pick me up. And now the church knows who ought to be doing the preaching."

Joseph grunted as he sat, "No, I'm not under any illusions about that. I loved it, and I think I did all right, but I'm not half the preacher you are. I know that, but if you ever need an assistant, somebody to fill in and help, I'm your man."

Amos looked down on him, hands on his hips. "If I can

ever reach the point where I can really do the job, you're in. We're a team. I know that now. God really did send you for me, and you got the job done."

"When you cross the line, you really come over, don't you?" Joseph beamed. "It does this old heart good to hear you talk like that."

Amos sat down between them and put his arm around them both. "Joseph, I believe. I said that over at the church, and I meant it from the bottom of my heart, but I know now that believing and understanding aren't the same thing. You said that yourself."

"Yes, I did."

Amos threw up his hands in a gesture of resignation. "Maybe you're right, Joseph. Maybe you've been right all along. It's just possible God really does want me working for Him. Only I can't do it the way I am; I'm a baby at this belief business."

"Yes, but it's all part of God's plan."

"Well, I wish He'd let me in on it. Right now life feels pretty uncertain."

Judy laughed. "When you two are through admiring each other, can we go get something to eat? I'm starving."

Amos stood to Joseph back to his living quarters in the jail. They linked arms as they went through the gate. Joseph gave him a pat on the arm. "You've come a long way."

"It feels like a long way, but I know I've still got a long way to go."

"We've all got a long way to go. Just so you don't beat yourself up so much, you understand that lots of ministers go to seminaries for years just to learn how to preach the Word."

"Is that what I'd have to do?"

They moved over in the street to let a rancher in a spring wagon pass. They waved. "No, we had this circuit rider come through some time back by the name of Peter Cartwright. I got the chance to talk to him about how he got started. He said most of those on the circuit, when they felt they had been called to preach, hadn't hunted up a college or biblical institute but had gotten themselves a good horse and some traveling apparatus instead. He said they took their Bible in hand and started out with a text that never wore out or got stale."

"So it isn't education that counts?"

"I'd think it would help, but the desire to carry the message, and having a message to carry, would have to be the biggest part of it. Some of the most powerful preachers carrying the Word today have never even finished the grades."

"I've got the desire. And I'm motivated. I've got a lot to make up for."

Amos stopped short of the boardwalk and let Joseph find it with his cane. The street was deserted.

Joseph said, "Only to yourself. You have nothing to make up to God. Your sins were forgiven as soon as you came under the blood. But I know how it is; sometimes being forgiven and forgiving ourselves are two different things."

"I don't think I can really forgive myself until I really can feel like I'm doing some good serving Him."

"Nothing wrong with that as long as you don't think you're earning what you're being given. There's nothing we can do to be worthy of salvation. It's a gift, given to us by a Father who loves His children. But works count, and we're going to have to be accountable for them someday."

They stopped in front of the jail. "Yes, I understand that," Amos said. "So what does He want from me? How do I know?"

"It's called the Great Commission. It's found in the last

three verses of the book of Matthew, and it contains our direct instructions from God."

Joseph put out a hand to find the rough plank door of the jail. He opened it, and the stale smell of unwashed prisoners wafted out. Amos lit the lantern and opened the Bible. *At last, direct instructions; God will finally tell me what I need to do.*

He leafed through the Bible with trembling hands, looking for the text Joseph had spoken about. Finally he located Matthew 28:18-20. He finished reading, then looked up with a puzzled expression on his face. "So that means what?"

"You tell me. There are many things I can't tell you, things only God can say. Those are His words; what is *He* telling you?"

"That He really does want me to carry the message?"

Joseph hung up his cane. "Don't put a question mark on it. He's either calling you to do it or He isn't, and only you know what He's saying to you."

"Then there isn't a question mark on it."

"Good. Anything else?"

He read it again. "It sounds like I'm also supposed to teach."

Joseph motioned him to a chair. "That's part of carrying the message. It says teach them to obey, because that's what God wants most of all. You haven't been a parent, but do you know what mothers and fathers want above all else? They want their children to mind them, to obey. That's what God wants too. He wants His children to mind Him as well, to obey."

Joseph held up a cup in an unspoken question. It took everything Amos had to choke down that coffee when it was supposedly fresh. The idea of a cupful that had been on the side of the fire for a couple of hours was too repulsive to contemplate. "No thanks. To obey what?"

"To obey what's in that book you have in your hands. That's God talking to us. He wants us to hear Him and to do what He asks of us."

Joseph poured his cup full. It didn't pour like coffee, but more like cold molasses. Amos tried not to think about it.

"I'm ready to take a shot at that, but I can't teach something I don't understand myself."

"You'll get there. Are you still thinking in terms of going on the road with the message?"

Amos watched as Joseph sat down and took a sip, studying his face closely for any sign of how it must taste. No response. *His taste glands must be permanently impaired*, he thought.

With a shudder, Amos forced himself back to the subject. "Not like I was. Joseph, in my mind I saw a tent show, selling God like hawking snake oil. I can't do that now; I know better. That Bible passage makes it pretty clear what He wants from me."

"How do you know, Amos? Millions of people read those words and interpret them only to mean that they are supposed to witness to people in their daily lives. How do you know God wants *you* to preach?"

Amos knew it was a test, but this time he knew the answer. This time the feelings were real. "It's not the words, Joseph, but what happens in my heart when I read them. It's what has happened between you and me and this whole town. It's where it seems to have been leading me all along. I guess I have no doubt about it."

"Congratulations, Amos. God just spoke to you. How does it feel?"

"Yes, I think He did, but I do know I couldn't do what He wants without you. I couldn't do it at all if it meant I had to leave Judy behind. I've got to make things right with her, otherwise my heart wouldn't be in it. That sounds bad, doesn't it?"

"You think God doesn't understand love? It's His favorite subject. But I don't think it's me you need to be talking to about this."

"You're right."

Thirty-Eight

Amos borrowed a horse-and-buggy rig and drove it over to Judy's place. Nothing could be right in his life until he had set things straight with her. When she answered the door, he said, "Judy, would you go for a ride with me? I really need to talk to you."

"Of course, Amos." It took her but a moment to put on a hat and pin it, then throw a shawl around her shoulders.

Amos hadn't driven the buggy the length of the street before he unloaded what was on his mind. "Judy, I've been a fool. Not just with you, but most of my natural life."

Her surprise was evident. "Well, what can I say? That's quite a statement."

He took his eyes off the road to make brief eye contact. "I'd take it kindly if you didn't argue with me about it because I know it to be a fact."

She cocked her head. "Very well, Amos. Go on."

He returned his attention to driving; it was convenient, gave him an excuse to not have to see how his words registered on her. "I just told you what you wanted to hear when we were out on that picnic. My father was a thief, and never around. I've had to make my own way since I stood knee high to a tadpole, and I had to do it with brains and by not being afraid to make my own rules as I went. I don't know how to do anything else."

"You know how to preach."

"No, actually I don't. I know how to give a good show if somebody else writes the appropriate words."

She took his arm and scooted closer. "That's a start. There are those who will help you get the words right. Joseph is still in your corner, and so am I."

"You couldn't be."

"Amos, I know Joseph told you that you can't be afraid to accept help. But first you have to admit you need it."

"I'm sure enough willing to admit that. I'm definitely Missouri-mule stubborn."

"But he said you'd listen to me."

"Listen to you how?"

She laid her head against his arm. "Amos, I suppose the truth of it all is I love you. I've fought it, and I know it's ridiculous for a girl to be admitting that under the circumstances, particularly when the man in question has yet to declare his love for her. In fact, when all of this started coming about I found myself wishing I didn't even know you, but there it is; there's no getting around it. Still, I could never be with a criminal, and I could never be with a man who wasn't a Christian. I simply couldn't."

He reached over and gently moved her hair out of her face. "My criminal days are over, Judy, I'm sure of that. This wouldn't be so hard for me to handle if they weren't. I could quietly slip out of here tonight, steal a horse, go somewhere far away, and just make money the way I always have. But here I am trying to figure out how to do it the right way, and truthfully the idea of running hasn't seriously entered my mind."

She raised her head. "You have no idea how glad I am to hear that."

He looked into her eyes. "And I love you too; I realize that now. I've fought it—oh, how I've fought it—but it's there, and there's nothing I can do about it. Now all I have to do is figure out where I go from here."

Joseph walked up behind Amos who was grooming his horse. "You have any idea who the Prescott brothers are?" Joseph asked.

Amos's head snapped around. "Why do you ask?"

"They were in today looking for somebody named Anderson. The sheriff didn't have any clue who they might be talking about, but I'll have to admit I had an inkling that you might know something."

Amos continued to brush the animal. "Yes, old friend, I know something. It's just more stuff left over from my old life. I ran a little land deal over in Dustin. It's going to take me a while to set things right for how I used to live."

Joseph felt around for a hay bale and took a seat. The questioning had a different tone than it had previously, not so much accusing but seeking to understand. "They said you robbed the bank."

"They lied."

"You have to give the money back."

Amos stopped brushing and made an open-handed gesture. "I don't have it to give back. It was part of the money you found in the hole."

"There wasn't that much money there. They said it was fifty thousand dollars."

"They lied about that too. It was only five thousand, and they did most of the work themselves because they were so greedy."

"Well, I can talk to the sheriff about it and he can get it

back to them. The money is still over at the bank. I just hope it makes the whole thing go away."

"Why wouldn't it?"

"I got the feeling the money wasn't as important as getting their pound of flesh from whoever did it."

"But they don't know it was me." He helped the old man to his feet to walk him back over to the jail.

"Nobody does. You stood trial for what you did at the church, not any of that other stuff. But I don't see that it serves any purpose to bring it out now with your trying to go straight and see all the money returned. Particularly with your life at stake."

"You think it's that serious?"

"No doubt in my mind. I think they mean to kill you."

"I'd have to say I'm basically opposed to that idea."

"I thought you might be."

This had to be done just right; the rest of his life depended on it. Amos made arrangements with the desk clerk at the hotel. There was a small private room off to the side of the main dining room. When the hotel staff found out what he had planned, the word spread like a prairie fire. *No way I'll be able to surprise Judy with this.*

It seemed to be true when he picked her up. She was beautiful beyond words. He was sure she *had* to know what was going on.

As she went back into her room to get a wrap, John elbowed Amos and said, "We're pulling for you." He had a grin on his face wider than a barn door.

"She knows, I know she does."

John shook his head. "Trust me, she don't know nuthin'. Ain't a soul in this town that wouldn't have their tongue cut out before they'd spoil this surprise."

"The whole town knows?"

John winked. "Every blessed soul. Half the women in town have been down there helping the cook, decorating the room, and getting everything right."

"Why would they do all of this for me after what I did?"

"You're the prodigal son. Church people love that better than anything. They're down there right now killing the fatted calf, so to speak."

"Amazing."

The short walk to the hotel took no time at all. When Amos and Judy walked in, the place was packed. "Oh my, there's no room," Judy said, sounding disappointed. "People are even waiting for a table. I've never seen it like this." She turned to Amos. "Are you sure you want to wait? I can fix us something at home."

"Let me see what I can do."

Andre, the headwaiter, spotted them and came over. "Everything is in readiness, sir."

"Readiness?" Judy looked at him with a question in her eyes.

"Trust me," he said. "Everything is under control."

"Yes, Amos, but have you noticed? No one appears to have even noticed we are here. That's a far cry from last time. Maybe we are no longer the center of attention."

As if every person in this room isn't here for exactly that purpose. "I'm sure you are right."

Andre led them to the small dining room and pulled the curtain behind them. Andre always had a lot of class, but this evening he stood there in one of the tuxedos shipped in when Marcie had gotten married.

"Amos, what is this?" Her eyes lit up as she saw the room. "It's beautiful."

"It's a very special evening, but you're going to spoil it if you don't quit asking so many questions."

Andre led them to the table for two. Candles burned softly in silver candelabras that had earlier been sitting along with the silver tea service at Splendora's house.

"Why, this is Helen's wedding crystal," Judy said. "And I think that's Mrs. McAfee's treasured Irish lace tablecloth. I've never even seen *her* use it. Amos, what in the world?"

"Must I say it again?"

She lowered her eyes. "No, Amos."

"I've already ordered for us. I hope you don't mind."

"Whatever you say."

Andre came in with a champagne bucket and stand. He produced a bottle and held it out for Amos to inspect the label. "Mr. Bigelow sent it from his private collection, sir."

"I'm very impressed." Andre began to open the bottle, but Amos put a hand on his arm. "But would you mind returning it to Mr. Bigelow with our most profound thanks?"

"Sir?"

"It's true I've been a drinking man most of my life, but I'm afraid it doesn't send the right message for a man of God to be seen partaking in public. Would you mind conveying that message to Mr. Bigelow for me?"

"It would be my pleasure. May I substitute a little punch then? It's nonalcoholic and is rarely available, but it has a most delightful taste."

"I think that would be very much in keeping with the plans for the evening, thank you."

Andre returned shortly with a cold pitcher and filled their glasses.

Amos held up his glass. "Here's to an extraordinary evening, Judy, and to us."

"To us," she echoed. As they each took a long sip, he held her gaze with his own.

They made small talk for a few minutes until Andre returned. He served them two bowls. "This is broccoli and cheese soup," he said, "a specialty of the chef, though he seldom gets to make it."

"My," Judy said, "where did he get the broccoli?"

"From Mrs. Tabor's garden, ma'am."

It tasted wonderful. They had hardly finished when the plates were cleared and a salad served. They picked at it a bit before the main course arrived.

"What have we here?" Amos asked.

"Prime rib, sir, compliments of Sam McDonald. Baked potatoes and asparagus in a garlic butter sauce complete the fare."

"Magnificent." They had taken the little menu he suggested to new heights.

Andre leaned over to Amos. "The best I've been able to serve since I've been here, sir."

They ate slowly, savoring it the way it deserved. It seemed the table had hardly been cleared when Andre appeared again. His face beamed in the glow of two bowls of flaming brandied peaches.

"Oh my," Judy said. "Do I blow it out?"

Andre inclined his head slightly, "If madam will wait a moment, the alcohol will burn itself out, and the peaches will be at the proper temperature."

They ate them slowly, partially to enjoy every succulent bite, and partially because they were getting very close to becoming totally stuffed.

Judy wiped her mouth daintily with her napkin, "Oh Amos, this is the most magical evening of my life."

"You have to know now what it's all about."

She reached over to take his hand. "Of course I do, Amos, and it's wonderful. The town is telling you there are no hard feelings. I think it's so very sweet."

"Perhaps you're right at that, but I assure you if that's the case it's very much secondary." He slipped out of his chair and knelt by hers. "Mostly they were setting the stage for this."

Amos opened the small box to show her the ring. She gasped. "Amos, I had no idea."

"Judy, I know I have to be the worst bargain to come down the pike any time lately, but I can't imagine my life without you in it. I don't have anything to offer you but the life of an itinerant preacher, but I don't think I can do God's work without you at my side."

"Oh, Amos, nothing would make me happier."

"Is that a yes?"

"It is, Amos. Oh yes, it is."

He pulled her to her feet to kiss her hard, then he threw back his head and yelled at the top of his lungs, *"Waahoo!"*

Andre burst into the room. "Did she?"

"She said yes, Andre. She said yes."

Andre stuck his head back out the curtain and announced, "It's yes!"

Suddenly there was a most remarkable noise coming from outside. The couple rushed to the curtain. To their amazement no one was dining any longer. All the tables had been pushed to the side, and the room had become a reception hall. *Everyone* was there.

Judy appeared stunned. There was no other word for it. "Amos, what does this mean?"

"It means you were wrong about us not being the center of attention tonight. The entire town has been watching us like hawks. Everybody knows I'm not worthy to tie your shoes, but by golly they all hoped you'd have me anyway, and you did. Although I have to admit it sure would have been embarrassing coming out to this if you hadn't said yes."

"There was no chance of that," she said. A small smile played with the corners of her mouth.

"Would you two quit jabbering and get over here," Sam Witherspoon said. "Hank, fire up that fiddle. We're gonna have us a first-class party."

Thirty-Nine

The party surged into full swing. Joseph came over to them. "Looks like you've decided."

Amos stood there with his arm around Judy's waist. "That kinda depends on you, old friend. I'm a long way from being able to do it without you, if I ever can."

"Well, God hasn't let me off the hook yet, so I guess I'm in."

Amos looked down at Judy. "We may have a family faster than we thought. Can we adopt him?"

"I rather had my heart set on someone a little smaller, not to mention younger, but I suppose he'll do until someone of that description comes along."

"They want you to continue to be the pastor at the church here," Joseph said. "And said to give you this as a wedding gift." He handed Amos a certificate of ordination. "Of course, you understand that also means you're off probation now."

"What a wonderful wedding gift," Judy said.

Joseph looked like a new father.

Amos agreed, then said, "I can't be their preacher here, you know that."

"Actually, you can. I talked to them about it, and they think the tent revival is a mighty fine idea, but you won't be on the road all the time. You can be the pastor here and still head out to do a revival a few weeks at a time. That's how it works."

"I didn't realize a guy could do both."

"Sure he can. Matter of fact, that's how it's usually done."

"Well, my goodness."

Judy moved over to take his arm. "It's like a fairy tale ending. This is where we all live happily ever after."

Joseph shook his head. "I sure wouldn't want to throw cold water on such a beautiful sentiment, but I'm thinking about all these folks you're about to start taking the message to."

"As am I, Joseph," Amos smiled at the thought. "I can hardly wait to start carrying the message to them."

"Aren't some of them likely to remember the shenanigans you pulled on them before?"

The smile dissolved, and the color drained from his face. "I hadn't thought about that part of it. Yes, I'd say they'll remember. Oh, will they ever remember."

"Perhaps we should go back East," Judy said. "You could go to a seminary, get better prepared."

He gave the hand on his arm a gentle pat. "You mean give them time to forget?"

Dropping her eyes, she said, "Well, that too."

"It's not a bad notion," Joseph said.

"No, I've got it to do. You know yourself people out here will give you the shirt right off their back, but they'll nurse on a grudge as long as the mountains stand. It ain't gonna get no better by waiting, and I couldn't hide back East forever."

"I was hoping you'd see it that way, son. The Bible promises us a lot of good things, but it also says we will be persecuted for our faith. If you want to walk the path of God, you need to make it right with the people you hurt."

"But we'll be right there with you," Judy said.

"That'll sure enough be a new experience." He shook his head slowly, looking into her eyes. "Judy, Judy, what have I gotten you into?"

Forty

Amos stood at the front of the church, his mind whirling. Married? That was a scary thought, but he loved Judy and simply couldn't figure out any way he could ever live without her. This was the final break with his old life. From this moment on nothing would ever be the same.

The benches in the little school/church were marked with white satin bows, and the pulpit had been set aside, replaced by two large candelabras of a dozen candles each. It was fortunate this event followed Marcie's wedding so closely, because the decorations and the beautiful red carpet runner that now ran down from the dais, across in front of the pews, down each aisle, and to the back, had been left from that magnificent event. It was a good thing nothing was too good for Sam McDonald's daughter. Sam had even had the piano tuned as well. Amos and Judy were the beneficiaries of all the money Sam spent.

The place had quickly filled to capacity, and everyone was waiting eagerly in their seats when the door opened and the best man, Joseph, walked in with Marcie as the matron of honor on his arm. They parted, and each went down the opposite aisle on either side to take their place at the altar. The process repeated itself with the groomsmen and the bridesmaids. They all joined Amos at the front. He and the groomsmen wore tuxedo coats shipped in special from Kansas City, again for Marcie's wedding.

The strains of the wedding march began, and the door opened for the bride to enter. Her gown was beautiful, white lace with a long train. Her Uncle John walked beside her to give her away. He looked like he'd been dressed with a board strapped to his back, then had his clothes stuffed.

The crowd "oohed" and "aahed" as Judy made her way down to the front. As she reached each row, the hats came off. It was the highest mark of respect a cowboy could pay.

As the bride approached the front, the groom and the groomsmen removed their hats and left them off, holding them in hands crossed in front of them. At the altar, John surrendered his charge and stepped back, leaving the happy couple up on the dais facing the crowd.

Mack Malone, the county judge, moved to his place in front of them, ready to play his part. Mack had been one of the ranchers who settled this area before he gave up active control of the ranch and decided to try his hand at politics. He had a red face with a huge black handlebar mustache, and was as undeniably Western as his heritage would suggest.

"Little lady," the judge said, then looking at Amos, "Partner ... we're gathered here as a herd of your friends in order to get you two hitched right good and proper. The days are gone for you to ride your trails alone. From this day forward, you'll be pulling in double harness."

He smiled a fatherly smile at them. "We talked before the ceremony, and I know you've both ridden some lonely trails, some of them pretty rough, to get to this point. And we know that there will be more rough trails to come 'cause that's just how it is in this old life.

"You'll be twice as strong now to face them though, as you

do it together. I want you kids to shut that door on the past and face the future with lots of love and understanding. If you do, the world will be yours and together you can face might near anything."

Opening the Bible, Mack continued, "In Matthew, chapter 19, verses 5 and 6, the Bible says 'For this cause shall a man leave father and mother, and shall cleave to his wife: and they twain shall be one flesh. ... Wherefore they are no more twain, but one flesh. What therefore God hath joined together, let not man put asunder.'"

He closed the book and held it to his chest, smiling a fatherly smile at them. "We've all seen many a good cowboy make a fast run, and a good throw, only to lose out because he didn't tie the calf with a good knot. I'm here to tell you when God ties the knot, it's solid."

They returned the smile as he continued. "Amos, will you this day lay your blanket down beside Judy, to share burdens and pleasures, happiness and pain, all you have or ever will have, to be one with her now and forever in the eyes of God?"

"Judge, I sure will."

"Judy, do you this day lay your blanket down with Amos, make his trails your trails, to be one with Amos now and from this day forward in the eyes of God?"

"I do."

"Reckon we can have the rings?"

The rings were produced and given to each of them. Then he said, "All right, here's the part I warned you about, the part we didn't practice. Instead of repeating after me, I want you to face each other and put those rings on each other's fingers. As you do, I want you to say what's in your heart. And eloquence don't count here, just sincerity. Amos, you're first out of the chute."

Amos slipped the ring on Judy's finger. He looked nervous enough to cut and run. "Ain't anybody in this whole building that doesn't know I don't deserve you. God has decided to bless me beyond anything I could ever expect; but then, I guess that's the business He's in."

Tears came to his eyes.

"Stay with it, Preacher," the judge said. "You can make this ride."

"Sure I can, Judge, only that fancy stuff I had in my head to say went right out of my head the minute they opened those doors and Judy came in."

He turned to look deep into her eyes. "That bright sunlight lit you up, and in that dress you looked more like an angel than anything I ever imagined an angel might be. It was like God had made me the best present He ever gave anybody. You're sure getting the cow's tail when you get me, but all of my shady dealings are behind me now, and it'll never happen again.

"I promise you, as I put this ring on your finger, that I'll be true to you, and I swear I'll love you and take care of you. You'll never have cause to doubt me."

There was a sound of muffled sniffling all over the little auditorium as Judy placed the ring on his finger. "Amos, the Lord knows you've been a hard one to convert, but your heart has been good all along. I'll marry you, and I'll stand beside you in what I know are going to be tough times to come."

They clasped both hands together as Judy went on to say, "I do know this. When those tough times do come, you look down by your side. You won't have to look far, because I'm going to be right there. I'm going to be there because I love you, and I'll follow you to the ends of the earth." She glanced back at the judge to indicate she was through.

The judge grinned. "I couldn't have got it said that good if I'd written all night." He cleared his throat, took his lapels in his hands, and said, "Since you've both said your 'I do's' and swapped rings all right and proper, then by the power vested in me I declare you legally and forever hitched in the eyes of God and this assembly."

He leaned forward and winked at Amos, "Preacher, I reckon you got some kissing to do."

Forty-One

The three sat on the porch of the hotel in the fading sunlight. Joseph smiled. "I'll bet you never thought you would have the chance for a fresh start."

"No, never thought it would happen. The only thing is, I don't know where to start," Amos said.

"The beginning is the only place to start." Joseph looked off into space as if he could see the answer there. "I know you plan on going to set things right, but it'll take quite a while to get the money together to get started anyway."

Amos gave a sheepish grin. "Not as long as you think."

Joseph turned as if Amos were looking at him. "That so? I don't understand."

"You were right, Joseph, I was still up to my same old tricks even after you quit catching me at it. I'm not proud of it."

"I was afraid of that."

"I did a saddle lottery, and I've got more than six hundred dollars in my room that I've saved up, including the proceeds from that."

Joseph closed his eyes and shook his head slowly from side to side. "How in the world did you get so much just selling off a saddle?"

Amos shrugged. "My mother was dying of consumption."

Joseph opened his eyes and laughed. "You were such a scoundrel. We'll have to go try to make it right with those boys."

"They'll be spread all over the country by now."

"Any drifters that were in the crowd will be. The regular hands don't stray far from the home range, and tend to water at the regular waterhole. They'll be there."

"It's not that black and white, you know. Such a gesture might result in me going to jail or worse. That could be their idea of setting things right."

"How do you feel about that?" Joseph needed to know what was in his mind, to find out how committed he was to a fresh start.

"I have to set the past right one way or another. If it has to be answering to the law, then that's how it has to be."

He smiled. "I was hoping you would say that."

"I'm afraid that's still not all of it."

"There's more?" The surprise on Joseph's face said he wasn't sure he wanted to hear more. Yet he knew he had to know.

"I went out to bilk Mrs. Cole out of a bunch of her savings."

Joseph hung his head. "Amos, Amos, what are we going to do with you?"

"That's behind me now, you know that." He looked down at Judy. "You believe me, don't you, honey?"

Judy had been listening in silence, her eyes getting bigger and bigger with each revelation. "Yes, dear, but we have to make it right. Did she give you any money?"

Amos produced the bank draft. Joseph whistled as Judy read the amount.

"We have to give it back to her," Judy said.

"Yes, we have to go make that right as well," Amos agreed.

"Amos," Joseph said, "I have to admit, misdirected as its been, you have the most amazing talent. We just need to figure out how to redirect it for the Lord."

"Well, I'll start with Mrs. Cole. I'll go see her first thing in the morning."

"Not without me, you won't." Judy gave his arm a tug to emphasize her point.

"Yes, dear."

They got an early start the next morning. The ride didn't feel nearly as long with company on the way. Judy sat on the spring seat of the buckboard with a frilly umbrella on her shoulder. The sun wasn't high enough to necessitate it yet, but it made a very appealing picture.

Amos searched for a way to prepare her. "You do know the lady we are going to see has, let us say, a checkered past?"

She gave him a frank look. "If you mean do I know she used to be a prostitute, the answer is yes."

"I guess it really ain't right for me to bring a lady like you to …"

She cut him off. There was no time like the present to set things straight. "Am I to be a partner in helping you with your work or not?"

"Of course you are."

She twirled the umbrella on her shoulder, feigning great innocence. "And will you be saving only decent, upright people, or will there perhaps be a sinner or two in the mix?"

"How can I argue with that?"

She dropped the act and got serious. "Besides, the way I understand it, even though she keeps to herself, Mrs. Cole has quite changed her ways."

"Yes, she has."

"I know there weren't all that many ladies out here when this country was settled, and many of those worked in dance halls or bawdy houses. Cowboys married them out of there right and left. Many a kitchen out in this country is run by a lady with a 'checkered past,' as you put it."

"I don't think you've led as sheltered a life as I thought."

Her eyes flared. *"If you mean ..."*

He warded off her sudden anger with an upraised hand. "No, of course not. I know your past is as clean as the driven snow, but I just didn't know you knew as much about how things were over on the other side of town."

The brief anger subsided. "I don't live with my head in the sand, you know."

"I'm learning that more and more all the time."

When they arrived at Mrs. Cole's house, Judy stayed on the seat as Amos knocked on the door. An inscrutable face peered out. "Missy not at home. You go 'way."

"Not again. Whey Fong, don't you remember what Mrs. Cole said about your pigtail?"

But the threat was unnecessary. The little man caught sight of Judy sitting in the buckboard. "Ah so, lady caller. Long, long time we no get lady caller. You come in, I tell Missy."

He left the door open and disappeared inside the house.

Amos turned to Judy. "I guess that means we're invited in."

"What a funny little man," she said. He put a hand on each side of her waist, lowering her gently to the ground. He kept his hands there for several moments, enjoying the closeness.

He let go reluctantly. "I don't think he likes me much. Or maybe he just doesn't like men coming here in general."

Amos took Judy by the elbow to escort her into the house, closing the door behind them. They stood in the darkened hallway.

"This is beautiful," Judy said.

"Thank you, dearie." A voice came from behind them. "My late husband was such a sweetie. He wanted nothing but the best for me, bless his soul."

Amos removed his hat. "Judy, may I present you to Mrs. Splendora Cole. Mrs. Cole, this is my wife, Judy."

"Wife you say? What a surprise. My dear, I don't know whether to congratulate you or console you, he's such a rascal."

"That he is."

"Well, I'm sure you can whip him into shape." She locked arms with Judy and led her down the hall. "Let's go into the drawing room. I've sent that worthless Whey Fong to set us up with tea in there."

"You shouldn't have bothered."

"Not bothered? Oh, pshaw, you have any idea how seldom I get company out here? And I've never had a lady caller. I'm delighted, just delighted, and I intend to keep you here as long as you'll stay."

"You should get into town more often." They turned into the drawing room.

"I don't need the aggravation. I'm sure a fine lady like you is not aware of my past, but—"

Judy cut her off with a wave of the hand. "No need to explain. I'm quite aware, and it doesn't make a particle of difference."

"Well, bless your heart, girl, but most people don't feel that way."

"Why don't you plan to come in next week, and the pastor's

wife will host a tea for you? I think I can prevail on my husband to preach on forgiveness tomorrow in such a way that you will find the climate quite different."

"Wouldn't that be a wonder?" She gestured to a seat and Judy settled into it gracefully. "Tea with the pastor's wife. You know I have half a mind to do it. Would it ever set the tongues to wagging."

"It had better be more than half a mind, because I will be making arrangements for it."

"And Judy is right, I think I can come up with a little something to pave the way," Amos said. "I do owe it to you, which brings me to the purpose of our visit."

"My donation wasn't sufficient? I suppose ..."

"No, no, that isn't it," he cut in. "Mrs. Cole, I've dealt falsely with you."

"I do wish the two of you would call me Splendora, and I know you did."

"You know?" Amos had often been surprised at the speed of the rumor mill, but this was astounding.

This time it was no rumor. "A lady who has worked where I've worked can smell a shyster a mile away. I know you put the bite on me. If you remember, I told you when you left that I knew I couldn't earn my way into heaven with a donation, but that's okay, it was for a good cause."

For a man accustomed to depending on his wits and having the confidence of many successes, learning to humble himself and apologize was a hard transition. "That's just it, it wasn't for a good cause. When I got a big enough stake together, I was going to light out. I wasn't even a real preacher."

"You stole my money?"

"I tried. Things have changed."

"In what way?"

Amos tried to read her face. There was something written there, maybe anger, possibly amusement, but he couldn't make it out.

"God really did get hold of me," Amos said. "I was about as worthless as a man could be, lying and stealing, yet He forgave me and took me in. Now He seems quite insistent that I serve as a preacher for real."

Whatever was going on in her face gave way to a broad smile. "Now that's priceless. Are you saying that you tried to steal from me and God wouldn't let you do it?"

"That's about the size of it."

Splendora broke out into a fit of most unladylike laughter, slapping her leg. As the fit subsided she dabbed at the corner of her eyes with a handkerchief. "And now you're here to return the money?"

"I am."

She composed herself again. "What you told me was that you needed it for a revival tent, a wagon, and a pump organ. Is that not true?"

"Yes and no."

"How could it be both yes and no?"

"When I told you that, it was just for the purpose of stealing your money. However, now I really am in need of just those items."

Mischief twinkled in her eyes. "So what you are telling me is that God knew what it was really for long before you figured it out?"

"I suppose you could look at it that way. I thought I was just coming up with a reasonable excuse to get the money. It just took God a while to get me on board."

Splendora fanned the air with a dismissive gesture. "I see

no reason for you to return the money. It is to be used for exactly the purpose I was told it would be used for. As a matter of fact, there is more there if it is needed, now that I know you are sincere."

"Oh, I couldn't do that, but it is comforting to know the help is available if we really need it."

Forty-Two

*T*he pair wasted no time telling Joseph about the reception they had received at the ranch. "It doesn't take a special gift to feel the Lord's hand in this, does it?" Joseph said.

They laughed, and Amos said, "No Joseph, it really doesn't."

Joseph was still having trouble believing his ears. "So all we have to do is put the rig together, and we are ready to go?"

"Apparently so. Isn't it amazing?"

"No, it isn't. When we get out of His way and quit trying to do things for ourselves, God provides."

"Well, old friend, He'd better be paying close attention when we get back to some of these places, because I don't look forward to the reception I'm going to receive."

Amos walked Joseph back over to the jail. On the way he asked, "Did you get the money back to the Prescott boys?"

"Yes, but they weren't happy. They wouldn't believe we didn't know who it had come from. You'd better watch out for them, Amos. They act like they've got something mean riding them and not sparing the spurs."

The jail stood empty except for Joseph. He hadn't been in bed long before he heard somebody in the outer office moving around, making little noise. "Sheriff? Is that you?"

Footsteps came closer, and he started to get up from his cot. He sat up on the side to slip his feet into the loose old shoes, but before he could rise, rough hands grabbed him and jerked him to his feet.

"Who's there?"

A surly voice answered, one he did not recognize. "None of your business, you old coot. We've got a few questions for you, and you had best come up with the right answers."

Joseph finally realized the voice had to be one of the Prescott brothers, probably Marcel, but thought he'd better not let them know he could identify them or he'd be in even bigger trouble, if that were possible.

"A man came by and turned in some money." The man was right in Joseph's face, and his hot, foul breath would fell a buffalo.

"Yes, I believe that's true."

"We want to know who he was."

Joseph scratched his head. "My mind isn't what it used to be, I don't recollect—"

A powerful slap spun his head around beyond where he thought it could go. His neck burned, and bright lights went off in his brain.

"Did I mention that every wrong answer is going to bring you some serious pain? And you better quit talking so uppity to me, or I'll take you down a peg or two."

Something in Joseph cried against having to do his act again, but something else told him he was facing pure evil here. He reluctantly resumed his subservient demeanor. "Naw, sah, I'm sorry, sah, I must still be half asleep. It's probably dark in here, Massa. So maybe you don't know I'm blind. If someone doesn't say who they are, how am I to know?"

The putrid breath was back in his face. "You tell me what he said, exactly."

"Yassah. The man came in and said he had found some money and old clothes out in the woods. He said he wanted to turn them in."

"How much money?"

"The sheriff counted it; you'd have to ask him. I know there was several thousand dollars, I heard somebody say that."

A powerful blow in the stomach took all of his wind. Joseph doubled over, gasping for air. "I don't believe you." Another followed, and a third.

"Naw, sah, why would I lie? I don't have nothing to gain by it."

"I don't know why you'd lie, but I'm not hearing what I want to hear."

"Massa, I just can't tell you something I don't know. I could make something up to save myself some pain, but you'd find out it wasn't true and would come back. There's not much I can do to protect myself."

"You keep that in mind, but I got to tell you I don't believe some drifter brought that much money in, and I sure don't believe he didn't even leave his name to get it if it wasn't claimed."

"Oh, if you mean do I think the guy really did find it, not for a minute. Neither did the sheriff, but that don't change the fact that he didn't say who he was, and I had no way to find out. I think he probably watched the place to bring it in when the sheriff wasn't here, because he knew I couldn't identify him."

"Would you recognize his voice if you heard it?"

"I doubt it; it's been—uhhhh." Blows rained down on him

again. Both men hit him. He couldn't protect himself because he couldn't tell where the blows were coming from. When they stopped, he dropped down on his cot.

"I told you it wasn't a good idea to lie to me. If you're thinking you can't admit to being able to recognize voices because I'm afraid you'll identify me, you're chasing the coon up the wrong tree. I don't care if you know who I am. I know you can't make it stand up in court, and you know what will happen to you if you try."

Joseph's ribs hurt very badly. He was sure that some of them at least were cracked, if not broken, and he could feel blood running down his cheek. His eye began to swell shut.

"You just keep in mind what will happen to you if I find out you've been talking about this little party. And if you hear that voice again, I better find out about it, and find out about it fast. I plan on killing that weasel for slickering me, and if you get smart and help me find him, you may get out of joining him."

A hard fist put Joseph on his back. "That's just to help you remember."

Just before Joseph passed out he entertained the thought that Amos was in trouble. These men would not give up and they liked to hurt people. Then the darkness closed in.

Amos found him the next morning. Joseph was bloody and bruised and couldn't seem to get his wits about him. Amos ran to the door to send a nearby youngster for the doctor, then the sheriff, in that order.

The doctor came and examined Joseph, then said that he had a concussion and the cracked ribs he had feared. He bound him firmly around the midsection and said he needed to get a lot of rest.

"Can he answer a couple of questions first?" asked the sheriff.

The doctor frowned at him. "If they are very brief."

"The big one is, who did this, Joseph?"

"I don't know."

"You don't know why, either?"

"No. They asked questions about the mysterious man who turned in the money."

"That'd make it the Prescott brothers."

"I didn't say that."

Wilson put his hand on the old man's shoulder. "No, you didn't, and when I go talk to them I'll tell them you didn't say, but I suspect they told you there'd be more where this came from if you did."

"I expect I deserved it. I *did* lie to them after all, something a good Christian shouldn't do, but it was that or set them on Amos."

"You don't have to worry, old friend. You get some rest. I need to take me a little ride." He paused at the door. "I intend to make it *real* plain what's in store for them if I find you've been mistreated again."

Concern came into the old man's face. "You're going to talk to them?"

The sheriff wasted a gentle smile Joseph couldn't see. "You just take it easy."

"You be careful, Sheriff; they're dangerous. And they have their own law in their town."

"That won't matter, not if I have a Texas Ranger with me anyways."

Amos got up to follow the sheriff out of the room but Joseph stopped him. "Amos, can you sit with me for a little bit?"

"Of course."

After everyone had gone, Joseph said, "Those men are crazy. They mean to kill you, and then I think they mean to kill me."

"I better go see them."

"No. You can't deal with them, and you can't set it right."

"But I can't let you take this kind of treatment when it's all my fault."

"Your getting some of it won't get me off the hook. There has to be another answer."

Forty-Three

*S*ergeant John David Slocum sat his horse outside of Dustin. He'd gotten the telegram down the line and waited on the sheriff at the junction north of town. The wiry little ranger had collar-length black hair and a full, flowing mustache on top of skin tanned to leather by the sun. It all added up to a dark, menacing look that he fully lived up to.

The sheriff rode up to stop beside him, facing him. "Bulldog," he said, using the nickname the ranger had earned from his dogged determination once he got on a man's trail. "I appreciate you coming." He extended a hand and they exchanged a perfunctory shake.

Slocum seldom showed any facial emotion. "I was in the area, following up on some questionable brands out east of here."

"East? That's Prescott range, isn't it?

"It is."

"Find anything?"

"Ain't through looking."

Sheriff Wilson cleared his throat. They had been friends a long time, but there were times the little man scared him. Slocum had never seen trouble he was willing to ride around and would ride hard half a day for a good scrap, as he had done now.

"I appreciate you siding me on this," Wilson said. "I ain't gonna be well received in these parts and my badge don't cut no ice here in Dustin."

Slocum knew Wilson was no pansy and if he needed someone standing behind him, there was a reason. He nodded once. "Well, we won't get it done sitting out here." He sharp-reined his roan and spun him in a tight circle. The pair loped into town and straight up to the town marshal's office.

Several deputies sat rocked back on the hind legs of straight-backed chairs on the boardwalk. One, a slim man with a marled eye said, "You're off your range, Wilson. That badge ain't no good over here."

Slocum turned hard eyes on the man. "You want to extend that remark to the badge I'm wearing?"

The man couldn't meet the ranger's glare. "I got no quarrel with a Texas Ranger."

"Then get off your tailbone and get your boss out here. If you make me climb down it's likely to make me irritable. You don't want to see me irritable."

The deputy didn't need convincing. He jumped up and headed into the office at a fast walk. He didn't come back out with the marshal.

"I don't take it kindly you coming into my town throwing your weight around, Ranger." Matthews was a potbellied little man with a two-day stubble on his cheeks and an odor that said it'd been a lot longer than that since he left a bathtub ring.

"Any town in Texas is *my* town, Matthews and it won't pay for you to forget it. Sheriff Wilson has a message for you, and I rode over with him to see you understood I'm backing his play."

"What's the message, Wilson?"

Wilson spit tobacco at the marshal's feet. "I know you're

bought and paid for, Matthews, but I'll give you the same message I intend to give your boss."

"And what would that be?"

Wilson turned in his saddle to see the speaker was Marcel Prescott. "Good, this'll save me a trip, Prescott."

Slocum did not even bother to look. He figured Wilson capable of handling Prescott, which left him Matthews and the three remaining deputies. If he had to take them, the fourth man would be a little bit of a stretch, but he didn't doubt the outcome.

Wilson reined his horse around to face Prescott, who stuck his thumbs in his vest pockets—a gesture calculated to show he was wearing no weapon.

Wilson spoke in a slow, even tone. "Two men, probably you and your brother, beat up a old blind man in my jail. I'm here to tell you if anybody lays one more finger on him I'm going to come over here and turn your hide inside out and nail it up on my barn. Don't try me on this; I ain't kidding."

"Marshal," Prescott glanced over at Matthews. "This man has no authority here. Are you going to allow him to ride into town and threaten your leading citizen?"

Matthews hitched up his belt. This was his bread and butter talking. "You come after Mr. Prescott, you got to go through me first."

"Reckon not," Slocum drawled. "This business is personal between Wilson and Prescott. Anybody else try to draw cards in the game and they take it up with me."

Prescott looked at his lawman. "I don't want to have to wonder whether they're coming back or not. They're here now; put an end to it."

Matthews's eyes darted back and forth between his boss and the ranger. Little beads of sweat broke out on his forehead.

"Your boy ain't gonna do a blessed thing," Slocum allowed himself a half smile. "He knows I'll drop him first, before anybody else clears leather." As Wilson had done, Slocum spat at the feet of the terrified-looking deputies as if marking them as targets. "Be plenty of time for you boys, too."

Matthews reached slowly with his left hand and dropped his gun belt. The deputies followed his lead.

"You spineless pig," Prescott said under his breath.

"I ain't pulling on Slocum, boss," Matthews whined.

"Just remember what I said," Wilson repeated. "Don't make me come back."

"Don't make *us* come back," Slocum corrected.

Wilson turned and rode out. Slocum tight-reined the roan to back him up until he was out of easy gun range before he spun him to ride alongside the sheriff.

"That was close," Wilson said.

"I'm disappointed," Slocum growled. "It ain't over, you know? Been better if we could have put it to bed right then."

It took several weeks to get the gear together, yet it seemed like no time at all before the little caravan was winding its way through the flat countryside.

The only other occupants of this desolate land were the stands of head-high mesquite bushes watching like amused onlookers, the occasional scurrying rabbit, and a never-ending variety of birds darting here and there.

It had been a dry year, and the grass grew tall, but quite yellow, beside the path. Occasional green patches of some hardier variety stood out like exclamation points.

Amos handled the reins on the freight wagon that carried the tent, pump organ, and lumber for the benches, while Joseph sat beside him on the seat. Judy drove the camp wagon. She looked out of place perched high on the wagon seat, a picture of femininity in her blue gingham dress and long chestnut hair wafting in the breeze. Her delicate and frilly appearance was deceptive, though, for she handled the reins of the spirited team in a most businesslike manner.

Amos handed the reins to Joseph and said, "It's all flat and there's nothing in the way. I need to see if Judy is ready to stop."

He stepped down and walked back alongside the camp wagon. "There's a little grove of trees over there," he told Judy, pointing to the east. "Nice little pond, too. It'll be dusk soon. Be a good place to overnight."

She gave him a weary smile. "That sounds nice. I'm pretty tired. I'm not used to all this driving."

Amos got back on board the freight wagon and the three of them maneuvered the wagons into position. Judy stopped her wagon to shelter the campsite from the wind. She immediately went to work getting something ready to eat. The light was fading, and they all knew their chores.

Amos strung a rope to the waterhole for Joseph to use as a guide. They always set the camp the same way, water to the front, wagons at a diagonal on the sides. Once he had that set, Joseph could navigate the camp.

As soon as they had walked out the site to help Joseph get it in his head, Amos gathered up firewood while Joseph went for a pail of water. Both wagons carried firewood and a water barrel, but they preferred to keep them until they were needed, gathering both fresh when available.

The camp wagon, which stood tall with hard sides, was painted as red as a barn. A small smoke pipe puffed a signal that Judy was making progress on fixing something to eat. Not commonly seen in these parts, Amos had bought the big wagon from a Gypsy sheepherder, and he thought it to be just the thing.

It had a table and chairs, the little wood stove that Judy now worked on, and a bed over a storage area. Joseph preferred to sleep alone in the freight wagon.

Amos returned with an armload of wood and soon had a modest fire going. Almost before he had finished, Joseph had three pieces of metal arranged over it like a tripod. A chain hung down the middle, and the fire-blackened metal coffeepot was hung on it before the flames had even started to lick at the bottom of it.

I'm so tired that a cup of that nasty stuff he makes might actually perk me up a bit, Amos thought. Just then Judy called, and the men went over to take heaping plates of food she passed out the back door. If the weather was decent, they didn't like to eat inside. They pulled logs by the fire to sit on, and Amos sat down holding both Judy's plate and his own. The aroma of the hot stew ran up his nose, exploding in his brain. He had no idea he was so hungry, but there he sat, both hands full, nothing to do but smell and salivate.

Then she joined him, carrying a big dish of hot cornbread and some fresh churned butter. She buttered a couple of pieces for Joseph and sat down. Amos went to work at once.

"Poor baby. Did I starve you to death making you smell that food with no free hand to work on it?"

"Smrunf dlesad."

"Don't talk with your mouth full, dear."

They ate in silence, content on the chore before them. "Dessert?" she asked, when they had finished. "I have a little cake left in there."

Joseph waved a hand. "Not for me. I'm not used to eating like this. After so many years of jailhouse food, you two are going to have to start rolling me around like a pickle barrel if I don't ease up a bit."

"Me too," Amos said. "Here I just thought I was marrying the best-looking woman in the West, and it turns out she's the best cook too."

"How you two carry on. Let me have those dishes."

"No such thing," Joseph jumped to his feet. "We might as well get this straight right now. If you're going to cook, I'm going to handle the dishes."

"Where does that leave me?" Amos said.

"The job of fetching and toting is still open."

"Well, I can fetch, and I can tote, so I guess the job is filled. 'Spect I better go stake those horses onto some fresh grass, too."

The chores were quickly done, and they were soon back by the fire. This time they sat on a blanket on the ground and leaned back against the logs. Judy laid her head back and looked up at the velvet sky. "Aren't the stars beautiful? There's always a lantern around at night back in town, so we just don't see them."

"Can put a fellow in his place," Joseph said around the pipe stem. "I mean, we wouldn't even make a speck on one of those stars, and there they are, as far as the eye can see. That is, if I had an eye to see them with."

Amos nodded. "The Boss has some mighty big ways."

Judy sat upright. "Wait a minute. It just occurred to me that I don't even know where we are headed. Where is our first stop?"

"Three Forks."

"I tried to talk him out of it." Joseph shook his head from side to side as if the very thought of it was exasperating.

"Why did you want to talk him out of it?"

"You want to answer that one, Amos? I don't figure it's my place."

"It was before I saw the light," he sat up where he could look at her squarely.

The question mark was still in her eyes. "You can skip the prelude every time you get ready to confess something new. You think I don't know how you were? What you were?"

"No, you know exactly how I was, which is why I constantly marvel as to why you are with me now."

"Are you trying to change the subject?"

"Just trying to get up the nerve to spit it out. Have I mentioned to you how nice you look in that dress?"

"Amos!"

Amos could hear Joseph quietly chuckling on the other side of the fire.

Amos rubbed his forehead as if it hurt, or he needed to massage the words out. "The problem was I needed to get up some money to make a getaway. That old bandit over there on the other side of the fire made me cough up everything I had."

Judy clucked her tongue. "You're one to call somebody a bandit."

He feigned being indignant. "Don't get personal now. You want me to tell this story or not?"

She inclined her head, pursed her lips, and folded her hands into her lap. There was no doubt she was toying with him. "As long as you leave Joseph out of it."

"It's hard to leave Joseph out of anything the way he treated me. He rode me like a green-broke horse."

Out and out laughter began coming from across the fire. In the dark Joseph disappeared, and a glance in that direction yielded nothing but a white beard and white teeth dancing in the air.

"At any rate, I had to have money, so I went over to Three Forks and ran a saddle lottery."

Judy frowned. "What's a saddle lottery?"

"You get an old saddle and sell chances on it. Somebody wins it. It makes a little money."

Joseph was having trouble talking the way his sides were heaving, but he managed to get out a few words: "To be truthful, something he finds very hard to do even with his new-found conscience, it's a way to sell a ten-dollar saddle for several hundred dollars."

"That sounds dishonest," Judy said disapprovingly.

"Funny thing, most sheriffs tend to see it the same way," Amos said. Joseph, who had collapsed against the log, was obviously having trouble getting his breath.

Amos tried to ignore him. "At any rate, those boys may still be a little testy about it when I get there."

"*Testy?*" Joseph howled. "Come on, tell her the rest of it."

She swiveled her head to bring her eyes full focus on Amos. "There's more?"

He gulped. "Well, maybe I did play on their emotions a bit to get them to bid it up."

She scowled, "I don't think I want to know this, but go ahead."

The words were hard to understand as Joseph could no longer breathe at all and was making strangling noises, like someone suffering from a severe case of pneumonia. "He told them his mother was dying of consumption and he was selling everything he had to get to her."

"Amos Taylor, your mother has been dead for years." Judy didn't see the humor.

Amos shrugged his shoulders. "There, see, it wasn't so far from the truth."

"How much money are we talking about?"

"About five hundred dollars."

Her eyes got wide. "Oh my goodness."

"Don't get all het up, I've saved it back, and I'm going to return it to them. That's why I'm starting there."

Joseph was starting to get his wind back. He held a hand on his ribs as if they hurt. "Seriously, he'll be lucky to get out of there with his hide."

Amos shook his head. "Now you don't know that. Cowboys are notional folks. They may be mad or they may think it's the world's greatest joke."

"If I was a betting man, I'd give long odds on mad."

"Well, so would I, but I have it to do."

Forty-Four

I'm going with you," Judy declared.

"A saloon is no place for a lady. They'd get me for sure if I took you in a place like that. They just wouldn't stand for it." He had one hand on her shoulder, looking her full in the face. "You've just got to trust me here."

"He's right there," Joseph said. "It wouldn't help for you to go in there. I'll keep an eye on him for you; not in a physical sense, of course."

Amos turned on him. "You aren't going either."

"I am so."

He put a hand on the old man's shoulder. "Old friend, you know I never even bring up your affliction, but I gotta talk straight with you on this one. You know I can't do what I have to do and keep an eye out for you at the same time."

"Oh, all right. I guess I'd be no help."

"Let's face it, Joseph, there has to be *something* a blind man can't do, though in your case it's sure hard to find much that fits in that category."

Joseph didn't answer. He just turned and walked slowly back to the wagon. His shoulders drooped, and the spring was gone from his step.

The short walk down the empty street felt like it was miles. Actually, the little town was comprised of one small dirt street with only a few buildings on each side. Amos straightened his coat, squared his shoulders, and walked into the saloon.

The bartender spotted him immediately. "We got us a Bible thumper, boys; everybody keep a tight hand on your wallets."

Amos held up a hand, palm out. "As a matter of fact, I'm not here looking for money. I'm here to give some back."

"Give some back?" The barkeep took a closer look at Amos's face. "Don't I know you?"

"I've been in here before; that's the problem."

The bartender quit wiping the bar and flipped the damp rag up over his shoulder. He put both hands on the shiny surface. "Why would it be a problem?"

"Last time I was in here I had a saddle to sell."

"A saddle?" He looked confused, and then gradually it dawned on him, changing his features ever so slowly as he comprehended. The change ended up in a wicked grin. "Well, well, you boys remember that shyster that palmed that old saddle off on us? Did you get there in time to see your mother before she died?"

"No, I missed it by several years, but that's why I'm here. I came to give you boys your money back."

"Give it back? This is a new dodge. How do you come out on this deal? Watch it, boys. I don't know what his game is, but he'll snake you again if you don't watch him mighty close. And what's with the preacher rig. You expect us to buy that?"

"It's the truth, I'm a new man. I figured to be too far gone to have any hope left, but God didn't see it that way. He forgave me. Then He put me to work."

"He may have forgiven you, but I figure forgiveness is going to be harder to come by around here."

"You said a mouthful there." A rough hand grabbed Amos by the shoulder and spun him around. "I can always get my hands on some money when I need it. I reckon I'd a whole lot rather even it up with a pound or two of flesh. You should have heard that saddler laugh when I took that old worn-out saddle in and tried to sell it. I ain't fond of getting laughed at. Ain't fond of it at all."

"Now wait just a minute, brother. I'm sorry you got laughed at, but if you'll just let me explain ..." A big fist caught Amos up under the chin and spun him around and down.

The man spit on the sawdust floor. "I ain't your brother."

Lights flashed in Amos's head, and he couldn't clear his vision. The big man was squared off, waiting for him to get up and come at him.

"Time was, I'd be all over you for that," Amos said, getting up slowly. "But now I have to follow different rules. The Bible says I have to turn the other cheek."

"That suits me right down to the ground." Amos tried to duck, but the next punch caught him on the temple. He went down in a heap again.

The big man pushed up his sleeves. "How many times you gotta do this cheek-turning stuff? This could get to be fun."

"I haven't had any instruction on that part of it; you see, I'm kinda new to this stuff," Amos said as he came off the floor, bringing a punch up all the way. It sent the big man sprawling back across a table. "I guess I've graduated from that to 'do unto others,' or maybe an 'eye for an eye.'"

"Well, all right," the big man growled, wiping blood from his mouth. "I was about to lose interest."

Two men grabbed Amos and held him firmly as the big brute advanced. "I'm going to enjoy this."

Suddenly a chair crashed down on the brute's head, and a cowboy said, "I got no dog in this fight, but I figure three to one is no kind of odds, no matter what that varmint's done." He threw a punch that took out one of the two cowboys holding Amos.

The room exploded. Once started, bar-room fights hold no loyalties and have no rules. When one breaks out, best friends find themselves punching each other. The reason for the fight doesn't matter or is quickly forgotten.

So it was with this one. Within seconds fists were flying, bottles were breaking, and furniture was being splintered. But regardless of who was hitting each other, Amos seemed to get the brunt of it. He went down again, and the big man found him and began to kick him in the ribs.

Suddenly there was a loud explosion, and dirt rained down from the ceiling. Cowboys ducked and dodged. They looked up to see an old black man waving a businesslike double-barreled shotgun. Next to him stood a very attractive lady with her hands on her hips. Her eyes looked more threatening than the shotgun.

"You stop that this instant," she ordered firmly. "The man next to me, as you may perceive, is blind, but he informs me that in this small a space all he needs to know is left or right. If I say either of those words, that side of the room will disappear, and I think you know enough about the weapon he is holding to know I'm not kidding."

A nearby cowboy whipped off his hat. "Ma'am, you don't need no gun to get me to do anything you want me to do." There was a chorus behind him as cowboys got up, dusted themselves off, and voiced their total agreement with that statement.

"Well, that's better." Her hands came off her hips. "To

start with, that big man over there can stop kicking my husband."

"*Your husband?* You mean to say that thieving varmint is your—"

Her gaze lanced them. "I would appreciate your helping him up."

A couple of cowboys helped Amos to his feet. One took his hat and began brushing him off with it, periodically shooting sheepish glances at Judy.

"Thank you. This is really most unseemly. He came in here in good faith trying to set things right, and you people went after him like a pack of wild dogs."

One puzzled-looking cowboy said, "You mean he really is a preacher now, ma'am?"

"He most certainly is, and you can come down by the wagon yard tomorrow to hear him deliver a whale of a sermon."

"Now I'd like that," said somebody in the back. "I ain't heard no real preacher in a coon's age."

"Has he got the power?" another asked. "I mean, can he shake the trees like my Uncle Ezra used to be able to do?"

"I think you'll find he is very talented in that direction."

"Don't that beat all?"

Once order was restored, Judy sat down at a nearby table and deftly handled the claims against the money Amos said he owed. As he had predicted, many of the drifters had moved on. A number of those who were present said to put their share in the collection plate, but to remember who they were so they could get credit for it at the service. The general consensus was that they wouldn't have money the following day if she didn't take it with her right then.

When Judy got ready to leave, they formed a receiving

line since all of them wanted to shake her hand and thank her for coming. "We don't get to see many gen-u-wine ladies out in these parts," one added. "It was a mighty nice to make your acquaintance, ma'am, a real pleasure."

Forty-Five

*D*own at the wagon yard, Judy and Joseph got the wagons ready to travel while Amos made a quick trip to the general store for a couple of items Judy said she was getting low on. As he tied up his horse in front, he saw Ford Fargo lounging on the boardwalk, leaning up against the wall. He nodded to him and said, "Fargo, what's up? Something going on?"

"I been hearing some strange tales, Amos. Something about you walking right into the saloon and coming clean on a dodge? Are you out of your mind?"

"I found religion, pard." He put his hand on Fargo's shoulder. "I'm retracing my steps trying to make it right with all of those I've taken for a ride in the past."

"I've seen jailhouse conversions before. They're generally just a way to convince people that somebody's changed so he can get out from behind bars. Nobody takes them this far. Nobody goes to these lengths."

"No, you haven't got the straight of it. They aren't all that way. For a lot of people it takes something as traumatic as hearing those bars close behind them to realize they're on the wrong road. An awful lot of them are the real thing. I know mine was."

"Even if it is, it ain't a smart play; you have to know that."

"It may not be, but I have to do it."

Fargo straightened up and got right in Amos's face. "I'll tell you what you have to do; you have to stay on your toes when you get back where some of these people are. I know about your trial. You got off on the church dodge, but you've got lots more you haven't paid for on your back trail. You start riding into towns confessing, trying to set things right, and you're going to be back in court. Believe me, you'll be doing hard time before it's all over."

"I just have to trust God to take care of it. He's made it clear I have to do this."

"You hearing voices now?" He jerked his hat off his head and threw it down on the boardwalk. "Your cinch strap is broke, Amos."

Amos bent to retrieve the hat, brushed it off, straightened the crease with a chop of his hand, and held it out. "Believe me, I know how it sounds if you don't have the faith, but what I'd like to do is to explain it to you. You need a little dose of what I've found."

Fargo put the hat back on his head and seated it with a tug. "Maybe I do and maybe I don't, but I'm not gonna hang around long enough for you to explain it. If you start telling people what you did, they're going to start remembering that I was with you when you did it. I'm heading down Mexico way."

"Funny, that was my dream for so many years. Now it doesn't even sound like something I want to do. I don't have much money, but I do want to give you most of what I have here. I did promise to take care of you if you'd watch out for me."

"Well, speaking of that, they're going to be coming, you know that. If they figure out how much I know, they may be coming for me too. I don't plan to be here. If you were smart you'd come to Mexico with me. Last chance."

"I know you mean well, but my path is clear now. You wish I was going to travel with you, and I wish you were traveling on my trail with me. Maybe I'll get a chance to share it with you. But right now I understand why you're going."

They shook hands, then Fargo mounted, and Amos watched him ride out. He knew the man wouldn't stop short of the border.

After getting the provisions, Amos returned to the wagon yard and the little caravan resumed its mission. Several hours later they rode slowly into the next town down the road. It didn't take long forFord Fargo's warning to come true.

Forty-Six

String him up!" a nearby man yelled as he spotted Amos. His anger made the big man's swarthy complexion even darker. It took even less time for a whole crowd of equally angry men to appear and back him up. *Why is it always a big man getting mad?* Amos thought. *Why doesn't somebody more my size ever get mad at me?*

Amos's mind was racing as they advanced on him. They weren't likely to listen to reason, or even listen at all. They were a scant fifteen paces away when a small man stepped between them. It was Slocum, the Texas Ranger.

"That's far enough."

"Don't listen to him, Hank. There's just one of him." The brave ones were always in the back of any crowd.

"Shut up, you idiot; don't you see that badge?" Hank said. "It's a Texas Ranger. Ain'tcha ever hear 'em say 'one riot, one Ranger'? They ain't kidding from what I hear."

Hank turned to face Slocum, putting on all the bravado he could muster. "Give him to us, Ranger; you know he deserves it." Hank shook his fist menacingly.

"Nobody deserves a lynching, you hear me? Nobody! And it ain't gonna happen, so you might as well go on home before I lose my patience."

"He does deserve it, Ranger. He skinned us. He took all our money. He didn't even leave us our pride."

Slocum eyeballed the crowd, seeking a target. "I heard about it. What he did ain't illegal; immoral maybe, sure enough rotten, but not illegal. He played on your greed. He showed you a chance to make a lot of money and you went for it."

"He still skinned us."

"That he did." The Ranger turned to look at Amos. "Taylor, you gotta be dumber than a bag of oats to come back here like this."

"What can I say, Ranger? You're dead right. Only problem is, I got no choice."

Amos stepped down from Biscuit-eater and tied him to the wagon Judy was driving. "You see, it's not my idea to come back. God is making me do it."

The look on the angry faces changed in an instant—but not all in the same way. Some showed surprise, some disbelief and maybe a little confusion.

Hank didn't change. He was still angry. "Don't listen to him, people. He's getting ready to run something by us again."

Amos smiled at him. "That's sure what I'd think if I were in your shoes."

The situation wasn't unexpected. Amos knew it was going to keep happening until he made peace with his past mistakes. "Hank, is it? Isn't that what the Ranger called you? Well, Hank, I have to admit that only six months ago I was doing a whole lot of things I'm not proud of."

The faces began to get angry again, but there was still a lot of confusion on them as well. An undercurrent of murmuring sounded like a flight of swarming bees.

"I gotta admit that's not the best training for a circuit-riding preacher, but that's precisely what I was doing when the Lord reached out and plucked me to serve Him."

"What?" Hank threw his hat to the ground as he thundered. "You got to think we're as dumb as a lightning-struck mule if you expect us to swallow that one."

"I know. I know. Believe me, if I'd come here to lie to you, I could think up something better than that in a heart-beat."

Amos picked up the hat and began to dust it off as he talked. It occurred to him that cleaning off people's hats was becoming a regular thing for him. "And it was a dodge when I first started doing it. I had me these preacher duds I have on now, and I used them to hide after I stuck up that stagecoach. I thought it was going to work at first, but then folks started expecting me to preach and do preacher stuff." He held out the hat.

Hank took it cautiously. "You're trying to talk circles around us again."

"No, I know it sounds that way, but it takes a bit of doing to explain this, and you got to hear me out."

"Oh, I got the time. This rope ain't going nowhere."

"How encouraging. Where was I? Oh yes, I didn't willingly come to take religion seriously, and that's a fact. But when God selected Paul, he wasn't a believer either. In fact, it was worse than that; he was actually persecuting Christians."

"I heared of this Paul fellow. He was some big Bible character. You comparing yourself to him now?"

Now that's a surprise. I wouldn't have figured you'd know who Paul was. Aloud he said, "You don't have a lick of patience, do you? I'd use any means I could think of to separate the sheep from their money, so maybe I was persecuting Christians too. Not that I'm proud of it; I'm just trying to explain."

"No, I don't have much patience for sure, and you're beginning to test it mightily."

"You gotta cut me some slack here; this would be easier if I were still the crook that I was then, or that you think I am now."

"Yeah, shut up, Hank," somebody behind the big man said. "This is starting to get downright interesting."

Ah, a sign of interest; that's encouraging. Amos moved over in front of the guy who had asked the question. He put his hand on the man's shoulder and looked him earnestly in the eye. "When they started really wanting me to preach, I hid behind the pulpit armed with a box of sermons that weren't mine while I robbed and swindled and basically made up my own rules as I went. When I looked out at those people, I'd only have one thing on my mind: What did I have to do to get them to fill those collection plates?"

The man grimaced. "Man, that was low."

"It was indeed." Amos removed his hand and turned as he paused to look around. This time there was no interruption. "Then I found myself pulled up short. The instruments of my conversion were an irresistible force, an immovable object, and a supernatural power. I'm married to the irresistible force now, Mrs. Amos Taylor, formerly known as Miss Judy Valentine. If you'll look to your right, she's the beautiful young lady sitting up on that wagon seat."

They seemed to notice Judy for the first time. Hats came off near where she was sitting, and there were some mumbled greetings. She gave them a nervous little smile.

Amos went on. "The immovable object travels with us in the person of an old blind man, Joseph Washington. If you'll look at the second wagon you'll see he's sitting on the seat, kinda back in the shadows. Joseph felt from the very first day he had been chosen to deliver me to my present circumstances."

They looked where he pointed. "Joseph is a black-and-white man, and it's more than just a description for his appearance. It sums up his interpretation of the Bible as well.

"The supernatural force? No doubt it was heavenly intervention, but it came in the form of an old, old Bible." Amos held it up, for it was never far from him these days. "Joseph gave it to me, and when he did, he told me a tale that rattled even a cynic like me. This Bible has power in it, the power of generations of hard-praying Christians that has seeped right down into the pages until it has covered every inch."

Amos smiled at his companions. "They delivered me all right, right into the Lord's hands. He put me to work, too. I still pastor the little church back in Quiet Valley, but what I really like is when the three of us load up the wagons and the big tent and take our show on the road."

Hank smiled a menacing smile. "That's a good story, Amos. One of your better ones, but I ain't buying it for a minute."

Amos moved back over in front of the big man. "I don't expect you to. Can't you see? The task the Lord has laid out for me is to go back to the towns where I plied my scandalous trade, back to the places where I cheated and swindled my way across the West, and apologize and try to carry His Word to those I wronged. I can't rest until I take the Lord's message back and face the very people who hate me the most."

Amos turned to address himself to the sheriff. "You see, I want you to know how big a sinner I am. I'm not hiding it. If God could save me, He can save anybody, and I don't expect you to take my word for it. I do want you to give me a chance to show you, though. Come to the meeting and let me give you the word God has put on my heart to deliver. I could never convince you ... but He can."

For the first time Hank showed some indecision. "Well, I guess there ain't no harm in listening. Like I say, this here rope is mighty patient."

The crowd turned and began to disappear.

"Thanks, Ranger," Judy said to Slocum.

"Comes with the badge. Gotta say I thought I heard a few things in all that talk I may have to check into a bit more later, though."

Forty-Seven

*T*he tent went up fast, thanks to the help of a couple of strapping farm boys hired for the purpose. They pulled the freight wagon across the end of it and unhitched the team.

Amos had figured out this little arrangement himself and was proud of it. The left-hand sideboard of the wagon dropped down, and supports went under it to create a little stage. The pump organ was permanently mounted behind the driver's seat, and Judy played it from there.

They slipped a couple of tall boards into their brackets, stringing up on them the cover that had protected the contents of the wagon on the trip. It had a scene depicting the cross on Calvary draped with a winding sheet.

They made appreciative noises, and Amos said, "Would you believe my wife painted that? I didn't know she had it in her."

"It's a fine painting," one of them said.

Amos gave each of them a dollar, and they left. He hefted the coin purse. He had no illusions about what the collection plate might yield on this trip, given the reception they were likely to find at every stop. Eating could become something of a problem.

"The Lord will provide," he told himself as he lit the lanterns. The soft glow reflected off the new canvas, making the entire tent glow. He looked over where they had pulled the lumber from the wagon and knocked the benches together. It made a very presentable little church.

Amos thought again how he had laughed when he had conned Splendora Cole out of her money. And when all the smoke cleared, what had the money gone for? A tent, a wagon, and a pump organ, just as he had told her it would be used. *Who says God doesn't have a sense of humor?*

He washed up and ate quickly as Judy brushed down his coat. Then it was time. Tucking the Bible under one arm, he walked out, feeling like those Christians must have felt when they walked into the Colosseum to face the lions.

He stopped behind the stage to compose himself and pray. Judy stepped up and got the organ going. Joseph led those who had gathered in several well-known songs, his rich baritone voice ringing over the sound of the whole crowd, not to mention the organ.

All three of them really hoped that the setting, the familiar songs, and the organ would make folks feel as if they were in a church. In fact, they hoped it would open their minds and help Amos with the task at hand.

Joseph gave the opening prayer. "Dear Lord," he said, one arm upraised, "we come to You this evening asking for Your presence here among us. Father in heaven, Amos is here in obedience to Your will. These people know what a sinner he is. He knows that without You, he is nothing. If he is to accomplish anything at all here tonight, it will only be if You fill him with Your Spirit and give him the words You would have him say. We turn the service over to You now and pray that You will move among us in a mighty way."

He turned and stepped to his seat next to the organ. Amos took a deep breath and walked out on the stage.

The reaction of the crowd was hard to read. The buzzing of the bees returned. Scanning the faces, he could see no support. No matter; he had expected none.

Amos stopped at the small podium and smiled. "I've already had to use some of my best stuff, trying to keep Hank from putting that rope around my neck." He gestured at the rope coiled at Hank's feet. "I see you're still prepared, Hank."

"You got that right."

Amos took another deep breath. "Well, it serves our purpose. I'm not here because I'm a good man. You know better. I couldn't fool you if I tried. I'm here as a really bad man that God decided to use anyway. I'm here not because of anything I have done, but because of what He has chosen to do through me."

Amos opened the worn old Bible. "Those of you who have your Bibles might want to turn to John 5:19." There was a gentle whisper as some, mostly the ladies, turned the pages.

After a couple of moments he said, "Let me give you a tip. When it's time to look up a Scripture, if you haven't found it by the time you hear all those pages around you stop turning, just stop where you are, nod, and look intelligent."

A small titter ran through the crowd. Maybe that was a good sign. He began to read: "Verily, verily, I say unto you, The Son can do nothing of himself, but what he seeth the Father do: for what things soever he doeth, these also doeth the Son likewise." Amos looked up and held the old book out to them. "You get what this is saying? Jesus Himself is saying that *He is nothing without God.* If He says that, how much less than nothing can I be? I mean that makes me feel like I could walk right under a snake with my tallest hat on."

He paused to let them get a good mental picture of that image. "You know, back when I was fooling people doing this,

I could never fool Joseph. I tried to. I did my best to make him think I had come to believe, but he never went for it. He said I couldn't fool him if it wasn't true, and that I couldn't hide it if it was. I hope that's true, because it's all that's standing between me and Brother Hank's rope. If you can see Jesus in me, then you know that it's Him reaching out to you, not me."

He went down from the stage and gave an altar call, but nobody came forward. When he finished, they left quietly.

Amos walked back to Joseph and Judy. "I didn't reach them."

Joseph smiled. "I wouldn't say that. You don't have a rope around your neck."

"Yes, I suppose that's true."

Judy took his arm. "You didn't take up a collection?"

"No, it's too early. I have to get them to trust me first. If I ask them for money, they'll start thinking about me shucking them out of their money again, sure as shootin'."

"We can't do this whole trip without any money coming in."

"I know that. God will provide. He'll let us know when the time is right."

The second night, following the sermon, a weather-beaten old cowboy limped down the aisle. "Preacher, I believe the Lord is working through you, and I reckon it's time for me to get right." They got down on their knees to pray together. As they finished, Amos looked up to find two others waiting.

It was a great night. In all, five souls came to the Lord, and when Amos closed the service people seemed hesitant to leave.

"Preacher," a man said. "Ain'tcha going to take up no collection?"

Amos was surprised. "I didn't want anybody thinking I was after their money. I wanted you thinking about the message, not sitting there watching your cash."

The man grinned at him. "I reckon we're past that now. You can't keep this up without no money coming in, can you?"

"No, in truth we can't."

He pulled off his hat. "Okay, people, give it up." He passed through those standing in the tent. They dug in pockets and coin purses, and more jingling than rustling of paper came from the hat as it was passed.

When he brought it back he said, "It ain't much. We're a poor town." He poured the contents into Amos's open hands.

"Don't worry, brother. God always sees that we get what we need."

The man inspected the contents of Amos's hands critically. "Looks to me like you lived better when you were a crook."

"No, I didn't. I may have had more money from time to time when I was doing that, but trust me, I've never regretted my decision for an instant."

The man gave Amos a sly look. "Not even when you were looking at Hank's rope?"

"Not even then."

Forty-Eight

The attitude in town was different. The people believed Amos had changed. At least, *most* of them believed. Hank was unconvinced. He had let the issue go after the first services because he felt that the shyster had pulled the wool over the townspeople's eyes again, and he knew he didn't have the backing to string him up. A lynching was not something one did alone.

He stood alone at the bar, sulking. There had to be a way to get even. A voice said, "I hear you have a problem with the preacher camped outside of town."

He looked at the man next to him. "What business is that of yours?"

"Could be a lot. Let me buy you a drink."

Hank pushed his empty glass toward the man. "I'll always listen to anybody willing to buy drinks. As long as his money holds out anyway."

"You couldn't stand to drink as long as my money would hold out." The man picked up the bottle and motioned toward the back of the room. "How about if we move to that table in the back? It'd be more private."

When they got seated in the back the man extended his hand. "I'm Marcel Prescott."

Hank took it in a half-hearted manner. "You said something about a drink?"

Prescott laughed. "I did at that." He poured a full measure. "Let me just set this bottle within reach. You help yourself to as much as you want."

The glass emptied in a single gulp, and Hank poured another full to the brim.

"Just as long as you continue listening to what I have to say, that is."

Hank looked sullen. "I'm listening. I said I would, didn't I?"

Prescott bit the end off a cigar and gave his vest pockets a pat looking for a match. "Fine, fine, just wanted the ground rules clear. If that preacher out there is who I think he is, I have business with him."

"If you have business with him, I may not want to listen to you as long as I thought." The sullen look didn't improve.

Prescott found a match and used it to toast the end of the cigar. "If it is him," puff-puff, "I have a great interest in seeing him dead." Puff-puff. "Does that coincide with your interest?" The cigar glowed cherry red and he shook the match vigorously until it went out. "I heard you were trying to string him up the other night."

Open interest toyed with Hank's features. "That's different. Go ahead."

"I'm looking for a shyster by the name of Jim Anderson."

"He's a shyster all right, but his name ain't Anderson."

Prescott blew a long cloud of smoke toward the ceiling, watching it rise. "Names don't matter much out here. He matches the description of someone who beat me out of a lot of money."

"Taylor would do that all right; he took me for all I had. You wouldn't have another one of them see-gars, would ya?"

"Mind if I ask how much?" Prescott fished another smoke out of his coat pocket and passed it over.

"I mind." He poured another glass full to the brim and emptied it. He passed the cigar under his nose, not used to one of that quality.

Prescott poured his own glass full again, but only sipped at it. "Let me put it this way, would a thousand dollars make it right for you?"

"*A thousand dollars?*" Hank froze in the act of lighting the smoke, an incredulous look on his face. "I ain't ever seen that much money in my whole life. *Yeow!*" The match burned down and he had to toss it and start the process over. A few tentative puffs to make sure it was going well and he reached for the bottle again. He stopped, looked thoughtful, then set it back. "I'm beginning to think I better slow down on this who-hit-John; I may need a clear head."

Prescott smiled. A practiced manipulator of men, he knew when he had one going his way. "That's a good idea. This Anderson, or Taylor, or whoever he is, beat me out of far more than that. I've gotten some of it back, but I don't consider the debt paid, not by a long shot."

"How do I fit in this?"

"I just had a visit from a hick sheriff. He had the gall to suggest that I had roughed up some old blind darky, and that law or no law, he was going to give me some of the same if it ever happened again. He also said he was going to be watching me mighty close."

"You mean the old blind man that's traveling with Taylor in that wagon out there?"

"The very same."

"You didn't do it?"

Prescott chuckled. "Of course I did it, but I certainly

wouldn't come right out and admit it. I had my own marshal tell him that he had no jurisdiction there. I made sure my marshal added that he didn't appreciate him threatening the leading citizen in his town. I'd have had him do more, but the hick had a Texas Ranger with him. Ain't no way I want to tie up crossways with one of them guys."

The astonished look returned to Hank's face. "You have your own marshal? Man, that's something."

"Is that all you heard in all that?"

"No, I heard it all. I just never knew anybody could have his own marshal."

"Money can make a lot of things happen."

"I still don't see where I fit in."

Prescott pushed his chair back on two legs and rested his forearms on the arms of the chair. He had noticed some people looking their way, and he didn't want the talk to appear too serious in nature. "It's just that I don't want to take direct action against Taylor with all of this attention focused on me. It's worth a thousand dollars to me for him to disappear, permanently."

"The old coot too?"

"If it's convenient. He doesn't matter as much. It needs to happen at a time when I am in full view of a large number of witnesses."

"When would that be?"

"I'm making a political speech Thursday night. Anytime along about then would do admirably."

Hank's face lit up in a crooked smile. "To be honest, I intended to settle up with him anyway. I might as well get paid for it."

"We have a deal then?"

"We do."

"We'd better not shake on it; too many roaming eyes in the room. Perhaps it would be best if we turned our attention to this bottle and just did a little sociable drinking."

"That suits me plumb down to the ground."

Forty-Nine

Hank sat in the dark of the livery stable, pondering on how to call out a preacher. He knew he couldn't do it on the street; the fool didn't carry a gun anymore. He could toss him a gun and tell him he was going to draw on him at the count of three, whether he picked it up or not. Hank pondered that one for a while, then dismissed the idea. He was sure Amos was playing the preacher game to the hilt and wouldn't pick it up. They'd get him for murder if he shot him.

He put his hands to the side of his head. It was tough trying to do heavy thinking with the pounding that was going on in each temple. He needed another drink to steady his nerves.

He left the livery on unsteady legs. He stopped at several porch posts during his journey to steady himself. He got even with the horse trough and stepped down off the porch to duck his head in it several times. The cool water felt good, but straightening up each time made his head pound all the more.

He made his way to the saloon only to find it locked. He pounded on the door. A voice said, "Go away; we're closed."

"Who is that?"

"I'm the swamper. I'm just cleaning the place up. Nobody else around."

"Ezra? Is that you? This here's Hank. I need a drink bad to clear my head; it hurts something awful."

The door opened. "Know how that is. I can snitch you one, but then you gotta go. If I get caught I'll get my hide tanned for sure."

He brought a full drink to the door and Hank gulped it down. As he took back the glass the swamper said, "Now you gotta go. I need this job."

Hank made his way on down by the creek. It was shallow, and he lay on his back in it stretched out full-length. It came up about half the breadth of his body. It felt cool and soothing.

Hank stayed there for more than an hour. His headache started to subside. He started to feel that the situation wasn't as complicated as he was making it out to be. He'd just walk into camp and shoot them, both of them. Nothing fancy. Neither man would be armed, so there would be nothing to it. He'd never shot a girl, but she'd be able to identify him, and the law would be on his trail before he could be sure of getting away. He shook his head in resignation as he realized that he'd have to shoot her too. No witnesses, no crime. Then he'd go pick up his money from that crazy Prescott and get a fast start to someplace far, far away.

Now that's a plan.

"Where to from here?" Judy ladled some enticing stew into bowls from the blackened pot hanging over the fire.

Amos accepted a bowl from her hands and looked into her eyes, measuring out the words he knew she wouldn't want to hear. "I've been thinking about making Dustin the next stop. I've got a powerful lot to set straight there."

Joseph choked on the stew he had in his mouth. "*What?* I thought we had that settled. That's mighty poor thinking. You'd get shot as soon as you hit town, and it'd probably be the law that'd do it for one excuse or the other."

Judy looked terrified. "Joseph is right. Prescott has it all his own way there. You wouldn't stand a chance. You sure couldn't preach your way out of it the way you did here."

"There has to be a way. I feel really strongly that I'm supposed to return to the site of all my old transgressions and set things right."

"I've been getting direction from the Lord a lot longer than you have, and I don't believe He wants you to walk right into the den of Satan like that," Joseph said. "I think when He is ready to help you set that situation straight He'll lead you to it, and He'll protect you."

Amos looked at the old man and said what he'd been thinking for several days. "I don't understand how you can be so sure all the time you are following the proper direction. But when I say I feel led you say it's not right."

"God knows how our minds work. He knows we'll get notions now and then and think maybe they are from Him, when maybe all we're doing is rationalizing something we really want to do."

Amos laughed. "You think going up against Prescott is something I really want to do? That's a hoot."

"It's something you feel like you need to do, which amounts to the same thing."

"So how do I know if I'm really being led?"

"As I said, God knows how our minds work. If direction is truly from Him, He'll confirm it. He'll speak to us in our minds, He'll speak to us in our Bible reading, and He'll speak to us in our daily contacts with good Christian people, but He *will* confirm it in more than one way. He always does. Right now it's just your head talking, and He might or might not have put it there. And right now you have a couple of good Christian people giving you some conflicting testimony."

"So I need to pray on it and get to reading the Bible?"

"That's what I'd say."

"I'd say you don't have the time for all that foolishness." A new voice cut in. Hank stepped into the firelight. "You aren't going to be around that long." He held a pistol trained on them.

Amos raised his hands, palms out, and got slowly to his feet. "We need to talk about this, Hank."

"Ain't gonna be no talking. I know how you are. You can mess up people's thoughts what with all that snake oil you spout."

"At least let me move away from them." He distanced himself from the fire with deliberate slowness.

The muzzle of the gun followed him. "Don't matter you do or you don't. You're all about to go meet that Maker you're so fond of."

"Why are you doing this, Hank? Surely you aren't so eaten up over such a small thing." Amos's mind raced. He was a dead man, he was sure of it, but there had to be a way to save Judy.

"It weren't small to me; besides, I stand to make a pile of money off this."

"Prescott. It's him, isn't it?" Amos inched toward the ax leaning against the wagon wheel. He'd have to take the bullets but make sure he reached Hank before he died.

"Don't guess it matters whether you know or not, since none of you are going to be around to tell anybody."

"You wouldn't shoot a woman, Hank." He was within arm's reach of the ax. He steeled himself. Even a man who knew what waited for him on the other side had trouble facing death.

Hank shrugged. "I didn't think I could either, but it turns

out I can. I may have to pleasure her a bit first. Would be an awful waste otherwise. I'd like to tie you up and make you watch, but that'd be too dangerous. I best just shoot both of you guys first."

He pulled back the hammer on his pistol. "I'd like to say no hard feelings, but it'd be a lie 'cause I'm up to my eyeballs in hard feelings."

Amos made his move, jumping to snatch up the ax. Hank fired, the shot going high with the unanticipated move. A second shot sounded and the clearing lit up with the pistol flash. It wasn't going to work. Amos took a quick inventory as he reached for the ax but he didn't feel a thing. He'd heard it was that way, that a person didn't feel any pain at first. He braced himself to try for the man when Hank fell over on his face.

"What the ... ?" Amos looked around to see Judy holding a smoking pistol. "Judy, what have you done?"

She was sobbing uncontrollably. "I had ... had to. He was going to k-k-kill you."

He let go of the ax. "But you've committed a terrible sin. God would have protected me."

Joseph said, "You really don't see, do you? He just did."

Amos looked stricken. "Using Judy? That's not right. The book says 'Thou shalt not kill.' Surely He didn't intend—"

"It isn't for us to understand the mind of God. Remember, all through the Old Testament God personally presided over a multitude of battles in which He personally empowered people to vanquish their enemies. He didn't want you to do it. He knew I couldn't do it, so He used Judy."

The pistol now lay at her feet. Amos picked it up. "This is my old gun. What were you doing with it?"

"I don't know. With all that has been going on, something told me I needed to put it in the pocket of my skirt."

He helped her to her feet and took her in his arms. Behind them Joseph said, "You can quit worrying about breaking that particular commandment. This jasper is breathing."

Fifty

*D*oc says he'll live, Mrs. Taylor," Ranger Slocum said. Judy breathed out a long sigh of obvious relief. "And you got my personal word he's going to prison for a long, long time. He implicated Prescott, too. You know anything about that?"

"He and his brother beat me nearly to death," Joseph said.

"That was you? I went with Sheriff Wilson to jerk a knot in his tail over that. Seems he might be a slow learner; he hired Hank to kill all three of you. I didn't figure Hank had come up with it all by himself; he's not the sharpest knife in the drawer. Anyways, I'm figuring on going over and rounding up Prescott for attempted murder. Maybe he can share a cell with old Hank there."

He walked over to the door and turned with his hand on the knob. "Guess I'll wire Sheriff Wilson to meet me. Reckon he'd like a piece of that action."

The telegram drew a quick response. Wilson did indeed want to go along, and he and two deputies would meet Slocum on the road to Dustin as quickly as they could get there.

As they met, and introductions were made, it was clear this was no sewing circle. The deputies Wilson had brought were hard-looking men, accustomed to trouble. Slocum didn't figure to require any help, but if he did, this was a group that could get the job done.

As they entered Dustin and rode up to the marshal's office, Matthews came out on the porch and eyed Wilson. "I see you're back again, still hiding behind Slocum."

"Don't make me peel that badge off you and use it to pin your ears back," Wilson said. "I got a gut full of you last time, and I'm not in the mood to hear much more of it."

Matthews wasn't impressed, "Like I said last time, you got no jurisdiction here."

Wilson's temper approached the breaking point. "I don't need no jurisdiction to lay a first class whuppin' on you."

Slocum had no time for foolishness. "That's enough of that stuff. I got all I wanted of you last time too, and I *do* have jurisdiction here. I'm toting a warrant for Marcel Prescott, and I'm here to serve it. Law requires me to check in with the local law before I do it, so consider yourself checked in with. If you'll get yourself back into that jail and stay there, I won't have to shoot you in the process." The sound of a door slamming echoed in the jail. "What's that?"

Matthews glanced inside. "Just the back door blowing shut."

Slocum's eyes narrowed, "Matthews, if one of your men has gone over there to warn Prescott, I'm gonna have your badge, and maybe your hide with it."

"One of my men? Not a chance."

Slocum didn't blink, didn't look away. The marshal felt trapped in the glare as Slocum said, "Where do we find Prescott?"

Matthews tried for an air of bravado, but failed miserably. "He owns most of these businesses; he could be in any one of them."

"Where's his office?"

"That'd be the same answer."

Wilson said, "His primary office is in the hotel, Ranger."

"Then that's where we'll be going." He looked over at the two deputies. "You boys would oblige me if you'd stake out that back entrance."

"You got it, Ranger," they said in unison.

Two sets of spurs jingled as they dismounted and crossed the boardwalk into the hotel. Slocum went up to the desk clerk while Wilson checked the saloon. He shook his head negatively as he returned.

"Marcel Prescott," Slocum said. "Right now."

"Ranger, I work for—"

Slocum reached across the desk and grabbed a handful of shirtfront to pull the little man completely off the floor, almost on top of the counter. "Being as how you seem to be a little hard of hearing, I said right now."

Sweat broke out on the clerk's forehead. "He ... he isn't here."

Slocum let him down, none too gently. "If you don't want a piece of this you better get to telling me what you know I need to hear."

"Yes, sir." He pushed his spectacles back up from where they had slid down on the end of his nose. "The deputy ran in a few minutes ago," he said, "and Mr. Prescott emptied out his safe into a valise before he hit that back door like his shirttail was on fire."

"I warned Matthews ..."

"He believed you," a new voice said.

Slocum turned around. "And who might you be?"

"I'm Sven Jorgenson," the old man said. "I run the general store, one of the few things the Prescotts don't own around here. I'm also on the town council." He held up a badge. "Since Marcel was the mayor, Matthews figured I was the only guy he could turn his badge in to."

"He coming back?"

"You talking about Matthews or Prescott?"

Slocum turned to face the storekeeper. For a relatively small man, the ranger had an intense presence. "Both, now that you mention it."

"Matthews and his deputies aren't. They're afraid they might catch some of this heat they think is coming down."

"Well, that shows more sense than I thought they had. How about the Prescotts?"

The shopkeeper thought it through before he answered. "We don't know that Leroy is gone, though nobody has seen him for a day or so. Marcel won't be back any time soon. I suppose I wouldn't rule out him trying to come back some day though."

Slocum agreed with the assessment. "Yes, I'd say so, particularly if he can do a little witness elimination in the meantime. We'll have to see that doesn't happen. I think we'll take one more step. You got anybody in mind to wear that badge?"

"No, in truth we don't."

"Sheriff Wilson, would one of these boys you brought with you make a town marshal?"

"Both of them would," Wilson said. "Homer's got some deep roots where he is, but I'd say Clarence would be very interested. I'd hate to lose him, of course, but it'd be for a good cause."

Slocum looked at the storekeeper. "That give you any ideas?"

Sven grinned. "I can arrange a council meeting in a matter of minutes, and I can guarantee Clarence will be wearing the badge within the hour."

"That all right with you, Clarence?"

"Sounds like a good job. How about this Leroy character?"

Slocum pushed his hat back on his head. "We don't really have anything on him. I guess as long as he keeps his nose clean you can let him be, but if Prescott shows up, I want him in your jail on sight. If you have a problem, you send a telegram and I'll come running. Western Union always knows where I am; that's how people get hold of me."

"You can count on me."

"I don't think you need to worry about Leroy, Ranger," Sven said. "Without Marcel to do his thinking for him, he's got all he can do to run his ranch. My guess is there'll be new ownership of most of these businesses before very long at all."

"That's assuming he's still scared to return, and that depends on our witnesses. He knows that, so we better hotfoot it back and take care of them."

"Aren't we going to try to track Prescott?" Wilson asked.

"I don't think we'll have to."

Fifty-One

They rode as hard as they could without endangering their mounts. As they entered town a man came running up to them. "Ranger, we're really glad you're back."

"What's the matter?"

"Hank's been killed."

Wilson looked over at Slocum. "We're too late."

"You sure he was killed?" Slocum asked.

"I am." They turned to see that the speaker was a little man with wire-rimmed glasses, wearing a tattered suit that looked as if he had been living in it, which he probably had.

"Oh, howdy, Doc," Wilson said.

Doc looked over his spectacles at the peace officer. "He had bruise marks on his face. Somebody smothered him with his pillow."

Wilson snorted. "I figure we know who that somebody is, Doc."

"How about Amos and his bunch?" Slocum asked.

Doc pointed in a westerly direction. "They left early this morning."

Slocum looked involuntarily, as if he expected to see them in the distance. "West? They say where?"

"They didn't say. Amos was talking about Dustin, but the other two were trying to talk him out of it."

"Yesterday that would have been a really bad idea," Slocum said, "Today it might be the smart move. They couldn't have known that, of course."

"Let's grab something to eat, get fresh mounts, and see if we can track them," Wilson said.

Slocum stepped down and started peeling his gear off his mount. "We sure have it to do, but let's get them to fix us something we can eat in the saddle while we remount. We got no time to lose."

Joseph was downcast. "Amos, this is a *big* mistake."

"Joseph, I've thought about this a lot. I feel so strongly that I have to mend my fences, and I sure can't get on with it until the biggest hole in the fence is fixed."

"It's not the right time." The old man was not going to let go of this.

"You said to read in the book. I just opened it and let my eye drop down. It was in Psalms, I think chapter 31. It said if I put my trust in the Lord, that He'd deliver me speedily."

Joseph shook his head. "You just opened it in the middle."

"It doesn't matter; I read what He wanted me to read. Sounds to me like He just wants me to trust Him, and He'll take care of me."

Joseph nodded slowly. "Yes, if it was me I think I'd believe that. Perhaps my concern for you is coloring my faith."

Amos put a hand on his arm. "I'm touched by that concern, my friend, but I have to do this."

"Very well. You had better go over there and explain it to Judy. I'll be pretty busy back here."

"Doing what?"

"Praying."

"What is this?" Marcel Prescott got down on one knee to study the tracks. It was clear that the people he was trailing were headed to Dustin. The idea repelled him; it just couldn't be. There was no way that they'd ride right into the middle of *his* town.

Only it isn't my town right now, Prescott thought, *and might not be again, unless I can dispose of those three, and Hank as well.* On the topic of Hank, Prescott hadn't thought that dead-between-the-ears drunk to be much of a threat, but he eliminated him anyway. The other three shouldn't be much of a challenge, particularly if they were still unarmed, but it didn't matter. One way or the other they all had to go. Then there wouldn't be any witnesses left. Whatever those law dogs thought they knew would be worthless without witnesses.

He swung back up on his horse. "Well, now that I know where they're going, I won't be slowed up any more by the need to track them."

He reined his horse around hard and took a line to intercept them before they got to town.

Slocum studied the tracks. "He got down here to look at the tracks." The Ranger stood and jerked a thumb to the northwest. "Then he remounted and rode off that way."

"He's figured out where they're going," Wilson said. "Back to Dustin, right?"

"Has to be unless they whup a ninety-degree turn up here somewhere," Slocum observed as he remounted. "Well, we can track two heavy wagons a lot faster than we can track one mounted rider."

They put hard heels to the horses, no longer trying to

spare them. It was a race now, and regardless of who won somebody was sure to end up dead.

Judy tried to talk Amos out of it. "I'm so afraid," she whispered anxiously.

He took her into his arms. "We just have to have faith."

Her voice was muffled against his chest. "I know, and I try so hard. I'm so proud that you have it that strongly now, but trusting God to feed and guide us is one thing, and facing the threat of watching you get killed is another. I'm afraid it takes more faith than I have."

"I won't lie to you; it's taking all that I have, but I feel strongly that I have to do it. Judy, I either have to go all the way or not go at all. I can't say I'll trust Him here but not there. I can't pick and choose."

She pulled away to arm's length. "No, I see that, but it's such a terrible penalty to pay if we are wrong about it being His will we are following."

"Yes, if I was more sure I was following His guidance, I could have more confidence. I'm just so new at this, but asking whether God will keep His promise to protect me is not the problem; I know He will. The problem is, am I trusting Him to do something He hasn't promised to do?"

Judy gave a jerky little nod. There was no color in her face. "If we could only be sure."

"It wouldn't hurt anything to pray about it." Joseph said as he joined them, and all three got on their knees to ask for guidance. They prayed, read some passages in the Bible, and talked about the situation at great length. In the end, they all agreed that Amos had it to do.

Amos helped Judy back up onto the seat. "It's in God's hands now."

"I can live with that," she smiled. "I'm scared to death, but I can live with that."

Amos and Joseph got into the front wagon and pulled out. There would be no stopping now. Their course was set.

"Is that them?" Slocum pointed at something moving in the valley below the ridge they had just topped.

Wilson looked through a pair of field glasses. "It's them. I guess they stopped for a while."

"Wonder why?"

"Dunno, but it's helped us catch up to them. Let's ride."

Prescott pulled his rifle as he dismounted. He slipped into the rocks overlooking the trail. He'd been afraid that he wasn't going to get there in time and would have to deal with them out on open ground, but luck had been with him. They hadn't made it as fast as he'd expected.

He rested the rifle barrel on a rock and settled in. He had a nice clear line of sight. They would never know what hit them. He sighted the rifle on Amos and waited for him to get closer to improve his shot.

The horses were running hard, reaching with their heads, giving their riders all they had. Wilson yelled above the pounding hooves, "There's somebody in the rocks!"

Slocum nodded. "Gotta be Prescott. We'll never make it. The wagons are almost there!"

Prescott had second thoughts. *No, this won't do. I want Amos to know it's coming, who's about to do it, and why. I want the satisfaction of seeing it on his face.*

The wagons rolled slowly forward. Amos drove slowly, his

arms resting on his knees, holding the reins loosely. He and Joseph were in animated discussion.

Prescott let them get into easy range before he stood from his place behind the big rock hailed them. They pulled up.

"Who is that?" Amos shaded his eyes against the sun that Prescott had made sure would be behind him.

"You know who it is. It's Marcel Prescott."

"What are you doing out here? We were coming to see you."

"I'll bet you were. I'll bet you didn't intend for me to see you first, either."

Amos stood and handed the reins to Joseph. He needed to buy time, to go up and be face-to-face with the man, to reason with him. "We were coming to try to make things right with you."

"I'm about to take care of that little chore for myself."

Apparently Amos wasn't going to be given the opportunity to make his case. "Your business is with me, Prescott. Let Judy and Joseph ride on." He began to fear he'd made a mistake.

"My business is with all of you. You're the last witnesses. With the three of you gone, I can return to my life as if nothing has ever happened."

"God won't allow it."

"Won't allow it? What has your God got to say about it?"

Amos bowed his head. *Lord, there's a rifle down here, but I probably couldn't get it in time. It doesn't matter. Either I trust You to protect me, or I don't. If it's Your will that this happen, then I pray for our souls.*

Prescott threw his head back and laughed. It echoed through the rocks. "Praying? You're praying? I have to hand it to you, Amos; this is a much better act than the one you did as a surveyor, but it ain't gonna do you no good. You think I won't shoot a man who's praying? You know I don't believe in that bull."

"It's no act, Prescott," Joseph said. "Amos is a new man in the Lord."

"You shut up, old man. When I get through with him I'm going to finish what I should have done to you last time." He looked back at Judy in the wagon behind. "Then I'll take my time with the little lady."

Joseph shook his head. "Amos is right. God won't allow it."

"And I repeat, what's your mythical God going to do, strike me down with a lightning bolt? Is He going to send down angels to pluck me up? Or maybe He'll just make the bullets disappear?"

"Or maybe He'll send a Texas Ranger to blow you off that mountain." Slocum rode in on a dead run, the horse sitting down on its haunches as it slid to a stop in front of Prescott, coming quickly back to its feet.

Prescott's face became a mask of rage. "What are you doing here?"

"You better let the hammer down easy." Slocum looked deceptively calm, and made no move toward his weapon.

"I don't see it that way. What I see is a rifle already out in my hands and a pistol still in your holster."

"You fire at him and I'll kill you where you stand. He's unarmed. You only got one chance and that's to take me first, but if that barrel starts moving toward me the tiniest bit I'm going to take it as you drawing on me and I'm going to drop you. If you want to try, you better hit it and you better hit it hard."

Prescott looked as if he was steeling himself. Sweat beaded

on his lip as his eyes darted from Slocum to Amos and back to Slocum.

Instead of turning and fireing, Prescott suddenly tumbled down the hill.

"What in the world?" Amos exclaimed.

Sheriff Wilson came out from behind Slocum. "I hope I didn't kill him. I hit him harder than I intended. Nice job of keeping his attention, Ranger."

"I was starting to hope you'd be late so I could just shoot the—" He glanced at Judy's white face as she came up from the back wagon, "—the so-and-so."

Slocum dismounted and walked over to where Prescott lay. He stooped to put his ear to the man's chest. "You can quit worrying about it. This bird is going to stand trial."

Judy walked over to look down on Prescott. "Ranger, is it over?" she asked.

Slocum removed his hat. "Pretty lady, you aren't going to have to worry about that cuss for a long time."

She looked embarrassed. "Amos said God was going to protect us. I'm afraid I really didn't believe."

"I don't mean to make light of your faith, ma'am, but it wasn't God that braced that varmint, it was me. It wasn't God that knocked him down the hill either. It was Sheriff Wilson. It was mighty lucky that you stopped though. He had quite a lead on us. If you hadn't stopped to let us catch up, we wouldn't have been here in time."

Amos walked up. "Perhaps you just don't recognize God's intervention when it happens. It was necessary for Him to put doubt in our minds so we'd stop and pray about it. That time apparently saved our lives. And God generally uses people, not angels, to accomplish His ends. A great deal of the time those people don't even know they are being used."

"Maybe you're right, Preacher. They do say God works in mysterious ways."

READERS'
GUIDE

**For Personal Reflection
or Group Discussion**

Readers' Guide

*I*s faith likely to be stronger in a person raised in the faith? Or in someone who has strayed far and suffered much?

In *Mysterious Ways*, our focal character, Amos Taylor, is a rogue and a scoundrel, yet he occasionally shows a spark of something that makes the reader hope he can be salvaged. His pronounced lack of faith leads the reader through a questioning process many of us may have long forgotten. His active resistance to the prodding of the Holy Spirit is a reminder of what all believers go through and need to be cognizant of when they talk with others.

The opposite side of the coin is Joseph Washington, an elderly, pious man who has enough faith for a dozen believers, and who, as a blind man, lives in a dark room alone with God. Joseph's stubborn refusal to give up on Amos is a wonderful testimony to the faithfulness of God, and his determination to hold Amos's feet to the fire to draw out the talent he believes is there is a beautiful picture of the patience of God.

The love of a good woman is generally the deciding factor

in the success or failure of a man, and this story is no different. Judy Valentine falls in love with Amos almost from the first. It's a rocky relationship as she finds out about his nefarious ways, but love wins out and she plays a critical role in Amo's coming to terms with his faith.

Which of these characters do you most relate to right now? As you reflect on the following questions, consider the path you are on. You may see a bit of yourself in all three of these characters, or in the townspeople. A closer look at their conflicting journeys can tell us a lot about our own walk, and the lessons of the late 1800s translate readily to our world today.

1. Joseph immediately saw something in Amos and felt a call to nurture it in spite of the outlaw's resistance. Do you feel this faith was justified? Or did Joseph leap to a conclusion that only by chance had a good outcome?

2. Amos often had attitudes uncomfortable for Christians. How do you feel when you encounter those attitudes in the book? Does it trouble you? Do you want to give up on Amos, or does it make you want all that much more to see him change?

3. How do you react to people in your life who exhibit these attitudes?

4. How did you feel about Amos's ability to preach and be very effective at it, even though he didn't believe in what he was preaching at all?

5. Does that tell you something about some so-called religions today? Do you feel all who are calling on the name of the Lord are genuine?

6. How could you tell if a preacher isn't a true believer?

7. How did you feel about Amos's sermons, other than the one that got him in trouble? Was the Spirit there even if he didn't believe? Would it be possible for someone's message to move you even if he wasn't sincere? Why?

8. What do you think about Joseph's feeling the need to hide his intelligence? Was it a foolish or wise decision, given the time period?

9. Do people hide aspects of themselves today for fear of what others may think of them? Do you hide parts of yourself? Why?

10. What do you think about the way Joseph handled his handicap? Did his attitude cause you to think about some of the things people with handicaps have to deal with?

11. Could you keep your faith with a burden like that? Discuss what that might be like for you.

12. What were some of Amos's actions that caused you to start thinking he had something in him worth saving? How did he show some redeeming qualities before he actually started reacting to the prodding of the Holy Spirit?

13. What do you think about the townspeople and/or church congregation? We get to witness their journey of faith as they cope with the chaos Amos caused. What are the stages they go through in this process?

14. Why was Judy so tempted by the bandit side of Amos? Can we be counted on to be logical when it comes to our love lives?

15. How was Amos able to swindle the Prescott brothers? What was in their nature that made them vulnerable to the scam?

16. Are all swindles dependent on flaws in our nature? Would you be vulnerable to this type of scam? Why or why not?

17. While different faiths and/or denominations may have different attitudes toward the consumption of alcohol, what do you think made the difference between Amos's eagerly accepting the bottle of champagne offered early in the book and his turning it down later in the story?

18. Was it simply fear of the law that kept Amos from running away from Quiet Valley or something more?

19. Could Amos really have killed Joseph to get free? He thought about it. What does your heart tell you about his ability to take a life? Do all of us have limits beyond which we cannot go, or is it a matter of temptation?

20. Is it possible to accurately judge the actions of others if we haven't actually faced the same temptation? Do you think it's possible to learn enough from someone else's experience to predict what you would do in a similar situation?

21. What do you think about Joseph's admonition to test responses from God to see whether they are real or simply a rationalization of something we want to do? Does God always provide corroboration if a message is from Him? Talk about a time when you tested God's word in your life.

22. What do you think about Amos's advice to the couple having trouble? Do you agree that putting the other person first is the key to success in a marriage? If Amos was a believer at this point, would he have added anything to that advice?

23. Judy's intuition kept telling her something was wrong even when she couldn't put her finger on what it was. Does that sound like a reasonable situation? Have you ever experienced uneasiness about a person or situation for no apparent reason? What did you do?

24. Did you get angry when Amos tried to swindle Splendora Cole? Were you surprised to discover that what he asked her for turned out to be exactly what he would need later? Does that encourage you to depend more completely on God for the needs of your life? How so?

25. What did you think about Mrs. Simpson's spending her last hours on earth reaching out to Amos? What effect did that have on Amos? Do you think he would have come to accept Jesus as his Savior if Mrs. Simpson hadn't ministered to him?

26. Amos recognized that both Mrs. Simpson and Joseph saw him for what he really was, and yet they loved and accepted him anyway. As Amos contemplated the reality of that, how did he begin to think differently about God?

27. To what degree do you think Mrs. Simpson represents a turning point for Amos?

28. Is it possible for you to be a turning point for someone and not even be aware of it? Are you comfortable with that? Why or why not?

29. Amos made virtually no progress toward getting real faith while things were going very well. It was only after God put him on his knees that he started coming around. Do you have to sometimes be put on your knees to see what God wants you to see? Why do you think that's true?

30. What do you think it means to say that the church "loved Amos more as a sinner than they ever did as a preacher"?

31. Do you think Amos was justified in his determination to go back and set things right? Would it have been better

for him to settle in and be a good pastor to the congregation that had accepted him? What is the basis of your answer?

32. When Amos started to atone for his sins, to say everyone was suspicious of his motives would be a great understatement. When we, as Christians, desire to make a change in our lives, do people tend to be critical of our sincerity? What can you do to assuage those suspicions?

33. Though Amos kept trying to turn things over to God, it was hard for him. Joseph counseled him to "do the prudent thing," fearing the consequences if they were not adequately interpreting God's will and His protection. How hard is it to turn things over to God?

34. The introduction to this readers' guide posed the question, "Is a person who had a long, hard trip to find Jesus more likely to have stronger faith than someone brought up and nurtured in the faith?" After reading the story and thinking about the questions, how would you respond? Does your answer reflect a change in your thinking? Discuss your thoughts about this issue before you read this story, and how those thoughts may have been reinforced or changed after you read the story.

35. Which characters or situations in this story have caused you to think differently or change your attitude about *your* walk with God?

The Word at Work Around the World

A vital part of Cook Communications Ministries is our international outreach, Cook Communications Ministries International (CCMI). Your purchase of this book, and of other books and Christian-growth products from Cook, enables CCMI to provide Bibles and Christian literature to people in more than 150 languages in 65 countries.

Cook Communications Ministries is a not-for-profit, self-supporting organization. Revenues from sales of our books, Bible curricula, and other church and home products not only fund our U.S. ministry, but also fund our CCMI ministry around the world. One hundred percent of donations to CCMI go to our international literature programs.

CCMI reaches out internationally in three ways:

· Our premier International Christian Publishing Institute (ICPI) trains leaders from nationally led publishing houses around the world.

· We provide literature for pastors, evangelists, and Christian workers in their national language.

· We reach people at risk—refugees, AIDS victims, street children, and famine victims—with God's Word.

Word Power, God's Power

Faith Kidz, RiverOak, Honor, Life Journey, Victor, NexGen — every time you purchase a book produced by Cook Communications Ministries, you not only meet a vital personal need in your life or in the life of someone you love, but you're also a part of ministering to José in Colombia, Humberto in Chile, Gousa in India, or Lidiane in Brazil. You help make it possible for a pastor in China, a child in Peru, or a mother in West Africa to enjoy a life-changing book. And because you helped, children and adults around the world are learning God's Word and walking in his ways.

Thank you for your partnership in helping to disciple the world. May God bless you with the power of his Word in your life.

For more information about our international ministries, visit www.ccmi.org.

Additional copies of *Mysterious Ways* are available
from your local bookseller.

❖❖❖

If you have enjoyed this book,
or if it has had an impact on your life,
we would like to hear from you.

Please contact us at:

RIVER OAK BOOKS
Cook Communications Ministries, Dept. 201
4050 Lee Vance View
Colorado Springs, CO 80918

Or

visit our Web site: www.cookministries.com

RIVEROAK®
Good News in Fiction